CW00822806

This book is dedicated to
Eve, for your warmth and affection
and to
My husband, Mick, for all your support and advice.

CONTENTS

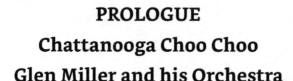

PROLOGUE
Chattanooga Choo Choo
Glen Miller and his Orchestra

Pat Thomas had many ambitions as a young girl. At first, she wanted to be a trapeze artist but a slight fall after swinging from the bannisters at the top of the stairs soon put a stop to that. A ballerina seemed a possible alternative and the fact that she had never had a ballet lesson in her life did not deter her, at least not for a few months. She could stand on her toes and all her family applauded her efforts, but no Pat abandoned this idea for an artist, a nurse, a singer, all in quick succession. At last, she settled on becoming an actress. Her favourite place in the whole wide world was at the local cinema and Pat would go and watch transfixed as the likes of Bette Davis or Katherine Hepburn lit up the screen. At last Pat thought I've found my true vocation in life.

The one thing Pat did not dream of being was a sewing machinist. For some reason this had never quite made it onto her wish list but when she left school at fourteen, just at the close of the second world war, that is exactly what Pat became. A sewing machinist in the Libro factory in Liverpool. It didn't take Pat long before she was one of the fastest machinists on the line, the women in front struggling to keep up with her. Pat no longer dreamed of a life different to the one expected of her. She realised they were only the silly day dreams of a young girl and had no actual basis in reality.

Pat's day dreams were now purely focused on looking forward to the weekend. It was only then that Pat felt as if life offered her more than the humdrum life of working in a factory. Pat now loved to visit dance halls such as the Grafton, just up the road from where she lived, or to the Tower Ball Room in New Brighton. New Brighton was fun and lively with tea shops, candy floss stalls, and fair ground rides.

Pat travelled over to New Brighton on the ferryboat, which would be packed to capacity at the weekend, full of young people, just like herself, who were off to visit the wonders and delights that New Brighton offered. The ferry ride alone was exciting in and of itself. Songs would erupt out of nowhere and everyone would join in. It was a happy time, the euphoria that followed the end of the war was contagious.

Everyone had had enough of misery and heart ache. Now young people let their hair down and Pat looked forward to the weekend, when she could put all her cares behind her. Pat and her friends loved their journey on the ferry boat as it crossed the Mersey, from Liverpool to Wallasey. They could eye up the young men and giggle when they caught their attention. The young men would shout over to them.

"Hey, where are you lot going? Can we buy you a drink when you get there?'

"Chance would a be a fine thing," they'd shout back, laughing amongst themselves.

The men would laugh and shout, "See you in the Tower Ballroom, gorgeous" and Pat and her friends would laugh uproariously and hoped that they would.

Although Pat's wages were meagre and she had to give her mum most of them she still had enough left over to buy herself some new clothes once in a while. Clothes which showed off Pat's slim figure. Pat turned heads. Pat was happy and carefree. As far as Pat was concerned, at the weekend, she had the world at her feet.

The one thing Pat was determined not do was not rush into marriage. The war had taken its toll and now it was time to have fun. Put the blitz behind them. Pat didn't want to be like her mother, old at forty, pregnant year after year with a gaggle of children. These days women could look forward to a brighter future. When Pat married it would be to someone like Tyrone Power or Gregory Peck, who would sweep her off her feet and treat her like a princess for the rest of her life. The trouble was though the Tyrone Power's and Gregory Peck's seemed to be pretty thin on the ground where Pat lived. Pat didn't want to settle for one of the mundane men who vied for her attention. They were too nice, or too rough, or too clingy. Pat held onto her dreams and knew one day her Prince would come.

Then one day Pat knew exactly what she wanted to do and after much arguing and cajoling her dad gave Pat permission to join the Land Army. At last Pat felt her life had some meaning and took to working the land as a duck took to water. For two years Pat found independence away from home. She lived in a dormitory with ten other girls. After a few months Pat was taught how to drive the tractor and it wasn't long before Pat was ploughing the fields. She was young, happy and healthy, and as she sat in her tractor with the sun shining down, Pat couldn't imagine anywhere else she would rather be.

Pat was eighteen when a letter from her mother arrived asking for her to come home. Her mother was expecting another child and needed all the help she could get. Her mother pleaded with Pat to return. At this point Pat was the oldest of six and now her mother was expecting her seventh. Please Pat, please come home. Pat returned home to Liverpool and her sewing machine.

Life settled down once more and jibes about her being an 'old maid' prompted her to finally accept the possibility of settling down and marrying. Harry was the first man she took seriously. Yes, Pat conceded he was loud and brash, but he was funny. He could make Pat laugh, and he was tough. Other men respected him. Harry gave her roses, took her out on romantic dates, told her how much she meant to him. Pat was smitten. Pat got married.

One marriage and five children later Pat returned to work and took up her sewing machine once more. Now she lived across the water from Liverpool and this time she worked at Biltons a small toy manufacturer and Pat sewed various patterns into teddy bears, dolls clothes or fancy-dress costumes. Pat worked happily enough, she liked her friends at the factory, the extra money helped with the household. Pat made do.

Her marriage would have to do as well. The debonaire Harry had long since departed. Pat remembered the time, not long after her first child Danny was born, when she'd had a particularly nasty row with Harry and had decided to leave him. She'd had enough. She bundled a few belongings into a bag, put Danny in his pram and returned to what she still considered to be her home, her parent's house in Liverpool. She had told her mum she couldn't live with Harry anymore, he was impossible, a nasty bully who put his friends before both her and the baby. Her mother's advice had been, 'You've made your bed, now you have to lay in it.'

It took a week for Harry to ask Pat to come back home. A week for Pat to contemplate bringing up a child on her own. Pat recalled her mother's advice and heeded it, even if it was a bitter pill to swallow. Pat went back with Harry, boarding the ferry boat, once filled with so many dreams, and began their journey back over the water to Wallasey. Pat cuddled Danny and watched as the Liver Building receded into the distance.

Harry behaved himself for a few years, but after her third child, Gary, was born Harry picked up where he left off. Harry expected Pat to be the perfect wife, mother and general dog's body. Pat realised she should have taken that chance when she had it. She could have managed with one child, now it felt impossible. Pat no longer dreamed of being a ballerina or an actress, she had never wanted to be a sewing machinist, but she was happy to be a mother, more than happy. It was the wife bit she was having a problem with.

CHAPTER 1

You To Me Are Everything

Real Thing

It was Eleanor Thomas's, or as she was more affectionately known by her family and friends Ellie's, last day at primary school. It was the summer of 1976 and although Ellie did not know this at the time it would be one of the hottest prolonged spells that had been recorded in England up until this point.

All Ellie knew was it was hot, there was no rain to stop her from playing out and it felt good. She didn't care that there were news reports warning about droughts, hose pipe bans, farmers complaining about their livelihoods and eventually there would be a Minister of Drought appointed, all of this went over Ellie's head. As far as Ellie was concerned, the heatwave was only there to add to the enjoyment of her long-awaited summer holidays.

What was far more important to Ellie was leaving primary school and going on to her middle school. The summer holidays in between were just an added bonus. Ellie's last few weeks of term had dragged by and the relentless heat over the last few weeks hadn't helped, it seemed to have made time stand still, every day was the same. The sun shined, the sky remained a perfect blue and the days were long and warm. Yet still finally, almost to Ellie's surprise, time passed, and the last day of term finally arrived but rather than feeling the long-awaited euphoria Ellie felt sad and a little bit afraid of what the future might hold. Ellie was a bit thrown by her own emotions. She felt happy and sad in equal measure and couldn't quite work out why she felt like this when she had been looking forward to this day for so long.

The last few weeks of primary school hadn't been so bad either, Ellie admitted to herself. The hot weather had brought with it a relaxation of the normal school rules. They had been able to play on the grass at break times, which was a rare treat, and some teachers had even taken them outside for lessons to offer some respite from the stifling heat of the classroom. So, although Ellie was looking forward to the summer holidays, and moving to her middle school it came as a bit of a shock to Ellie to realise she would miss her old school and her teachers. It had brought an unexpected lump to Ellie's throat that she was finding hard to gulp down.

Ellie's last day of school had been agonisingly slow, the heat in the classroom was unbearable and Ellie had stared despondently out of the classroom window, watching a faint breeze ruffling the leaves of a tree outside. Now and then she would turn her attention to the hands of the clock, in her classroom, which seemed to be moving at a snail's pace. It wasn't only Ellie who was waiting for the end of the school day, all of Ellie's classmates were waiting in anticipation and Ellie could almost feel the excitement fizzing in the air around her. The children sat with a mixture of fear and excitement, waiting for that final ring of a bell, little understanding it would bring a significant chapter of their lives finally to an end.

At long last, the bell rang, and they all jumped up from their desks and rushed out into the playground. They ignored their teacher who remonstrated with them to slow down, pick up their bags and a dozen other things which all fell on death ears. Outside beckoned and with-it freedom but after their initial rush into the playground, once outside Ellie and her classmates wavered, unsure what to do, surely there should be some kind of celebration, they couldn't just leave as if it was a normal day. They all stood in groups their initial excitement melting as they stared at one another expectantly. Suddenly as if on cue they formed into ranks, linked their arms through one another's and paraded around the school yard singing:

We break up

We break down
We don't care if the school falls down
No more English, no more French
No more sitting on the old school bench

With such gusto and with such exhilaration that Ellie thought her heart would explode with happiness. It was the caretaker who told them to leave in the end. It was then that they realised that there was no one left to hear their chant but still, Ellie thought, she heard it and sang it and even though in the past she never really wanted the school to fall down, now she wished it would, now she was no longer part of it.

Once outside the school gates Ellie split up from her classmates, shouting to one another that they would meet up in the holidays but knowing that they probably wouldn't, even so it was nice to pretend that they would. It was only as Ellie walked away that she felt the heat of the day hit her with full force. She looked up at the perfect blue sky and noticed how the seagulls slowly ducked and dived as if they too had been sapped of all their strength. Then Ellie noticed how the sunlight gave the grey tired buildings of her town a bright vivid colour that they usually lacked. The pavements glistened as if jewels were set inside the concrete and even the tarmac seemed alive, bubbling in the heat.

Ellie's thoughts wondered, as they had a habit of doing. She laughed at a silly joke one of her friends had told her and tried to remember the punch line so she could tell it to her mum when she got home. She picked up bits and bobs from the day, replaying them back to herself as she slowly made her way home. Suddenly she heard her name being called and looked up to see her best friend Billy waving to her from the other side of the street.

Billy was the same age and in the same year as Ellie, but he was in another class, so although they lived across the road from one another, it never occurred to either of them to hang round together in school. Ellie had even spotted Billy in the melee in the playground but had hardly taken any notice of him. In school Billy had his friends and Ellie had hers but now that was forgotten. Outside of school they were as thick as thieves, it was the summer holidays and Billy would be an integral part of that.

Ellie ran across the road to Billy and as she neared him, she could see how hot he was. Ellie wondered why he still had his jumper on in all of this heat but didn't think to ask him as Billy was just Billy and he had little peculiarities that Ellie was quite used to. The sweat stood out on his forehead and made his thick brown hair stick out at odd angles. She did not notice that his uniform was too small for him, or that his jumper was dirty with holes at the elbows or that his shirt was off white and had seen much better days. Or even that his head seemed too big for his small frame. Billy was Billy and she could not remember a time when she had not known him.

They fell in line with one another automatically and talked about what they would not do for an ice cream or a lolly ice, or a cold glass of lemonade. They dawdled both dragging their feet, chatting happily about the various things which had happened to them that day.

Then as if it had suddenly occurred to him Billy said, "Just think seven weeks of no school!"

Ellie stopped dumbfounded, "Yeah, seven whole weeks."

"What shall we do?"

"All sorts, all sorts of things."

"Like what?"

"Like go to Newbo baths, down the Prom, up Biddie Hill!"

"Yeah, or we could go down to Moreton shore!"

"We can do anything. We've got seven whole weeks off school."

"Yeah, just think no school for seven whole weeks, it'll be great!"

It was then that it struck her. The school holidays stretched out before them. Endless days filled with fun and excitement. School was forgotten. She jumped in the air and Billy laughed.

"Race you home?" Ellie shouted as she began to run.

She need not ask. Billy was ahead of her before she had time to finish her sentence, his little legs at full pelt and she knew she would never catch him. Billy Whizz they called him but still she persevered and ran after him shouting his name and telling him to watch the traffic as they crossed the main road. She heard a screech of breaks but then to her relief saw Billy dodge the car and run ahead once more. Happy she followed with the one enduring thought flowing through every inch of her being, seven whole weeks and they all belong to me!

When they turned into their road she could see her dog, Benny, standing to attention outside their front door staring down the road waiting for her. She noticed his ears pricking up as he caught sight of her and then he made a mad dash towards her. He jumped up at her, his tongue hanging out and his tail wagging furiously. She and Billy made a big fuss of him. Benny always waited for them after school and every reunion was as if Benny hadn't seen her for a whole year.

Elle said goodbye to Billy, promising she would be out soon, and her and Benny ran towards their house together. Benny barely able to keep up as his tail was wagging so furiously and Ellie kept having to stop as he jumped up at her demanding yet another stroke. Ellie felt as if she was glowing inside. It was good to be home, she couldn't wait to tell her mum all about her day and the singing outside in the playground. The lump in her throat had disappeared and all her earlier apprehensions disappeared as if by magic.

Ellie loved her street. It was where Ellie felt at her happiest and although this street was not remarkable in any shape or form for Ellie it was the centre of her universe. Her street was filled with terraced houses and was replicated right across her neighbourhood. A labyrinth of houses filled with people playing out their lives amongst the bricks and mortar. The small houses, painted in various shades of colour, some gleaming and others with peeling, blistered paintwork but as a whole, to an unobservant eye, they would be called shabby or neglected but Ellie saw none of this. Ellie only appreciated it for what it was, a vibrant community full of life and vitality.

If Ellie could have expressed how she felt, it was the essence of the place that she loved. The shouting and arguing, the poverty and neglect passed Ellie by. When Ellie walked her streets, with its familiar smells and sounds, Ellie felt safe and secure. It was the instinctive feeling that she belonged here. It was the place she called home.

To Ellie her neighbours were her extended family. Some she liked others less so. Mrs. Rogers was nosey and never left her front window, in case she missed some juicy bit of gossip she could regale the neighbourhood with. Mrs. Berry called the police on her and her friends if they pinched flowers from her tiny front garden or played football outside her door. Mr. and Mrs. Robinson across the road were kind and patient. Billy's family were by far the worse, always fighting with everyone but Billy was okay, well most of the time. There were the Simpson's made up of her other best friend, Karen and her two little sisters. The Farrell's, whose mother was having an affair with one of the Nolan's sons, who lived next door.

There was a whole host of characters of one shape or another who kept her amused or on her toes or out of trouble. It was a myriad of people which represented home to her and if she had tried to explain it in words she would have failed dismally. She just knew that they were part of her, and she was part of them, and it was as simple as that.

CHAPTER 2
Get Up and Boogie
Silver Convention

Ellie's family loved music and during the day the radio would take centre stage but the family's most treasured possession was the radiogram which sat in the front parlour. This allowed them to play all their own records from Motown to the Beatles, from Elvis to the Eagles. These were Ellie's older sister, Fiona and older brother Gary's preference. Ellie's mum, Pat, loved the big band numbers, particularly Glen Miller but she also adored Ella Fitzgerald and Nat King Cole.

It was only Ellie's dad, Harry, who didn't share their passion. If he was in, he would tell them to 'turn that load of garbage off' and turn on the television to watch the news or some boring documentary. Even then they would sneak off into the front room and play the music quietly so as not to disturb him. Ellie loved her dad but couldn't understand why he didn't share the rest of the family's love of music.

Lately though, a new development had occurred which made playing outside in the street even better for Ellie and that was because, due to the hot weather, her older brother or sister had begun to open up the front room window so when they played their records it could be heard outside. As far as Ellie was concerned the hot weather had made everything so much better. Everyone seemed to be happier and the music blasting in the street added to her enjoyment of playing out. Music was the backdrop of Ellie's life but she barely registered the fact, it was just there.

Walking in through the open front door of her home Ellie could hear the radio playing the latest hits. Ellie found her mum in her usual place, the kitchen. Ellie's intention was to grab a quick salad cream butty, her favourite and then join Billy outside. Ellie's mum, Pat, was in her mid-forties. Pat was a slight woman and not very tall, all of Ellie's older siblings Danny, Gary and Fiona, were already head and shoulders above their mum but for all her diminutive stature they all knew not to give their mum too much cheek. Pat had olive skin, brown eyes and short dark permed hair, going to the hairdressers on a Friday to have it set was the one small treat Pat allowed herself.

Pat was older than Ellie's friend's mums, in Ellie's eyes at least, she was by far the prettiest, even if she didn't dress up and wear lots of make-up. Sometimes Ellie thought her mum looked a bit like the Queen and when Ellie had told her this her mum had laughed and said, 'I don't think so, love but I wouldn't mind having her money.'

When Pat saw Ellie she opened up her arms for a hug, kissed her and asked, "How was your last day at school?"

"It was great," Ellie said enthusiastically, "We all stood round singing 'we break up we break down' until Mr. Murphy threw us out of the playground!"

Ellie skipped past her mum and began to raid the cupboards for the salad cream to make herself a butty. Pat smiled at Ellie. Ellie had left for school this morning looking quite respectable but now her blue chequered summer dress which had been neatly ironed was now creased, with an array of what looked like soil and grass stains all over it. It looked as if Ellie had been rolling around the ground in it, which she probably has been doing, Pat thought. Suffice to say Ellie's socks and shoes were now full of dirt and one shoe buckle was undone which Ellie hadn't seemed to notice. Ellie's dark hair so neatly put into plaits this morning now hung loose past her shoulders.

Pat knew it was a losing battle with Ellie. Ellie could never stay tidy unlike Sally, her youngest daughter, who always looked so pristine. Sally had come home looking as spotless as when she walked out the door this morning. Sometimes Pat dressed Ellie and Sally in the same clothes but in different colours to compliment the fact that they were so dissimilar to one another. Ellie's hair was as dark as Sally's was blonde, Ellie's eyes were blue whereas Sally's were hazel. Ellie was tall for her age and robust and Sally was petite like herself. Pat was proud of her two daughters; in her eyes they were both lovely in their own unique way but as different in both looks and temperament as chalk was to cheese.

Pat remembered that Sally had been complaining about Ellie, so thought, for all the good it would do her, to tackle Ellie about it. "Sally said you told her this morning not to walk home with you after school and she had to walk home on her own."

"Well, it's not like it was her last day."

Ellie had no remorse about telling her younger sister to 'get lost' earlier on. It wasn't as if Sally didn't have anyone else to walk home with, Ellie reasoned with herself. She was fed up with Sally always hanging round with her at school, why didn't she play with her own friends?

Pat tutted and said, "You should be nicer to your younger sister." But she knew the two were close and both were as bad as each other.

Pat's words fell on deaf ears. "I'm going out to play," Ellie told her mum as she walked out taking a big bite out of the butty she had made.

"Change out of your school clothes, first, Ellie," but it was too late Ellie was already running out the door. "Don't go far, Ellie, as your tea will be ready soon." Pat said in a last attempt at some kind of parental control.

"I won't mum," Ellie shouted as she rushed back out onto the street.

Outside the street was full of parents out on their respective steps and children playing. Karen and her sisters were skipping, and Billy was kicking a football. There were other kids around, but they were not her best friends. Ellie was so happy with the thought of her holidays stretching out in front of her and knew it would be wonderful. With not a cloud in sight she couldn't imagine that anything could spoil it for her. She finished her butty and shouted to Billy to pass the ball. Skipping was boring, Ellie would much rather play football.

CHAPTER 3

Heaven Must be Missing an Angel
Tavares

Ellie was watching a cartoon on the tele, it was early in the morning and she was still wearing her nightie and hadn't dressed even though her mum kept telling her to. She was eating toast. Fiona, her older sister was sitting next to her and looking through wedding brochures, oohing and ahhing at the pictures. Ellie older sister was getting married and as far as Ellie was concerned, she was bored of it. It was all Fiona ever went on about.

Pat had the ironing board out and was busily ironing various articles of clothes whilst Fiona, sitting on the settee, poured over the various magazines laid out in front of her. Every so often Fiona would stand up to show Pat another picture and her mum would glance at it, smile encouragingly and then return to her task at hand.

"Oh, mum, have you seen this?" Fiona said once more.

Fiona held up one of the wedding brochures for her mother's inspection. Pat peered over to see what Fiona was looking at.

"Mmmm." Pat said and went back to her ironing.

"What do you mean Mmmm?"

"It's lovely Fiona."

"What you don't think that dress isn't absolutely gorgeous?"

"Yes, it's beautiful."

"Well, you don't seem to be that interested."

"Look Fiona I've got more things to worry about than your wedding."

"Like what?"

"Lots of things, Fiona."

"Like what? Don't you understand this is the most important day of my life?"

"Of course, I do."

"So, what's the problem then?"

"Nothing."

Fiona was looking up at her mum with an angry expression on her face. It seemed to Ellie that Fiona was brewing for an argument and her mum was trying her level best not to play ball. Ellie thought her mum had the patience of a saint when it came to Fiona.

"Yes, there is you haven't shown the slightest bit of interest in my wedding for weeks now."

"I've had a lot on my mind."

"What's more important than your eldest daughter getting married?"

"Well, when you put it like that, lots of things."

"Oh my God mother I can't believe what I'm hearing. Don't you care about me?"

Fiona had knocked the magazines onto the floor in her haste to stand up and was now standing up, facing Pat with her hands on her hips.

Pat raised her eyes to her daughter, picked up another shirt to iron and at last said, "Of course, I care about you but the world doesn't begin and end with you. You can see I'm busy."

"If you cared. You would be interested in helping me pick a dress. I don't understand you, what can be more important than that?"

Pat put the iron down and stared at Fiona.

"Do you really want to know?" Pat glared at Fiona.

Ellie thought, up oh, here we go.

"Well to be honest I think you're rushing into things."

"Rushing into things? God mother I've been engaged to Simon for six months."

"Six months that long? Well, I never."

Even Ellie recognised the underlying sarcasm of her mother's words.

"Mother, what's got into you?" Fiona said, her tone becoming slightly less aggressive in the face of her mother's wrath.

"Well, I'm sorry Fiona, but I just don't share your enthusiasm for your impending nuptials."

"What? What do you mean? Why are you being like that?"

"Because you're only nineteen years of age and you've got your whole life ahead of you. Why the big rush to get married?"

"Because I love Simon, it's as simple as that."

"Then move in with him. Have a test drive before you make such a huge commitment."

Fiona looked at her mother in shock.

"My God mother as if I'd do that."

Ellie also stared in shock at her mother but more because of the expression on Fiona's face and the tone of her voice than any real understanding.

"Why not, I wish I would have then I would have avoided the biggest mistake of my life."

Ellie or Fiona was not shocked to hear their mum talking about her own marriage in this manner, it was ongoing theme for their mum.

"Oh, wonderful and then you wouldn't have had us, thanks a lot mother," Fiona said staring at her mum.

"That's not the point Fiona, what's done is done but you've got your whole life ahead of you and I don't know what the rush is."

"There's no rush I just want to spend the rest of my life with Simon."

Pat raised her eyes to the ceiling, the ironing seemed to have been forgotten, "You do now but you mightn't in a few years' time, especially when you have a couple of kids tied to your apron strings, it mightn't be so wonderful then."

"I can't wait to have children."

"You've got years before you should be thinking of having children."

"What at nineteen don't be daft most of the girls my age are already married and have kids."

"That doesn't mean you have to."

"I know that, mother, but me and Simon aren't like you and dad. Simon loves me and he'll be a lovely husband and father."

"Yes, I know it all sounds wonderful now and believe it or not I felt like that once but..."

"But what mother? Do you have a problem with Simon?"

"No not as such."

"Not as such. What does that mean? So now you don't like Simon? What's wrong with Simon? I thought you liked him. I knew you had a problem. I can't believe this, why can't you just be happy for me?"

"I am happy for you but you're so young once you have a child you won't be able to move."

"God, you make it sound like it's some kind of prison sentence." Pat grimaced but did not reply. "No, I know what your problem is you don't want me to be happy because you're not. My dad's right about you. It's those stupid women in those stupid meetings you go to that are putting stupid ideas into your head."

Ellie watched as her mum smiled inwardly.

"No one's putting ideas into my head I just feel that I've woken up at long last."

"Oh, there's no talking to you. All you're interested in is going to those stupid meetings and talking about burning your bra or whatever it is you talk about. You don't care about us anymore."

"It's because I do care that I feel I have to say something to you before it's too late."

Fiona stood facing her mum, and although she was angry, she was trying hard not to cry.

"I just can't wait to get out of this horrible house, away from you and me dad. Do you know what it's like to live with the two of you constantly arguing all the time?"

"I know it must be horrible and I'm sorry about that but it doesn't mean you have to get married."

"It does. I love Simon and he loves me and I can't wait to get married and leave you all to it."

With that Fiona ran out of the room, her magazines left strewn on the floor.

"I don't know," Ellie's mum said with a sad expression on her face and went back to her ironing.

There was silence and Ellie looked at her mum appealingly.

"It's all that Simon's fault," Ellie said.

"It's not Simon's fault," her mother said, "It's this world which we live in. Look at me. I have to work, look after you, your sisters, brother and your father. Feed, wash and clothe you and be the perfect housewife, mother and wife all at the same time. I'm worn out with it all. I can see it all mapped out for our Fiona and I just can't bear the thought of it." Ellie stared at her mum in confusion. "Oh. just ignore me Ellie when you're older you might understand."

Ellie felt sad but did not know why. It was Fiona's fault for upsetting her mum and this pathetic 'Wedding of the Century' as her dad and her older brother, Gary, called it. No wonder her mum was angry. Her sister's wedding, mood swings and tantrums seemed to rule the house. Ellie hated the way it had taken over everything. No wonder her mum was unhappy.

Ellie sat brooding for a while. Fiona was spoilt. She had a wardrobe of beautiful clothes. She was lovely looking with long blonde hair and stood out like a sore thumb in their district. Fiona was always jumping in and out of taxis, laden with bags with yet more clothes in them. Her hair was always immaculate, her make up picture perfect and her fingernails polished. For years there had been a string of admirers vying for her attention but no she had to go and ruin it all and choose Simon and now he was the centre of her universe and she didn't care about them anymore.

It was all Simon's fault. Once he came on the scene, he and Fiona had commandeered the parlour as their own private love nest and never let her and Sally in. Fiona would sit in there night after night with the doors locked and soft music playing. What made it worse was that Fiona would take Simon in little treats of food that her and Sally were not allowed to touch. It had been melon the other night and Fiona hadn't given them any. They tried to peep in through the front room window but ran away when they heard Fiona shout:

"Mother there at it again!"

Ellie smiled when she thought about it. When the coast was clear they sneaked back with all their friends and they all started to sing: -

Fiona and Simon up the tree KI – KI
Fiona and Simon up the tree
K I double S I N G!

Fiona had opened up the parlour window and swore at them. This had made them laugh all the more but in the end their mum came out and chased them away. It was still funny though but they knew when they'd pushed their luck too far so left Fiona in her 'love nest' as they called it and went looking for something else to amuse them.

CHAPTER 4
Mamma Mia
ABBA

Pat was sitting at her machine. It was only eleven o'clock but already there was a pile of her work sat in a basket next to her. The radio was playing, and she hummed to herself as she worked. She thought back to her argument with Fiona the day before and sighed to herself. She should not interfere. It didn't matter what she said, Fiona would not change her mind. She did not dislike Simon she just thought her daughter was rushing into things. Oh well, she thought no one could have told me what to do at that age either.

She could hear Sandra Tweadle's loud voice above all the noise and her laugh as she screeched at her own jokes. Sandra was a bit rough round the edges, but Pat liked her. Pat shook her head at her latest story but couldn't hear the gist of it due to the sound of the machines all around her. She had heard a snippet about some bloke Sandra had met in New Brighton, something shocking about a wife who made a surprise visit to Sandra's. Pat blanched at the thought of anyone tackling Sandra, but Pat hadn't been able to hear all the gory details so did not know how it all ended.

Sandra had no shame. She would talk about the most intimate details of her life to anyone who listened and anyone who was within hearing distance would be privy to them too. Sandra was now regaling their supervisor Tina Brown with her weekend exploits. Whilst everyone worked Sandra seemed to get away with murder. Pat was relieved their Fiona wasn't like that. My God the thought of having a daughter like Sandra Tweadle gave Pat nightmares.

Pat's friend, Joan, sat next to Pat and they both looked at each other and raised their eyebrows.

"What's she been up to now?" Joan mouthed to Pat and Pat shrugged her shoulders.

"Who knows Joan, I wouldn't put anything past her," Pat whispered back, and they both laughed.

Pat looked up as she heard a door bang. Young Debbie Walters had run out of their boss, Mr. Kinnear's office and past their machine. Pat frowned if she wasn't mistaken, it looked as though Debbie had been crying.

Pat looked back to see Mr. Kinnear standing at his office door. His face was red, and he was staring after Debbie.

"Bloody women," Mr. Kinnear shouted and went back into his office, slamming the door behind him.

Sandra Tweadle's voice could no longer be heard and the noise on the floor had quietened as the woman paused in their work.

"What's up with him now?" Sandra Tweadle asked.

"Who knows," Joan said, meeting Sandra's eye.

"Come on now, get back to work," Tina Brown shouted, clapping her hands.

"Where not in fuckin' school now you know Tina," Sandra shouted, laughing uproariously even though what she had said wasn't particularly funny.

Tina laughed despite of herself. Sandra had a way of swearing that did not cause offence, it was just a part of her everyday language, and everyone was used to it. Even Tina Brown, who used any excuse to exploit her authority, allowed Sandra Tweadle far more leeway than the other women who worked there.

"Come on you lot," Tina shouted, ignoring Sandra's remark. "Chop, chop."

The women sighed and after a few moments returned to their work.

"Anyway," Sandra said to Tina, resuming their conversation, "I said to her, he didn't tell me he was married, how was I to know?"

Pat continued with her work, but a worried frown creased her brow. Finally, Pat shouted over to Tina, "Just going the toilet."

"Make it quick will you Pat, it looks like he's got a bee in his bonnet about something," Tina shouted over as Pat rose from her machine.

Pat was a bit surprised by Tina's response. Tina was a real jobs worth. She usually refused this simple request, saying that's what their break was for. Tina must have been distracted by Sandra Tweadle's gossip but as long as Pat could go, she didn't really care what the reason was. Probably trying to stay on the right side of Sandra Tweadle more likely, Pat thought, because for all of Tina's bluster she still would not like to get on the wrong side of Sandra, like most of the bosses. Sandra was a law unto herself and as long as she got on with her work, she was pretty much left to her own devices unlike her co-workers.

Pat forgot all about that as she quickly made her way to the toilet. She was worried about young Debbie Walters and was hoping she would find her there. Debbie was fresh out of school and seemed a bit lost in the rough and tumble of working life. Debbie only lived in the next street to Pat, so Pat had known her since she was a toddler. Realising that Debbie hadn't returned to her machine Pat thought it was best if she went to see if she was alright. Pat wondered what on earth had made Debbie so upset. She was a timid little thing and Pat thought maybe she could give her a few words of advice to toughen her up a little.

"Debbie, love," Pat shouted as she went into the toilets. There was no reply, but Pat noticed that one of the cubicle doors was locked. Pat went over and knocked lightly on the door. "Debbie, love are you in there?"

Pat thought she heard a snuffle.

"Come on love what's the matter. You can tell me." Still no answer. "Debbie I'm worried now. Come on if you don't let me in, I'll bloody well climb over the door," Pat said trying to make a joke to put Debbie at ease.

"It's okay, Pat, just got a headache. I'll be out in a minute," Debbie at last replied.

"Just open the door, sounds like something is upsetting you more than a headache. Has that Mr. Kinnear upset you?"

"No," Debbie said quickly.

"Come on Debbie love, he's renowned for it. What's he done now?"

Pat waited patiently outside the door. Finally, she heard the lock and Debbie came out wiping her nose.

"What's up love?" Pat asked putting her arm around the young woman's shoulder.

"It's nothing Pat, just feeling under the weather."

Pat could have let it go but she knew there was more to it than that and she was annoyed at Mr. Kinnear riding rough shod over a young girl like Debbie. He was a bully and took advantage of the timid workers. If you stood up to him, he soon backed down, but Pat remembered when she was young and how intimidating the bosses had been. Pat would just tell Debbie to take no notice of him and it would all blow over. Debbie was still wet behind the ears; she wouldn't be able to handle someone like Mr. Kinnear until she was a few years older.

"What's he done?" Pat asked thinking Debbie had been reprimanded for some silly misdemeanour.

Suddenly Debbie said, "He put his hand up my skirt."

"What?" Pat said, not believing what she had heard. Pat had assumed that maybe Mr. Kinnear had said something untoward to Debbie, but not this. Pat was shocked.

"It's okay Pat it's nothing. I don't want to lose my job. I'm just being silly."

"What do you mean he put his hand up your skirt?"

Debbie's face grew red. "He asked me to get something from his filing cabinet and I was a bit confused because I'm not an office worker and when I went over his hand shot up."

Pat noticed Debbie was shaking. "I pushed him away and he just got rougher. I had to run out in the end. I didn't know what else to do."

"The dirty bastard," Pat said. "I can't believe this. I thought he was a lot of things, but I didn't think he was capable of that."

Pat then recalled the rumours which had circulated for years about Mr. Kinnear but it had all been treated like it was a bit of a joke really but Pat realised, obviously it wasn't funny if you were on the receiving end of it.

"Look Pat, it's not your problem. I'll just keep out of his way," Debbie said trying to smile at Pat.

"Keep out of his way? And, how long do you think that's going to work?"

"I will though Pat, he said something about my skirt being short and I was asking for it."

"Asking for it, I'll give him fuckin' asking for it." Pat stormed out of the toilet leaving Debbie in her wake.

Later on, Pat realised she had acted instinctively, she hadn't actually considered what she was doing. All she could think of was yet again here was another man using his power to get away with murder. A young girl who was young enough to be his daughter. Pat was sick and tired of it all.

Pat walked back onto the factory floor. All of the women had their heads down, even Sandra Tweadle, and were concentrating on their work. A few looked up as she passed them, and walked towards Mr. Kinnear's office, his inner sanctum as they all called it.

"Hey, you," Pat said as she opened his door without knocking. Mr. Kinnear looked up in surprise. "I thought you were a piece of work, but I didn't think you would assault a young, naive girl like Debbie Walters." Pat said, surprised at how calm her voice sounded when inside she was seething.

Outside the machines fell silent.

"What? I did no such thing. What's the little tart said?"

"Tart," Pat shouted her blood boiling over, "You call that young innocent girl, a tart? You have the cheek."

"Cheek," Mr. Kinnear rose from his seat, his face was red, and he was stammering. "I don't know what she's been saying but it's a pack of lies."

"Oh, come of it. I thought you were a lot of things, bully being the worse but this? How many other girls have had to put up with you and your hands everywhere?"

"I did no such thing."

"She's not making it up."

"Oh, she comes across as the innocent, wearing short skirts like that for work, that's no innocent believe you and me. She's been giving me the cow's eyes since she started."

Pat could have laughed if it wasn't so serious. Instead, she said, "Are you joking, why would a young girl fancy you? Have you taken a good look in the mirror lately and as for wearing short skirts, it's the fashion. All young girls dress like that. It doesn't mean anything you silly little man."

Mr. Kinnear stared at Pat as if he couldn't believe his ears, at last he said, "It's her word against mine and I'm telling you she's lying, and she can get the fuck out of this factory if she doesn't retract what she's said."

Pat was speechless, "You what?"

"You heard. There should be some dress code round here. Accusing me when she flaunts herself around the place like that." He turned his attention to Tina who Pat hadn't realised was standing behind her. "Do you know where Debbie Walters is?" He asked Tina, resuming an authoritative manner.

"I'll go and find her Mr. Kinnear," Pat swung round to stare at Tina. Tina had a smug expression on her face and her arms were folded across her scrawny chest as she waited for Mr. Kinnear's approval.

"Did you hear any of that?" Pat asked Tina.

"A bit but I'm sure," she said looking at Mr. Kinnear, "that Mr. Kinnear would do no such thing."

Pat was too shocked to reply to her and could only shake her head at the woman. Mr. Kinnear grew in confidence, now that he had Tina's support, his voice rose likewise, "In fact what am I playing at. Go and tell her to pick up her things and get the hell out of here. I won't stand for a whipper snapper like her, spreading lies about me."

Suddenly as if he had warmed to the idea, he stared pointedly at Pat. "And as for you. It's only because you're such a good worker and have worked here for so long I'm willing to overlook this but if you go around repeating any of this to those lot outside, you'll be next..."

He stopped as Pat made a dash towards him. Later Pat didn't know what she would have done if Tina had not interceded and grabbed her by the arm. It gave her enough time to take stock of the situation. Pat stopped in her tracks and stared at the fat, little man in front of her.

"You low life piece of work," Pat said, "I don't know how I'm going to do it but I'm going to have your guts for garters you snivelling little excuse of a man."

That's it," Mr. Kinnear shouted, "I've had enough. You can collect your things as well. I've had enough of all this."

"You can stick your job. I wouldn't work here for a big clock."

"Pat don't be hasty now, I'm sure we can work this out." Tina turned to Mr. Kinnear, "Bob Pat's one of our best workers, she'll be hard to replace."

"I don't care Tina, I'm not being spoken to in that manner in my own office, I'm not going to stand for it." He looked at Pat, "Go on, you heard me clear off."

Pat smiled at him, "Go fuck yourself Turnip Head." Later on, Pat would giggle to herself wondering where on earth she came up with that remark but as she stared at him that is exactly what he looked like, a fat, turnip with a spattering of hair on his head.

"In fact," Mr. Kinnear said to Tina, "Tell Debbie she doesn't have to leave, it's this one that has caused all the fuss. I'm sure Debbie said no such thing and this one just took it out of context."

Pat snorted at him and turned on her heel. She walked across the factory floor and picked up her bag by her table, ignoring the women all around her who were staring at her in shock.

"Pat love," she heard Joan call to her, but Pat walked on oblivious of her surroundings.

When Pat walked through the main gates she began to calm

down. Oh my god, she thought what have I done? It's one thing making a stance but it's another thing losing her job. Pat wondered how Harry would take it, they were struggling as it was. Pat's anger evaporated in an instant and she brushed away the tears, which up until that point she had not realised were falling in a steady stream from her eyes.

CHAPTER 5
The Boys are Back in Town
Thin Lizzy

Ellie was standing outside when she heard the sound of a scooter coming along the street. She looked up to see Simon perched upon it and watched as he slowly pulled to a stop outside their house.

"Hi, Simon," she said but he did not even acknowledge her.

Ellie watched as he hopped from his 'love machine' (well that's what Gary called it) and marched right past her and into her house. Ellie couldn't see what Fiona saw him, so what if he had dark wavy hair to his shoulders, was quite tall, dressed quite fashionably and rode a scooter. All he ever did was scowl. Not once had he tried to be nice to her or Sally. Gary couldn't stand him and said, 'he was full of himself' and Ellie was inclined to agree with him, which didn't happen very often.

Billy Whizz sidled up beside her and they both stared at the disappearing figure of Simon.

"Don't know who he thinks he is," Ellie said.

"Thinks he's great," agreed Billy, "cos he's got a scooter."

"If our Danny was home, he'd kill him." Danny was Ellie's older brother, who was away at sea and since his departure had taken on almost mythical proportions in both Ellie and Sally's eyes.

Ellie and Billy stared at Simon's scooter, his pride and joy perched on the pavement.

"Fancy a seater?" Billy asked.

They jumped on to it but of course they couldn't get it started. Billy tried to move it but it was too heavy for him so they called over to Karen and her two little sisters, Tracie and Melanie, who were standing on their front. Next thing they were taking it in turns to wheel each other up and down the road but soon they were bored. It wasn't much fun in the end and they couldn't go very fast.

"Let's hide it," Ellie said and the others laughed.

They took Simon's moped up the back entry and hid it behind some bins. Ellie thought this was a great joke and so did the others. She didn't care what Simon thought.

As the night wore on most of the mum's came out and stood on the front doorstep watching their children as they played in the street. Billy's mum, Carole, was there stick thin with long, lank hair and a face that looked far older than her years. Karen, Ellie's other best friend, mum, Debbie, was on her step laughing and gossiping with the other neighbours, her loud raucous laugh echoing up and down the street. Ellie's mum was not amongst them, she was never one to stand on the step. For some reason Ellie could not quite fathom her mum did not quite fit in with the other mum's. Her mum was more world weary, harassed and did not seem to have the time to stand around and gossip.

Some of the parents were drinking beer and someone was playing Fleetwood Mac with their windows wide open so everyone could hear it. As it got later some of the mum's started joining in with the skipping. All too soon Ellie realised it must be time for bed when she noticed her mum standing on the front calling her and Sally's name.

Sally was with her and without thinking they threw themselves behind a parked car. It wasn't fair all the other kids were playing out, why couldn't they?

"Ellie! Sally!"

Ellie looked up to see Billy's mum, Carole, looking over at them with a malicious smile playing on her lips.

"They're over here Mrs. Thomas."

"Sally, Ellie get here now."

"It's not fair Billy's still out and he's younger than me." Ellie said.

"Even Karen, Tracie and Melanie Simpson are still out," Sally joined in.

"It's the summer holidays. It's not a school night," Ellie finished for good measure as they walked discontentedly to where their mum stood.

"I don't care. You both need a good wash before you go to bed. I'm not Carole bloody Patterson who doesn't wash her kids from one week to the next!"

They were still arguing with their mum as they walked into the front room dragging their feet.

"Oh, for Christ's sake what's going on?"

They jumped at the sound of their father's voice. It was rare their father was in at this time. He was normally in the pub but tonight for some reason there he was sitting watching the television. They appealed to him as their outrage knew no bounds.

"Everyone's playing out and me mum's dragged us in. It's not fair."

"It's still light and we have to go to bed."

Their diatribe continued until suddenly Harry shouted:

"Get out the two of you!"

Ellie and Sally needed no further encouragement and headed for the door.

"You stupid man it's just taken me twenty minutes to get them in and you undermine me like that. One night you stay in and this is what you do. I have to put up with this every night while you sit in the pub with your mates..."

Ellie went back outside oblivious to the ensuing argument of her mum and dad but it seemed different somehow now that the spell had been broken. Soon it started to get dark and the other kids started being taken in followed by their parents. Then most of the front doors were closed and lights started to go on in each of the houses and still their mum had not come out for them.

"Shall we go in?" Sally asked and at last Ellie reluctantly agreed. It felt weird being in the street all alone.

When they skulked back into their house their dad was still sat in front of the television and their mum was in the kitchen.

"Sorry mum." Ellie said.

"You two listen to me the next time I tell you to come in or I'll lock you out all night and we'll see how you like that."

Ellie and Sally hung their heads in shame. Their mum tutted and set about getting them ready for bed. Soon they were bathed and laying in their beds. Ellie still felt hot even though the bedroom window was open and a gentle breeze picked at the nets. Ellie listened to the noises creeping in through the window and at a strip of light which travelled across the ceiling every time a car went by. It wasn't long before Ellie fell asleep. She did not know how long she slept but it seemed as if it was the middle of the night when she was awakened by the sound of Simon shouting:

"Someone's nicked me fuckin' scooter!"

Ellie smiled to herself and snuggled back down to sleep.

CHAPTER 6
Let's Stick Together
Bryan Ferry

Pat sighed as she placed Ellie and Sally's dinner on the table. Her youngest son, Gary, was lying on the settee; thankfully he had had his tea and seemed content watching the television. The house was calm, the only noise came from the television, but Pat could barely hear it from the kitchen.

Pat still hadn't told Harry about losing her job. She just knew he wouldn't understand. She felt sick to the bottom of her stomach at the thought of broaching the subject. It was only that he was out at work every day that he hadn't noticed her change of routine. Maybe tonight, after he had his tea, she could have a quiet word with him.

Pat felt as if her world was closing in on her. Her life seemed to be fraying at the edges, falling apart at the seams. It's a pity it couldn't all be overlocked like the edges of the material she'd worked with all her life. Tidied up, neatened out so it would stop unravelling but unfortunately there was no way of doing that. Pat felt as if she was slowly suffocating, life kept on piling more and more pressure on top of her and there were some days when Pat actually found it difficult to even draw breath.

Pat sighed and began to wash the pots and pans. Harry's tea was in the oven; he still hadn't come home from work, but they had been married long enough by now for her to know he must be in the pub. Pat decided not to think about this, she had enough on her plate at the moment. Instead, she looked forward to seeing her friends on Thursday night. That's where she would find the support she needed. She hadn't seen any of the 'girls' since leaving her job. They all had busy lives and she knew any worries she had would keep till then,

It was because of the reaction this group evoked in Harry that Pat was afraid to tell him about her job. She knew he would blame the group. She shook her head at the way her family reacted to her Thursday night out, predominately egged on by Harry. Harry thought she had joined some radical feminist liberation movement; it could hardly be called that. She could hear him now telling her they were putting ideas into her head, but Pat knew even if she had not joined the group, she still would have reacted in exactly the same way to Mr. Kinnear's actions.

The irony was Pat mused it was the introduction of the Sex Discrimination Act the year before which had raised the groups awareness of how things could change but maybe they had been naive to think it was a fundamental shift for women. After losing her job Pat wondered how effectual they could really be. It was one thing discussing these issues, but it was a different matter living in the real world. Really what had they achieved if Mr. Kinnear could assault a young woman and sack her all in one day and still get away with it?

She remembered how excited they had been when they discussed the Dagenham Women's Strike, the way the women had fought for equal pay illustrated that they could fight back but that was a different scenario compared to what had happened to her. Had she been kidding herself? At the time it had given her a feeling of power but now Pat felt it had all been a waste of time.

Pat thoughts turned back to Harry. She wasn't immune to how hard he worked. She knew his lot in life wasn't great, but she felt as if she had a double burden. She had gone back to work once Sally started school and the money helped a lot, but she was still left with all the housework, cooking and cleaning and sometimes she felt as if she just couldn't cope. It wasn't fair and slowly she realised that for a long time she had resented Harry his freedom. Yes, he brought in the majority of the money into the house, but it wasn't her fault she was paid buttons. It shouldn't mean that he couldn't help her sometimes. Share the burden a bit more. He even resented her for going to her meetings, but it was the only time she could express herself. The only time she felt she was listened to and respected.

Pat tried to shake these feelings of despondency. There was a black cloud threatening to engulf her and Pat tried to encourage herself that although she felt disillusioned at the moment, she knew the women in the group would be there to support her. She tried to summon up her usual enthusiasm for this week's meeting and to convince herself that at least there she could discuss Mr. Kinnear's actions. Sadly, Pat acknowledged to herself, she received more support there than from her own husband. It was a sobering thought.

Pat was brought back from her reflections when she heard the living room door opening. She felt her heart contract. She looked up to see her husband walking unsteadily into the living room. Pat noticed his face was red and with him came the unmistakable smell of alcohol. Her own worries and concerns were put to the back of her mind with Harry's arrival. She knew instinctively he was in a foul mood.

Harry was a large man, but his once fine figure had turned to mush, and a beer belly now protruded from behind a too tight t. shirt. Harry had never been what would be considered a handsome man, but he'd had a strength to him that Pat had been attracted to but it wasn't his beer belly which repulsed Pat, it was what he was as a person which turned Pat's stomach. She hated herself for thinking this way but these days if there were any redeeming qualities still remaining in Harry Pat was finding it very difficult to find them.

She sucked in a sharp breath as she watched him stopping to peer over the settee at Gary. Gary was lying on the settee and if there was thing Harry hated was Gary lying on the settee. Gary was different to his father in so many ways, although he had his father's stature he looked more like her side of the family. He was dark and unlike her husband quite good looking but he had Harry's temperament. Gary was just like his father, belligerent and hated authority. Gary liked fighting, he hated school, he bunked off and unlike his older brother Danny, had no ambitions other than hanging round with his friends. The irony was, Pat knew Harry was exactly the same when he was his son's age.

For all of this or because of this Gary and Harry had always clashed. Harry had always been hard on Gary. It had been difficult for Pat trying to support her husband on the one hand whilst protecting her youngest son from Harry's perpetual condemnation but lately Harry's behaviour was becoming worse. Pat realised that even when Gary was a child Harry had been disappointed in him. Pat asked herself, what type of man hated his own son?

Danny on the other hand could do no wrong. He was Harry's blue eye, the eldest son, who was small, slighter than both Harry and Gary, who didn't like to fight and made friends easily. Somehow Danny earned everyone's respect without the bravado both his father and brother had to display to the outside world. Danny was bright and funny and could charm the birds out of the trees.

Pat shook her head. She watched her husband warily. Pat was no fool, she knew Gary didn't help himself either but Harry was far too hard on him. She looked over at them now and tried to diffuse the situation.

"Your teas in the oven, Harry, if you don't have it now, it'll be ruined," she said hoping it would distract her husband sufficiently to pull his attention away from Gary.

"Sit up you lazy bastard." Harry said to Gary ignoring her.

Gary stared up at him but did not move.

"Sit up, I said, lying there all day. You'll never make anything of yourself. You're nothing but a parasite."

Pat walked into the living room slowly, she did not realise it, but she was staring at her husband with a look of pure loathing on her face.

"Leave him alone, you've only just walked into the house and you're already picking a fight."

Pat looked at Ellie and Sally who continued to eat their tea, although not oblivious to the sudden change in atmosphere, her two youngest were so used to the constant arguing that they carried on eating, regardless. It was this which hurt Pat the most.

"Are you sticking up for him?" Harry said, looking at Pat.

Harry's words were slurred, and he stood swaying whilst staring at Gary with such hatred that Pat thought Harry should thank his lucky stars, she didn't have a blunt instrument in her hand as she wouldn't have trusted herself not to hit Harry right over the head with it the way he was acting.

"Why can't you be more like your brother?" Harry asked, "At least he's out there working, doing something with his life."

"Maybe because Gary's still at school," Pat said quietly.

Pat was finding it hard to keep her temper at bay as she knew it wouldn't help matters.

Gary sat up. She could see he was scared but he was trying hard not to show it. Gary had learnt the hard way not to show fear to his own father, it only made him worse. Gary continued to ignore his father, and Pat knew this was infuriating Harry even more. No wonder her oldest son, Danny, joined the merchant navy. He couldn't get out of the house fast enough but, Harry wouldn't admit this. Danny had now gone up even further in his father's estimation and Gary had become the epitome of all that was wrong in the world.

"Do you think it's alright do you?" Harry said addressing Pat, "That he can laze around all day, and you think it's perfectly normal?"

Here we go thought Pat, he's found his excuse to have a row but at least he's focused on me now rather than Gary.

"What do you mean, a man of his age, he's barely fifteen."

"Yeah, and at his age I was already working and paying keep to my mother."

"Why don't you just sit down, and I'll get your tea for you." Pat said still trying to remain calm.

"I suppose that lazy bastard's already eaten, has he?"

"Does it matter?" Pat asked.

"Yes, it does, I've been at work all day and I expect my tea to be on the table when I come home."

"It was but then I realised you must have gone the pub, so I put it in the oven."

"Are you begrudging me a pint now?"

"I don't care what you do but do you think I'm some sort of a mind reader, how am I supposed to know when you're going to waltz in here?"

This flummoxed Harry Pat noted but then it wasn't hard. Harry stood swaying; trying to stare at his wife but Pat knew he was finding it hard to concentrate.

"Yeah, well I'm here now and I'd appreciate it if I could have my tea."

"Well sit down and I'll bring it in."

Gary stood up, "I'm going out."

"Don't let him drive you out, son," Pat said.

"You're joking, aren't you? I'm not staying in here when he's in one of his moods."

Gary left the room, and she heard the vestibule door bang shut as he left the house. Harry stood contemplating his next move but then eventually he sat down next to Ellie and Sally and smiled at them.

"Hey kids, you been having a nice time?"

The mood changed and Pat sighed with relief and retreated back into the kitchen.

CHAPTER 7

These Boots are Made for Walkin'
Nancy Sinatra

Ellie and Sally were trying on Fiona's 'real' rabbit skin slippers that Fiona had recently bought. She had told Ellie and Sally that under no circumstances were they to go anyway near them. It had been a constant source of consternation in the house ever since because every time Fiona went out Ellie and Sally took turns to wear them. Even, Benny, the dog, seemed fascinated by them too and was constantly sniffing at them warily, trying to decide what they were.

"Let's have a look at those things," Harry said, and Ellie picked the slippers up and handed them to him. "Real rabbit skin hey?" Harry said and began to goad Benny with the slippers. "If they're real then our Benny will know."

"They are real dad," Sally said, "Our Fiona said she paid a fortune for them."

"Oh, did she now? Here's the real test. Let's see if our Benny thinks if they are."

Soon Benny was growling and biting the slippers. He even ran off with them at one point and hid beneath the settee growling and chewing at them. After a while Pat came in and saw what they were up to.

"Give us them, this minute," Pat said, "Our Fiona paid a fortune for them."

Pat tried to get them from Benny, and it took her a few good tugs before he released them. Benny stood wagging his tail and looking at Pat with his tongue hanging out and Ellie could have sworn he was smiling. Pat ignored Benny and put the slippers in the in the cupboard under the bureau. Benny kept sniffing at the door and whining.

"I don't know who's worse you or the kids," Pat said to Harry and left the room.

"Oh well," Harry said, "at least we now know they are real rabbit skin slippers."

Ellie and Sally snickered and Harry winked at them.

After a while Pat came into the living room. She had changed her outfit and was wearing a bit of makeup. Ellie and Sally stared at her in surprise. Their mum never used to go out but lately, every Thursday, she went out to 'one of her meetings'. They hated their mum going out, it did not feel right.

"Right, I'm off, Fiona's in the parlour; she's going to look after you."

"Where are you going?" Harry asked sullenly.

"You know quite well where I'm going."

"What to one of your Mother Reunion meetings?"

"Oh, you might put us down but at least I get to talk to people who actually listen to what I have to say."

"Whining no doubt about how bad you've got it, I suppose."

"Don't flatter yourself I've got more important things to talk about than you."

"Oh, have you now? Ever mention your kids stuck at home while you're out gallivanting."

"It's a pity you're not thinking of your children's welfare when you're in the pub." That seemed to stump him, Pat thought as he stopped and stared at her sourly.

Pat picked up a book that had been lying on the table and Harry, snatched it from her and stood looking at the title.

"Who's Kate Millet when she's at home?"

"A very intelligent woman who talks a lot of sense," Pat replied and snatched it back from him.

"That would be a first then."

"What do you know," Pat retorted.

"Load of nonsense if you ask me, wasting your time with a load of bloody feminists. They're all a bunch of lesbians if you ask me."

"Well good job I'm not asking you."

"You've got kids to look after and a house to run. They're just filling your head with a load of rubbish."

Pat smiled at him, "Do you think so? I've never heard so much sense in my life. Makes more sense than the rubbish you come out with."

"What do you mean by that?" Harry shouted but it was too late, Pat had kissed Ellie and Sally quickly and walked away. "What about the poor kids?"

"They're your poor kids too you know."

"You should be ashamed of yourself," Harry shouted after Pat.

Pat did not answer. Ellie and Sally looked at their dad expectantly.

"I'm going the pub," Harry said and with that he too left the house.

CHAPTER 8
You Should be Dancing
Bee Gees

Pat was the first one in the pub. She bought a round of drinks for her friends and took them over to their table. Once Pat had made herself comfortable Lisa Bancroft walked in. Pat hardly knew Lisa before the group, she was younger than Pat, so their paths hadn't crossed until Lisa came to work at Biltons. Unlike the rest of the women in their group, who were sewing machinists, Lisa worked in the packing department, so they rarely had a chance to talk to each other in work.

Lisa was a great laugh; she could see the humour even in the most serious of situations. Pat hadn't realised how intelligent Lisa was either, she was widely read and carried out most of the research for their discussions. Lisa would give them books or pamphlets to read, a lot of which went over Pat's head but then Lisa would explain them and made even the most complex of subjects seem simple.

"Hey, you," Lisa said coming over to her, "What's this I hear about you causing all this trouble at work?"

Pat sighed, "Where do I start? Do you know what went on?"

Lisa looked at her concerned, "I know that Kinnear one sacked you. What for?"

Pat said, "Wait till the others get here and I'll tell you the full story."

"Can't wait," said Lisa. "Are you okay though? Caused any problems at home?"

"I haven't even told Harry yet. I can't bring myself to do it as I know there's going to be all hell to pay."

Lisa shook her head, "Well he's going to find out sooner or later

Pat. Best take the bull by the horns. At least then you can give him your side of the story," Lisa said and then added, "Whatever that is."

"I know you're right, Lisa, but I just feel like such an idiot now."

"Oh, don't be like that Pat I don't know what's got on yet," she paused, "but I'm sure you did what you thought was best."

They were interrupted as Joan Meadows, Steph Smith and Paula Brown came in. The Group as such only comprised of five permanent members. Others joined them from time to time, but family and work commitments made the group sporadic, but it was the five ladies who were there tonight, who were its core members. Eventually they all sat down, staring at Pat expectantly, waiting for her to tell them exactly what had happened.

Pat took a huge breath and began to tell them. They gasped when she told them what Debbie accused Mr. Kinnear of doing, "That dirty bastard," Paula said but she was shushed so Pat could continue and then Pat told them her parting shot to Kinnear had been to call him Turnip Head. The women burst out laughing and Pat, for the first time in what seemed like weeks, began to laugh too.

Pat said, "It just came out."

"Sounds like that wasn't the only thing that just came out that day," Lisa said.

Steph who had been taking a sip of her drink nearly choked as she burst out laughing.

"Oh, you would have to lower the tone," Joan said tutting at Lisa.

Lisa banged her hand on the table. They all looked at her up expectantly as she stared at them with a stern expression on her face.

"Members of the Committee, order, order. Is this any way to behave?"

They all looked at Lisa giggling, waiting to see what the punch line would be.

"Thank you," Lisa continued, "Now that I have your undivided attention. I hereby declare that Kinnear hence forth should only ever be referred to as Turnip Head. Under no circumstances can he be called by any other name unless it is Pervert, Knob Head or in extreme circumstances Gob Shite."

They all laughed.

"Have you taken that down honourable secretary?" Lisa looked at them all in askance, "Is no one minuting this meeting? Steph weren't you the designated minute taker?"

"I forgot my pen," Steph shouted, as they all began to laugh in earnest once more.

Lisa continued, "I have made a decision and I want it to be duly noted and put on record." Lisa tried not to laugh, "How are we going to overthrow this patriarchal society if we don't have a bloody pen?"

"The pen is mightier than the sword," Pat shouted.

Maybe it was the relief of telling her story at long last or just having her friends with her, but Pat suddenly saw the funny side of her encounter with Mr. Kinnear and was finding it difficult to control her laughter.

"I have an eye liner and I have a beer mat. We will not be thwarted." Steph said grabbing the pencil from her handbag and waving a beer mat in the air.

This caused them all to laugh some more but eventually they calmed down and Lisa said, "No I'm sorry, we shouldn't joke about this, it's bloody serious."

"If you don't laugh, you'd cry," Paula said smiling at her friends. "It does the heart good to see the funny side."

They became serious once more.

"You did well, there," Joan said.

"I'm glad you think so, Joan, but I didn't achieve anything did I?"

Joan ignored her, "Did your Fiona say I called round the other day? I wanted to see if you were alright?"

"Our Fiona's in a world of her own, Joan she doesn't pass on messages." Pat said raising her eyes, "The mere suggestion." Once again, they all laughed.

"Anyway, I knew I was seeing you tonight, so I just left it. I thought it was best if we figured this all out together," Joan added.

"My God," Paula said, "The story Tina's been going around saying is that Kinnear," she stopped, "Sorry Turnip Head."

"Duly noted," Steph acknowledged.

Paula smiled but continued, "Is that Turnip Head reprimanded Debbie Walter's for wearing short skirts to work and she then became upset. You then went in all barrels blazing saying women can wear what they want for work and all hell broke loose."

"So, she didn't mention the words Turnip Head, at any point?" Lisa asked.

"No, funnily enough Lisa omitted to mention that little snippet of information," Joan replied.

"Funny that," Pat said sarcastically, "She didn't mention a lot of things, did she? I don't know what little respect I had for that woman has totally gone out the window now but obviously I'm not surprised at her behaviour but it's one thing not saying anything but it's another thing going round and spreading downright lies about the place."

"Obviously she's going to cover up for him," Lisa said shaking her head, "What happened to sisterhood, that's what I'd like to know?"

They all raised their eyebrows and shrugged.

"Has anyone seen Debbie?" Asked Pat. "I called round but her mum said she was out. I'm not too sure if I believed her but I only wanted to see if she was okay."

"She's still at work," Steph said, "but she's creeping round like a little mouse and looks on the verge of tears if anyone goes near her."

"Yes, and what's given credence to Tina's story is Debbie's wearing long pants for work and tops buttoned up to her neck," Paula said shaking her head.

"But now we know the real reason for that now, don't we," Joan sighed.

"It's sickening, isn't it," Lisa said. "No wonder he thinks he can get away with it."

"Well, he can, can't he?" Pat said, "In fact he has and all I'm left with is no job and a husband who's going to hit the roof when he finds out."

The women consoled Pat as best they could.

"We've got to do something about this," Lisa said her eyes shining with excitement. "I'm not going to let that bastard get away with it."

"But it's his word against Debbie's and she's only young. The fact of the matter is I'm not going to get my job back even if Debbie was to tell the truth. I don't think anyone would believe her even if she shouted it from the rooftops."

"I do," the women said as one.

"Yes, we do but where will it get us?" Pat asked feeling defeated.

"I don't know," Lisa said, "but there must be something we can do."

"I've never trusted him," Steph said. "I remember when I first started at Biltons and he had the cheek to ask if I wanted him to give me driving lessons after work. I knew what he was after."

"You never told me," Paula said. Steph and Paula were best

friends.

"I probably did, Paula, but it was years ago, when I first started." Steph carried on ignoring the confused expression on her friend's face. "I just said I'd ask my Albert to see what he thought of the idea and Kinnear backed off."

Albert, was Steph's husband. He worked at Biltons as a driver and had always had a reputation of being a bit of a hard knock, so it was no surprise to hear that Kinnear had not pursued the matter.

"It's funny isn't it," Joan said, "I've heard these rumours about him for years but I never really took them seriously. Thought it was all a bit like a Carry-On film, chasing his secretary around the desk, if you know what I mean."

"Yes, what's the expression," Lisa said, "A bit of slap and tickle, doesn't do any harm."

"I know it's disgusting really isn't it." Pat said. "I just saw red. Maybe I should have thought about the implications a bit more."

"No, I would have done exactly the same," Joan said, and they all tried not to smile as Joan, as lovely as she was, was a bit of a walk over and never said boo to a goose.

"That's the problem though isn't it," Lisa retorted, "they think they can get away with murder and it's up to us to show them they can't."

"Easier said than done," Steph said grimly.

"If we all have that attitude," Lisa said sincerely, "We'll never get anywhere. If we don't make a stand, we might as well be back in the dark ages."

"Yes, but what can we do?" Paula asked exasperated.

The women talked and the drinks flowed freely. The pub was becoming more packed, but the women were oblivious as they discussed the ins and outs of Pat's plight. They sat huddled in the snug, a room at the back of the pub away from the bar and the men, deep in conversation.

Smoke filled the air, and someone was playing the piano in the bar. For all of their talk there was a lively atmosphere and Pat felt better being surrounded by her friends. Some men they knew sent over a couple of rounds of drinks and the women shouted over their thanks, waving their drinks in the air at them. The women quickly turned away, too engrossed in what they were talking about to give them any more attention.

"The Mother's meeting in full swing then," one man shouted over.

"Of course," Lisa shouted back, and they all laughed.

Last orders rang and Lisa playfully shouted, "Meeting convened."

They all promised to meet the next week, hopefully with some ideas on how to proceed.

"If there's anything you need in the meantime, Pat, just let us know," Joan said.

"I'm okay don't worry, you're just what the doctor ordered, so thank you once again for being there for me."

"Oh, don't be daft," Lisa said seriously, "you know we've always got your back."

"I know," Pat said hugging her, "I don't know what I'd do without you lot."

Pat stopped as she felt tears coming into her eyes so laughed and pushed Lisa away so she could hug each woman in turn.

They parted with Pat, Steph and Paula saying Goodbye to Lisa and Joan who lived in the opposite direction. Pat walked arm in arm, with Steph and Paula on either side of her.

Pat felt a little bit lightheaded walking out into the fresh air. She breathed in, it was a lovely summer evening and a bit cooler compared to the heat of the day. Maybe my problems aren't as bad as I thought, Pat tried to convince herself. Biltons and all its problems hardly seemed important as Pat walked home with her two friends.

They turned into the main road toward Pat's. It was busier here with people walking back from the various pubs of the district. Pat saw some of Harry's mates and wondered where he was. Harry's probably gone for a Stay Behind in one of the pubs along the Dock Road, Pat thought but beyond that she did not give him another thought. At last, they reached the top of Pat's Street and parted company.

"Keep y' pecker up, Pat." Steph shouted as they walked away.

"I'll try my best," Pat smiled and watched them until they were out of sight and then turned into her street. Pat took a deep breath as she walked along. She knew seeing her friend's tonight was just the tonic she needed.

In the distance she could see the lights on in the front parlour where, no doubt, Fiona and Simon were sat listening to records. As Pat neared, she saw that the front door was standing open, it wouldn't be shut until she arrived home and she closed it behind her. Harry had a key, it was closed if he wasn't home before the pubs shut. Benny was on the front doorstep waiting for her and her heart swelled at the sight of him. She patted him as he jumped up at her.

Pat stopped before going in, savouring the warm night air. She looked at her front door, with its peeling paint work where Benny had scratched at it, on the few occasions it was closed. She sighed deeply to herself. Pat had wanted so much more for herself and her children but she had accepted her lot in life a long time ago. It mightn't be Buckingham Palace but it was still her home, and for better or worse she had to make the most of it.

All it had been a good night, Pat thought. She had been able to get a lot off her chest but in the great scheme of things she was still left with no job and she wasn't looking forward to the prospect of telling Harry the reasons why. She walked into her home and the warmth of her friends evaporated as she opened the vestibule door.

CHAPTER 9

Young Hearts Run Free
Candi Staton

Ellie and Sally were sitting watching the television when they heard a knock on the door. Ellie and Sally looked up at their mum. It was quite early and they were still having their breakfast. Ellie and Sally had still not ventured outside, otherwise the front door would have been open.

Pat stopped what she was doing whilst they all listened.

"Sshhh," Pat said as she peeped round the living room door, "I think it's your grandmother."

Ellie and Sally's eyes opened wide with fear. There was another rap on the door.

"Cooeee is anyone in?"

Ellie and Sally loved their grandmother. She wasn't like their mum's mum, their nan, who cuddled them and made jokes and dressed 'normal'. Their grandmother dressed as if she was going to church every day. She always wore a hat, sometimes with flowers on it and basically, in Ellie's mind at least, dressed like the Queen Mother.

Their Grandmother had been brought up in the country and this seemed to explain why she was so different to their Nan. Why they had to call her grandmother, and why when they went to visit her, she brought tea out on a tray and shortbread biscuits on a saucer. Why they had to sit quietly while the adults talked or Ellie corrected herself, whilst grandmother talked and boy could she talk. Ellie's grandmother talked incessantly and once in she stayed all day and did not go home until it was dark. The horror on their mum's face said it all.

"That's all I need," Pat said.

Three knocks this time.

"Now be quiet kids. I'm too busy today to have your grandmother in. She'll get fed up in a minute and go round to your uncle Terry's." Uncle Terry was their dad's brother.

The knocking continued and then stopped. They waited for a couple of minutes, hardly daring to breathe when Ellie and Sally noticed a movement in the back yard. Ellie watched as the back door slowly opened.

"Mum."

"Sshhh, I think she's gone."
Pat was still peering down the hall.

"Mum."

Their grandmother was now stood in the backyard and was approaching the window.

"Cooee."

Pat jumped. Ellie and Sally waved to their grandmother and then turned to watch their mum as she slowly turned around to see their grandmother waving at her through the window.

"Oh grandmother," Pat asked innocently, "What are you doing there?"

"Pardon?" Their grandmother mouthed through the window.

Pat shouted, "Didn't see you there."

"Yes, I'm fine," their grandmother shouted back, obviously not hearing what her daughter in law had said, "Just thought I'd pop round to see you. Didn't you hear me knocking?"

Pat's eyes opened wide. "You were knocking?" Pat shouted loud enough for their grandmother to hear. "No, we didn't hear a thing, did we kids?"

Ellie and Sally shook their heads.

"Hey, you two don't leave your grandmother in the backyard go and let her in."

Once grandmother came in, she said to them, "I thought you might have gone out for the day and then I remembered that you might be in the back room with the tele on and hadn't heard me and there you were just as I thought."

"Oh, that was lucky grandma. Good job you checked." Pat said through gritted teeth, "Would you like a cup of tea?"

"Oh yes please. I was only saying the other day that I hadn't been here for a few days and must pop in, in case you thought I was neglecting you. Now I have some sweets for Sally and Eleanor..." Ellie grimaced; it was only her grandmother who used her full title but she knew better than to ask her to call her Ellie. There would be a lecture for half an hour that Ellie wasn't a real name. So, Ellie ignored it and accepted the sweets gladly. They were about to make a sharp exit when their grandmother said, "Come on now kiss your grandma."

Ellie gulped as she watched her grandmother's pink wet lips pucker for a kiss and realised, she would have to succumb. Ellie couldn't believe what she had to do for a few sweets; she seriously considered it wasn't worth the sacrifice.

Their ordeal over Ellie and Sally started to make for the front door.

"Where are you two going?" Pat asked them.

"Going out to play, mum," Ellie said.

Pat's eyes narrowed.

"What? When your grandmother's made such a big effort to come and visit us?"

They squirmed. They knew their mum did not want to be left on her own. They were the diversion she needed.

"But mum," Sally ventured, "it's lovely outside, we want to go out and play."

"That's OK, Pat," grandmother said, "its fine. We can have a nice little chat while they play out."

"Oh no," Pat said, "that would be rude and anyway they love it when you visit. Now sit-down kids. They love to have a good old chin wag with their grandma, don't you kids?"

Ellie looked at her mum and Pat smiled. Ellie looked at her mum shrewdly, sometimes her mum could be so mean it was unbelievable. To make matters worse Ellie was sure that for some reason her mum was trying hard not to laugh.

An hour later and Ellie and Sally had still not orchestrated an escape. They sat patiently whilst their grandmother told them about her shopping trip over to Liverpool, about what she bought on her shopping trip over to Liverpool. How much it cost her when she went on her shopping trip over to Liverpool and how the price of things had shot up since the last time, she went on a shopping trip over to Liverpool. It never occurred to their grandmother that they were not remotely interested in her shopping trip over to Liverpool and the only thing on their mind was to go out and play.

Ellie was just about to put her foot down and demand she be allowed out when their mum said the magic words, "Why don't you two go out and play."

Ellie and Sally did not need asking twice as they raced for the door. Pat gave them one last tormented look as they left her to her fate. Still, it was not going to be that easy as just as they were about to make it to the front door they heard:

"Do you two know anything about Simon's scooter?"

Ellie looked up to see Fiona coming down the stairs. She was wearing a matching pink chiffon nightdress and nightgown. Her hair was in curlers but her make-up had been applied and even at this time of the morning Fiona still looked as if she had just stepped out of the pages of a magazine. Ellie and Sally noticed that she was wearing her 'real' rabbit skin slippers. They were grey and white with a tiny, little mule heel. Ellie noticed they looked a little ragged round the edges, but it must have escaped Fiona's notice or they would have known about it.

"What?" Ellie asked playing for time.

"Simon's scooter. It was found up the back entry the other night. It took Simon hours to find it." Ellie tried desperately not to smile. "Did you have anything to do with it?"

Ellie was astounded to see that Fiona's question was solely directed at her.

"Me?" Ellie said in mock innocence, "No of course not. Why me?"

Fiona's eyes narrowed as she watched Ellie's expression carefully.

"Because you're never far away from trouble."

"I don't know anything about it."

"Are you sure?"

Ellie had to think quickly.

"Grandma's in there," she said and watched as Fiona physically blanched.

"What?"

"Grandma, Fiona's here," Ellie shouted through to the back room.

"I'll kill you Ellie, keep your voice down."

Fiona turned to go back up the stairs, for some reason forgetting her cross examination of Ellie.

"Fiona is that you?" They heard their mum say, "Come in and see your grandma. She's dying to hear all about your wedding."

"Is that you Fiona, oh I'm dying to hear all about it..."

Ellie and Sally watched as Fiona stood standing on the stairs, her knuckles white as she clutched hold of the banister. Fiona's body was half turned as if ready to flee but she stayed deathly still as if she was caught in headlights.

"You wait till I get my hands on you," Fiona said.

Their grandmother popped her head round the living room door and Benny sneaked past her and stood looking at Fiona. Fiona was smiling at her grandmother.

"Hi, grandma, lovely to see you I was just getting ready."

"Oh, don't worry about that, you're lovely as you are."

Ellie smiled up at Fiona and did not notice Benny's hackles rise. She watched with quiet satisfaction as Fiona slowly walked down the stairs. Fiona shoved past Ellie and Sally and was about to enter the living room when suddenly Benny pounced on Fiona's feet.

"Benny! What are you doing?" Fiona squealed as Benny playfully bit at her slippers. Fiona kicked out at Benny. "Get this stupid mutt off me."

"Don't kick our Benny," Ellie shouted.

"What? What the hell's he doing? He's gone mad." Benny had clenched firmly onto one of Fiona's slippers, trying to wrestle it away from her.

Their grandmother came into the fray, "Benny get off Fiona's slippers." No one was surprised when Benny ignored her request. "Benny you naughty dog, get off Fiona now."

"Grandma, it's the slippers. He thinks they're rabbits," Sally shouted. Ellie tried not to laugh.

"Why would he think they were rabbits?" Their grandmother asked.

"Because their real rabbit skin slippers, grandma," Ellie and Sally shouted as one.

Fiona was now screaming, kicking her legs back and forth and shouting, "Benny get off me, do you hear."

Grandma shouted, "Quick Pat, come out here, Benny's attacking Fiona's feet."

Pat ran out and tried to pull Benny away from Fiona but by now Benny thought it was a game.

"Benny, I'll bloody kill you if you don't stop," Pat shouted.

"What's got into him, Pat? He's gone mad." The grandmother asked quite calmly under the circumstances.

Fiona continued to swing her foot wildly, clinging hold of the sides of the door as if her life depended upon it. Benny was growling and chewing at the slipper, jumping backward and forward with every movement of Fiona's foot. Fiona tried to run away and Benny slid across the floor and would not let go. At last Benny made one last effort and was able to wrestle a slipper from Fiona's foot. He ran to the corner of the hall and hunched up he began to gnaw and growl at the slipper, his tail all the while wagging like mad.

"Mum," Fiona wailed her curlers in disarray and her nightgown hanging forlornly around her arms, "Benny's got one of me real rabbit skin slippers."

Ellie and Sally ran into the sanctuary of the street their laughter uncontrollable. They did not notice Benny following them, his prey still firmly gripped in his mouth.

CHAPTER 10

Tonight's The Night (Gonna Be Alright)

Rod Stewart

Ellie and Sally were lucky in the fact that their Fiona had taken them out a few times to New Brighton Baths and Harrison Park whilst some of the other kids just hung around the street all day but apart from these little excursions, they could generally please themselves. They filled their time by climbing walls or mooching around, mostly down the prom. They had loads of places to go and there were no restraints on their movements. As long as they all stuck together and were back for tea no one asked where they had been.

It seemed perfect but for the rumours that their street, in fact their whole neighbourhood, was going to be knocked down. Ellie noticed that as each house became vacant workmen would turn up and brick up the doors and windows, but Ellie chose to ignore these tell-tale signs and concentrate her attention on the fact that one of these abandoned houses would make a perfect den.

Ellie, Sally, Billy and their other friends, Karen, Gavin Farrell and Joanne Farrell were stood outside the front door of where a Mr and Mrs. Hughes used to live. Benny of course was in attendance and stood amongst them as they all stared at the bricks where once the front door had stood. This, they had decided, would be their den as it stood at the top of their street away from the prying eyes of their parents. Various toolboxes had been raided, hammers quickly acquired and were now being used to knock a sizeable hole into the bricks.

Benny was the first to squeeze past them and peered inside, then the children followed suit and gathered around him so they too could take a closer look. Their initial thoughts concerned ghosts of one description or another. It was dark. It had never occurred to them that behind the brickwork the front door would still be intact and be a further deterrent for entry, but it stood open hanging from its hinges, and they were able to glimpse the dark recesses of the hall. They had thought ahead, this had been a well-planned execution, candles and matches were at the ready.

"Go on Gavin you're the biggest you go in first," Billy said.

"Why me?"

They all looked at Gavin. None of the children actually liked him. He bullied his younger sister and brothers mercilessly and every time anyone allowed him to play with them it did not take him too long before he started to grate on their nerves. They found it a bit odd as well that at his age, he was at least three years older than Ellie, that he wanted to hang round with them, but they all knew that older lads in their neighbourhood would not put up with him so unfortunately, he inevitably ended up hanging round with them.

Gavin tried to think, he did not want to be the first in the house and the argument Billy used was compelling enough for him to consider. Consider how to get out of it. Gavin looked at the opening and then an idea occurred to him.

"No, Billy you're smaller than me. I might get stuck and then none of us will be able to get in."

Billy stood tall, "Alright Gavin I'll go in but it's you who's the chicken.

"It just makes sense," Gavin muttered.

Billy scrambled in and a candle was soon lit. The hall became brighter, and Billy felt slightly cheered by the fact.

"Come on then. What you waiting for?" He asked everyone.

Suddenly Gavin became very brave and squeezed himself in.

"What you waiting for scaredy cats?" Gavin sneered at them.

"Shut up Gavin," Ellie said, "you're already getting on our nerves as it is."

Once inside the hall was bright with their various candles. It seemed spooky and unreal. They began to inspect their new abode. Some furniture had been left. The film 'Calamity Jane' came to Ellie's mind, the one where the two women fixed up their cabin and put nice clean curtains up on the windows and flowers in a vase. They could have this place looking lovely she thought, her imagination on over drive.

They were all excited. It was quiet and peaceful in the house and with the window's boarded up it was cool and tranquil compared to outside. Gavin started to stomp around, looking into all the rooms and had even gone upstairs not the least bit afraid all of a sudden.

Gavin came back down and looked at Ellie and said, "I know we can be mum and dad and they can be our kids."

Ellie's face was a picture, "Ew, get lost Gavin."

"Ah," Sally said, "Gavin fancies you, Ellie."

"No, I don't it's just that we're older."

Billy was laughing his head off, "Gavin wants to play mummy and daddy. How old are you?"

"Shut it Billy or I'll knock you out."

"Yeah sure."

Billy laughed and although he was only little he never backed down from Gavin and for some reason Gavin never carried out his numerous threats of 'knocking him out', 'beating him up', 'kicking his face in' however much Billy wound him up.

Half an hour later and they were bored.

"It needs some more furniture, there's nowhere to sit down."

"So, where we going to get that from then?" Joanne, Gavin's sister, asked.

"There're loads of empty houses round here. There's got to be some furniture in them. It's not nicking or anything," Billy said.

***

A few days later Billy and Karen came running into the den to say they had found a settee in a house in Gladstone Road. Gladstone Road didn't have as many bricked up houses as their street, it was still more or less intact. When they arrived at the house Ellie was amazed to find out that there was still a lot of furniture inside, but it was the settee, they were interested in. They all stood staring at it. It was a bit old fashioned, Ellie thought but it would do.

"It's ok in here, isn't it?" Ellie said and everyone agreed.

"Why don't we make this our den?" Karen asked.

Although they were all tempted to move dens for some reason, they felt a sense of disloyalty for their original den so decided against it.

They all agreed the settee was in quite good condition. In other words, it was perfect. Between them they managed to get it out of the living room, through the kitchen and into the back yard and were just taking a breather when they heard a shout.

"Oy, what are you up to?" A man stood looking at them from the door of the kitchen. "That's my settee you've got there."

They all stared at him in surprise. Where had he come from?

"I don't think so," Billy said, always the cheekier one out of all of them and they were all spurred on by his attitude. "No one lives here."

"Yeah, we found it," Karen added.

"Finders keepers," Ellie said not to be left out.

"Yeah," Sally joined in, "loser's weepers."

"You cheeky sods. Put that down now."

The man looked angry, and they quickly realised they had taken the wrong tact with him. Ellie stared at the back yard door, she wondered whether they would be able to run whilst carrying a settee between them but knew they wouldn't get far.

"What on earth do you think you're doing?" The man asked staring at them one by one.

They stared at him in silence until eventually Ellie said, "It's for our den."

"You're what?"

"Our den, we want it for our den," Billy said meeting the man's stare.

"Well, you can't bloody well have it," the man said stepping towards them. "It belongs to me so put it down now." They all stared at him feeling less sure now of their possession rights. "Do you want me to phone the police? I could get you done for burglary?"

"We haven't done anything?" Billy said his voice more subdued, "We haven't nicked anything. We thought the house was empty."

"Well, it's not and how on earth did you get in here?"

"The kitchen door was open," Billy said.

He had in fact squeezed himself through the kitchen window but he was not going to mention that under the circumstances.

The man looked puzzled and then said, "The door wasn't open when I left," but then he raised his voice and said, "That doesn't matter anyway. This is my house and I live here."

They looked at each other shocked, Billy said, "Like we said, we thought it was empty."

"Well, it's not." He seemed to gather his thoughts and asked, "Have you taken anything else?"

"No, Sally said affronted, "We only need a settee."

To their surprise the man laughed and said, "Oh is that all?"

"We didn't know anyone was still living here," Gavin at last joined in.

Ellie whispered, "How do we know it's his house. He could be anyone."

The man shot a look at Ellie, "Hey you cheeky little thing I'm telling you it's my house. Do you want to see what the Police have to say?"

"No," Ellie mumbled looking at her feet.

"We didn't know," Billy said pleadingly. "We honestly thought it was an empty house."

"Wait there," the man said and walked back into the house. They stood still holding the settee until he came back and said, "Well it doesn't look like anything else has been taken, apart from the settee that is."

"We haven't taken anything Mister, we just thought the house was empty and we needed a settee for our den," Billy tried to explain once more.

"Look kids," he said his manner seeming to soften, "you've got it wrong. I live here. I'm in the middle of moving out and the removal van's parked up outside."

"Well, we didn't know, honest." Billy said.

"You know I really should call the police."

"Oh, don't do that. We didn't know, honest," Gavin said cutting in.

The man shook his head, "I can't believe this I've only been away for a couple of days and this happens."

They all looked at him, realising he was telling the truth and they could be in serious trouble. As one they all started to put the settee down and stood away from it as if it was no longer any of their concern.

"Oy Mick," the man shouted, "come and have a look at this."

Another man appeared and he told him the story and for some reason the two men began to laugh.

"I can't believe it," the first man said, "five minutes later and they would have had it away."

Although they hoped they weren't going to get into trouble Ellie looked at the settee longingly. They had been so close to having it and she felt aggrieved that they had lost their prize possession.

"Sorry," they all said.

"I don't know I must be going soft in my old age," and much to their delight he dug his hand into his pocket and took out a fifty pence piece. "Go and get yourself some sweets but leave my settee alone for Christ's sake."

Ellie couldn't believe their luck but her delight turned to disgust when the man handed the fifty pence piece to Gavin.

"Thanks mate," Gavin said and pocketed it quickly.

They all went to walk away, "Where do you think you're going?" The man asked. They stared at him in confusion. "You can bloody well help me get it in the van. That fifty pence weren't for nothing you know."

"Oh okay," Gavin said. "Come on you lot, heave."

They all lifted the settee, with lots of giggling and laughter they managed to get it into the hallway. The two men watched them for a while, laughing at their efforts until at last they took hold of either end of the settee and told them they could go. He didn't have to tell them twice and they turned on their heels deciding it was best to leave before he changed his mind.

"Now I don't want to see your faces round here again or I really will call the police," the man shouted after them as they ran back through the house and towards the back entry.

"We won't," Ellie shouted as they retreated.

"Sorry," Billy said for good measure.

"Hey Gavin," Ellie said when they were safely out of earshot, "Don't think you're keeping that fifty pence all to yourself!"

"Never said I was."

"Yeah, well we all know what you're like."

"Yeah, so hand it over Gavin," Billy said, "or I'll knock you out."

The two men watched as the children left.

"You're too soft," Mick said.

"Bleeding hell we got up to worse when we were kids."

"Did we? I don't ever remember trying to nick furniture right from under people's noses."

The two men shook their heads and began to laugh once more.

CHAPTER 11
Lean on Me
Bill Withers

It didn't take too long before Ellie and her friends were bored of the den. There was only so much sitting around indoors they could do. Especially when the weather was so lovely and warm with not a cloud in sight. The den abandoned they were back where they were happiest. Outdoors, playing games or riding their bikes, they had a neighbourhood to explore and adventures to be had. However, Ellie's carefree days were marred when she began to notice that Karen seemed out of sorts.

At first Ellie didn't pay too much attention, if Karen wanted to mope around that was up to her but all the same it would be nice if Karen cheered up a little. Karen didn't seem to want to come out and play with them anymore and had taken to sitting on her step looking glum. Still, it came as a shock to Ellie when Karen eventually made her announcement. Karen and her family were moving. The Council had offered them a house in an estate a few miles from where they lived, but as the news sunk in as far as Ellie was concerned it might as well be in Timbuctoo.

"That's miles away," Ellie said to Karen accusingly.

"It's not that far and you can come down and see me all the time and we'll have a garden and a bathroom and everything."

"So, what it won't be as good as being round here."

Karen looked sad. Ellie had always known Karen and apart from Billy she was her closest friend.

"It's not fair," Ellie said.

Karen looked confused. She had tried to convince herself that Ellie would be pleased for her but obviously she had been kidding herself. Initially Karen hadn't wanted to move but when her mum and dad had told her she had no choice in the matter she had tried her hardest to look on the bright side. It hadn't worked though. Karen would miss all her friends and she knew it wasn't fair.

Karen felt disloyal towards her friends, as if somehow it was her fault. That was why she had found it so hard to tell everyone.

Karen tried to reason with Ellie and said, "It's not like you haven't got anyone else to play with."

"I know but it just won't be the same without you, your Tracie and Mel."

"It's not my fault," Karen said and decided to go in. She didn't want to see the look of hurt on Ellie's face. Karen felt like crying. "I'm going in," Karen said and walked quickly away from Ellie who was left staring after her. Ellie's mouth left wide open, catching flies, her mum would have said if she had seen her.

Ellie went in. Her mum was in the kitchen and Ellie sat down at the table with her head bowed.

"What's up, Ellie?"

"Karen's moving and they say the whole street is getting knocked down."

Pat sighed and sat down opposite her.

"Nothing's definite yet Ellie but the Simpson's haven't even got a bathroom, so they have to move out. There's talk of all the houses being knocked down but it's not for certain. They could be getting renovated."

"Renovated?" Ellie asked encouraged by her mum's words. "What's that?"

"It's when they do the houses up. Put in bathrooms with hot water and a toilet inside."

Ellie thought of Karen's house compared to her own. Ellie had never appreciated the fact that they had a bathroom. Harry had put an extension of sorts on their house after they'd moved in. It never occurred to her that Karen did not have a bathroom and for the first time she wondered how they kept clean. She knew Billy did not have a bathroom but he went down the local swimming baths where they had rooms with baths in. Billy was always made up when he was going to take a bath and never hid the fact. In fact, Ellie wanted to go with Billy to see what it was like and always felt envious of him when he went.

"We're alright though, mum, aren't we? We've got a bathroom and everything."

"Well yes if you can call it that."

Ellie's bathroom was more of a lean-to running from the kitchen. The roof leaked and the tiles on the floor were cracked and worn but Ellie saw none of these faults.

"So do you think they'll do up Karen's house up and then she can move back in?"

"No, they're going for good Ellie I'm afraid you're just going to have to get used to it."

"But why are they going miles away?"

"That's the only place available if you want to move out quickly. You've got to wait otherwise."

"Are we waiting to move then?"

"If I had my way we would."

"Why mum, I love it here?"

"Well, it's not exactly ideal Ellie. It's too small for us all for a start and it's falling down around our ears."

Ellie looked puzzled. She did not know what her mum was going on about.

"I don't think it is," Ellie said, "I love our house. I don't want to move."

"Well, you'll be alright then," her mum said, "because neither does your dad."

"Doesn't he?"

"No."

"Why not?"

"Well, in his eyes," her mum put on a gruff voice and Ellie conceded that it did sound like her dad, so she laughed as her mother continued, "because we, no that's wrong, because *he* bought this house and the council can't tell him what to do. And, according to the Oracle none of us are moving. Using your father's own words, *a man's house is his castle and no one is going to tell me what to do.*"

"But that's good then isn't it, mum?"

"Is it?" Pat asked and then she looked at Ellie and said, "Look love it hasn't happened yet, so no need to worry."

Ellie felt a deep sense of relief. No one was going to brick up her house, not if her dad had anything to do with it and her mum had told her not to worry. Ellie failed to notice the sad expression in her mum's eyes or the worried frown that creased her brow. She ran out happy to play now that her mum had put her mind at rest so did not see her mum crying in the kitchen.

Pat had dried her eyes by the time Harry came in. He looked tired she thought but her sympathy for him was waning. He had changed. The man she married had a sense of humour, looked after her and cared how she was feeling. This man she barely recognised. They rarely talked, all he seemed to do was come in and argue if not with herself then Gary or Fiona. Ellie and Sally still adored their dad and for the most part they were able to avoid the worst of his moods. Pat felt sad, this was not the life she envisaged for herself and she was sure Harry hadn't either.

Pat was worn out with all the arguing and the day-to-day struggle but if they worked together, it would make life easier. Make it all worthwhile. She didn't even know if she loved him anymore. Harry was difficult to love these days. All he seemed to care about was his mates and the pub. He gave her keep but the rest of the money he spent on himself. Would it kill him to give her a bit extra? The kids needed new shoes and she dreaded asking him for any more money. She would usually buy them out of her wages but she didn't even have that anymore. She looked at him and realised that not only did she not love him she didn't even like him anymore.

Harry sat down in front of the television and could see Pat pottering around the kitchen. He was bone tired. He had been working on a building site all day and his back ached. He looked at his wife. When had she changed? She looked tired and worn out, why didn't she make an effort anymore? Would it kill her to dress up a bit, do her hair and make him feel that she was still attracted to him? God, he worked hard enough was it too much to ask that she paid him a bit of attention? She was more interested in her stupid meetings than him these days.

Harry was relieved that the living room was empty for a change. Normally Gary was sprawled out on the couch watching tele like the bone, idle lazy bastard he was or Fiona was flapping around doing her hair and asking him for money for this idiotic wedding. What did she want to marry that waste of space Simon for anyway? She could do much better.

He was proud of his daughter but she was wasting her time on a gob shite like Simon. What annoyed him the most though was that Pat encouraged it all. She should be telling Fiona that there was no rush to be married and as for Gary, he dreaded to think what would become of him.

As far as Harry was concerned it was all Pat's doing. She spoilt the children, stuck up for them, and belittled him in front of them. Pat undermined everything he did. He had had enough of it all. The only place he was respected was in the pub with his mates or at work. He certainly didn't receive any respect at home.

"What's for tea," he asked.

"Pie and mash," Pat called in.

"Is that all?"

"No, there's veg and gravy," Pat said exasperated.

What did he expect her to provide with the money he gave her? She had spent ages cooking that pie, it was homemade not shop bought. Sometimes she wondered why she bothered. There was a time when he used to love her homemade pies. He hadn't bothered to answer her and she heard him switching over to watch the news. She put his tea out on the table.

"Here's your tea," she said.

Harry stood up and turned the television up and sat at the table. He didn't thank her and Pat walked into the kitchen wondering where it had all gone wrong.

CHAPTER 12

Show Me The Way

Peter Frampton

Ellie and Sally had been woken up by a huge row. They could hear their mum and dad shouting at one another downstairs.

"What's up now?" Sally asked her voice still slurry with sleep.

Ellie shrugged, her heart was beating fast, she had woken up before Sally and had been listening to her mum and dad in a daze. Ellie was worried about her mum. Her dad was always shouting at their mum.

"Where are you going?" Sally asked as Ellie got out of her bed.

"I'm going to see what they're arguing about."

"I'm coming with you," Sally said slipping out of her bed and joining her sister.

Ellie and Sally crept along the landing and sat huddled at the top of the stairs frightened in case they were heard and chased back to bed. They could now hear their mum and dad quite clearly.

"You did what?" Harry shouted. "Why on earth did you get involved?"

"I only went into have a word with him but his attitude just made me mad." Pat sounded exasperated.

"Oh, come of it," Harry said sarcastically, "It's these stupid meetings. Who do you think you are, some kind of radical feminists out to defend the rights of all of your repressed sisters?"

Ellie and Sally heard their mum laugh, "Don't be so bloody ridiculous. No woman should have to put up with that in the workplace, but it doesn't make me some kind of radical feminists. Even if you do know what that actually means."

"Don't be putting me down with all your clap trap. The point is you didn't even have the respect to tell me. If Sam Cummingham hadn't told me, when would you have got round to telling me?"

"I was waiting for the right moment."

"The right moment, I felt a right lemon when he told me. My own wife had lost her job, attacked her boss and I knew nothing about it. I don't know what's got into you. I really don't."

"Why would you have patted me on the back and said, well done?" Pat asked.

"No and why would I? It's not up to you to go round fighting other people's battles."

"So, you think it's perfectly acceptable behaviour then?" Pat asked.

"I'm not saying it's acceptable, but you've only got Debbie Walters word that's what's gone on. She could have been exaggerating."

"Exaggerating? You've known Debbie Walters since she was a baby, I don't even think she's even had a boyfriend, let alone enough experience to make up a story like that. She's scared of her own shadow. You know that as well as I do."

"Well, you don't know what gets into these young girl's heads. Maybe he'd been nasty to her, and she wanted to get her own back or something?"

"Oh, don't be so naive, you didn't see the state she was in. She'd have to be a damn good actress to put on a performance like that."

"What do you know?" Harry said losing ground but then his voice rose once more, "But he's right, isn't he?"

"Who's Right?" Pat was lost for a moment wondering what Harry was talking about now.

"Mr. Kinnear. He was right."

"Right about what?" Pat asked bewildered.

"What is she doing going to work with a skirt right up her arse if she's that bloody innocent?"

It was at this point Pat's voice rose in volume to match her husband's.

"So, she asked for it did she?"

"Yes, if you want to put it like that. Putting all her wares on the table what did she think would happen?"

"I don't believe you, maybe he should have just raped her there and then and you could have stood round and applauded him."

"I didn't say that." Harry shouted back, "you're putting words in my mouth but whatever happened you've lost your job, defending some young girl, who if she didn't like it should have just left."

"That's not the point, she shouldn't have to leave. He should behave himself. Does he think he has the god given right to put his hand up a young girl's skirt just because he happens to be her boss?"

"Oh, he was probably only messing around, if you ask me, she sounds like she was just being hysterical."

"Well, good job I'm not asking you isn't it." Pat paused, "Don't you get it Harry, he's got no right to act like that. I mean what type of world are we living in if a young girl can't go to work without some lecherous bastard manhandling her?"

"Oh, behave yourself, with your feminist boloney. It's gone on for centuries, it's not the end of the world, is it. Certainly not enough to lose your job over."

"I think it was. I couldn't just stand there and do nothing."

"That's exactly what you should have done," Harry shouted.

"I was so angry I didn't know what I was doing." Pat paused for breath. "All I know if it was our Fiona would you be so bloody complacent then?"

"But it's not is it. It's bloody Debbie Walters and she's still working there and you're not. You have a family. She's still living at home, getting wages and with a mother and father to support her."

Silence reigned and Ellie and Sally strained to hear their mum's voice.

"Look Harry, you should have heard him. The things he said. I just lost it okay. You would have knocked his lights out, if you'd been there."

"That's not the point, you've lost your job and the way things are going I could be losing mine soon."

"Why what do you mean? Has something happened?"

"No, but I could and then where would we be? Money doesn't grow on trees you know."

"Well, if it's that bad why don't you stop going out so much?"

"You're begrudging me a pint now?" Harry's voice had raised once more.

"I'm just saying if things are that bad, then maybe we'll have to start tightening our belts until I find another job."

"Piss off, it's the only enjoyment I have."

Silence.

"Well, that's nice to know," Pat said.

The voices died down and Ellie and Sally returned to their bed. They whispered to one another.

"No wonder mum's been in a terrible mood lately," Ellie said.

"I know I wondered what had happened. Especially when she didn't go to the hairdressers last Friday."

"I know I thought that was odd too."

"So, what do you think has happened and what's it got to do with Turnips?" Sally asked.

"Turnips?" Ellie asked.

"Yes, I heard something about turnips as I woke up."

"I don't know but Debbie Walters has got something to do with it and it's got something to do with short skirts and filing cabinets, that's all I know."

"When did you hear that?"

"I heard mum and our Fiona talking the other day but I didn't know what they were going on about, I didn't know she'd been sacked for hitting her boss."

"She hit her boss?" Sally asked impressed.

"I think so," Ellie didn't seem quite so certain now.

Ellie and Sally mused about this for a few minutes.

"All I know is all our Fiona was worried about was her stupid wedding."

"Yeah, but can you blame her. Mum was moaning about not being able to afford buying our bridesmaid dresses and everything. I was looking forward to choosing my bridesmaid dress," Sally grumbled.

"You're as bad as our Fiona." Ellie said.

"No, I'm not."

"Yes, you are. You're going to grow up just like her. All you'll want is a boyfriend and to get married."

"What's wrong with that?" Sally asked incredulously.

"There's more to being a woman than getting married and having kids you know, Sally."

"You're sounding just like me mum now," Sally hissed back.

They stopped as the bedroom door opened. Ellie and Sally looked up to see their mum standing looking at them.

"Are you two still awake," Pat asked knowing full well they were.

"Yeah," they mumbled.

"Have you lost your job mum?" Ellie asked.

Pat sighed, "Yes love but it's nothing for you to worry about. I'll find another one, don't you fret."

"What's dad so mad about then mum?" Sally asked.

"Me standing up for what I believe, I think."

"I thought it was because you'd called your boss Turnip Head," Sally said.

Pat laughed, "Should have called him a lot worse than that Sally but yeah that was part of it." Pat sat down on Sally's bed and stroked her hair and looked at her two youngest daughters. "Now go to sleep. I'm sorry if we woke you up, I've tried to stop rowing with your dad," Pat said.

"But it's hard," Ellie answered.

"Yes," Pat laughed, "but I shout too and it's not fair on you two."

"We're alright mum," Sally said, "We're used to it."

"I know," Pat replied, "and that's the worst part." Pat paused and took a deep breath, "Now come on get some sleep, it's getting late."

"Maybe now you're not working we can go out more mum," Ellie said as it occurred to her that now her mum wasn't working maybe they could.

"Yes, that would be nice, Ellie. Maybe when I've got a bit more time we can go over to Liverpool and get you your uniform for your new school."

"Yes," Ellie squealed, "I can't wait."

"And, me too," Sally said.

"Yes, and you too Sally. Now come on get some sleep. I'm worn out with it all. I'm having an early night too."

Their mum kissed them and left them, their eyes growing heavy and before they knew it, they were fast asleep.

CHAPTER 13
Born to Run
Bruce Springsteen

Ellie was bored and was kicking a ball despondently against the pavement when she spotted Billy riding his back towards her.

"You know that Turnip Head?" He asked as he skidded to a halt beside her.

"Yeah." Ellie said, she'd told Billy all about Turnip Head sacking her Mum.

"I know where he lives."

Ellie looked at him as she couldn't believe her ears.

"How do you know that?"

"My mum knows a woman who cleans for him," Billy said.

"Is it far?" Ellie asked innocently.

"It's in New Brighton. We could bike down there."

Now, this was a cool idea. She'd like to see where Mr. Turnip Head lived. He was now Ellie's arch enemy after she found out he had sacked her mum. For some reason he chased young women round his office all day and although Ellie didn't know why he did this she did know it upset the young women involved. She was sure they could get their own back on him.

Suddenly the day had taken on a whole new aspect and Ellie was no longer bored.

Ellie got her bike from out of the hall and joined Billy outside. He and Ellie rode up to the small park which had recently been built on a bit of scrub land at the top of their street, to see if Sally was still there. They found her there playing with Joanne Farrell. After explaining what they were planning to do Joanne decided to come along too. Sally and Joanne ran home to grab their bikes.

Joanne came back and told them she had seventy pence she had saved up and would buy them all some sweets and lemonade along the way. They all thanked her and Joanne's face lit up. Ellie thought, she's good like that, Joanne, not like her older brother Gavin but then Ellie remembered, she'd always called Joanne a wimp and maybe she shouldn't any more.

They decided they'd bike along the prom and when they got to New Brighton, they'd find Turnip Head's house from there. They rode along the prom with the sun shining down. It was a long journey and they tried not to become distracted by the sea and the sand, and the million and one things they passed along the way.

They eventually arrived at New Brighton pier and turned off towards the houses. The fun fare beckoned them and they could hear the screams and laughter coming from out of the Palace fair ground and chose to ignore it. They were on a mission and nothing was going to stop them. At last, they stopped to have a look around and felt as if they had stumbled into an alien world.

The houses they rode past were very imposing, most of them had gardens in the front with driveways and the streets were trees lined, it was very different from where they lived. It seemed quiet and deserted as they rode along.

Billy had written down the name of the street on a piece of paper he had tucked into his jeans pocket but by now they all knew the address by heart. Unfortunately, they still weren't sure exactly where it was, and it took them a while to build up the confidence to ask someone for directions. Thankfully they were told it wasn't too far away so they all rode along laughing and joking and shouting:

"Turnip Head we're coming to get you."

"Let's get a drink," Ellie shouted at last. "I'm dying of thirst."

"Me too," Billy shouted.

So, it was decided before they went any further, they'd best buy a drink. They rode along scouring the streets until at last they saw a row of shops with a few kids milling around outside. They all looked at one another wondering whether it was a good idea to approach, as strange kids weren't tolerated in their own area and these kids may feel the same but their thirst got the better of them, so they decided to brazen it out. The other kids barely moved so they had to walk through them to enter the shop. The other kids stood back eyeing them suspiciously. Billy scowled at them, but Ellie told him not to in case they were beaten up.

Joanne bought them a drink and a chocolate bar each and warily they walked back out of the shop and onto the street. The kids were still outside, in fact it looked like a few more had joined them.

"Where you from?" One of the kids asked them as they walked back through them.

"Seacombe," Billy said with pride.

"What you doing round here?" Another asked.

"What's it to you?" Ellie said without thinking of the consequences.

"Just asking"

They stood facing one another.

"My cousin lives in Seacombe," one of the other kids said at long last.

"What's his name?" Billy asked.

"Jason Price."

"I know your Jason dead well," Billy said. "He goes to our school."

"Next time you see him tell him his cousin, Tim, was asking about him," Tim said.

"I will," Billy said.

They walked away their hearts pounding knowing they had avoided a tricky situation.

"Good job he was Jason Price's cousin, or I would have kicked his head in," Billy said and they all laughed, as Billy couldn't fight his way out of a wet paper bag.

They sat on a bench with their bikes laying in a pile in front of them whilst they drank and ate their chocolate bars. They all felt better after that and before long they all picked up their bikes and resumed their journey. They knew they were close but they still had to ask someone else for directions before they eventually felt they were on the right track.

"I think this is it," Sally said at last.

They looked down yet another quiet cul-de-sac. They felt as if they had been wondering around in the heat for hours and it must be some kind of mirage.

"Sycamore Drive. That's it," Billy said.

They rode slowly up the street, looking to their left and right. The street was quiet and empty with not a soul in sight. It was not until they were half way up the street that they saw a yellow sports car on one of the drives.

"That's his car," Ellie said. "I've seen it in the car park at Biltons."

"You sure?" Joanne asked.

"I'm sure of it. It was bright yellow like that one. You don't see many of them around, it has to be his."

"It must be the right address then," Sally said.

"What do we do now?" Billy asked.

"We'll sit and wait. See if we can spot him."

They waited, hiding behind a hedge in a neighbouring garden, no one came out to ask them what they were doing so they felt safe for the time being.

"Look there he is."

They could see a short fat man standing at the front room window.

"He does look like a turnip, doesn't he," Joanne said laughing.

"Yeah, he's horrible," Ellie said.

They waited and realised he was on the phone, at last he moved away.

Billy whispered, "I'm going to go over and see if I can see in."

"Be careful," Sally said.

Billy scuttled across the road, hid behind the yellow car and then ran towards the window. After a few minutes he beckoned them over.

Once they were next to him, Billy said, "Look they're all in the back garden."

They looked through the front room window and could see right through the house to large patio doors leading out into a garden. There seemed to be quite a few people milling around and they were holding glasses.

"They're having a party," Sally said. "I've heard posh people have what you call garden parties, that's what they must be having."

"He's having a garden party after sacking my Mum, I hate him," Ellie said.

"So do I," Billy said.

"Me too," Joanne added not wanting to be left out.

"What shall we do?" Billy asked.

They thought about it and then Ellie said, "Why don't we let the tyres down on his lovely yellow car."

They all started laughing, they'd done this before. Sally has two hairclips in her hair and carefully while Joanne and Sally kept guard Ellie and Billy, with the help of the hairclips, began to let the wheels down on the yellow sports car. It took some time but at last their job was done.

"Now for the finale," Billy said and started to knock on the door and ring the doorbell.

They jumped on their bikes and started to ride away but stopped when they were at a safe distance away and waited. Turnip Head himself came out, looking up and down the road.

"Oy Turnip Head," Ellie shouted.

He glared over at them. His bald head was gleaming in the sun and his face was red and puffed up.

"Hey," he shouted over to them, "Have you lot just rang my doorbell?"

"Yes, we did," Sally shouted. "You fat pig."

He started to run over towards them, other people had come out of the house and were shouting at them as well. A woman ushered him back and Ellie presumed that must be his wife.

"Tell your husband to keep his hands to himself," Ellie shouted.

"I'm phoning the police," the woman shouted.

Ellie, Sally, Billy and Joanne started to peddle away. They knew they had out stayed their welcome.

"Nice car," Billy shouted as a parting gesture. "Hope you enjoy driving it, Turnip Head."

They carried on peddling as fast as they could. When they felt they were far enough away they stopped and began to laugh.

"That'll teach him," Ellie said.

They all felt better getting their own back on Turnip Head, as far as they were concerned, he deserved it. They stopped to buy another cold drink and celebrated by clacking their bottles together. Getting back on their bikes they picked up speed, desperate to get back home to their familiar neighbourhood, pleased that a successful mission had been accomplished.

CHAPTER 14

Love Hurts

Jim Capaldi

Pat sat in the kitchen, Ellie and Sally had been in asking for something or other and Pat had spoken to them but she couldn't remember what they had actually been asking for. She felt as if her head was in a cloud and somehow, she was floating outside of herself, looking down at a poor woman, who was sat in a chair with a sad expression on her face. Pat had tried to clear the fog that was clogging up her mind but hadn't been able to do so.

At the same time Pat felt as if the walls were caving in on her. Her heart was beating and although she knew she had to go out shopping she felt unable to sum up the energy to do so. She didn't know what she was going to make for tea. Whatever she decided would be eaten. Eaten or discarded. Discarded or eaten. For some reason Pat kept saying this mantra in her head until at last she heard herself and with a puzzled frown stopped.

The heat was stifling. It weighed heavily on her and she felt too hot to move. Was it the heat? Pat asked herself. What is up with me? Why can't I summon up the energy to take charge of myself. Stop feeling so sorry for myself? Count my blessings?

She looked at the cup sitting on the table in front of her. The tea she had made earlier had now gone cold. She noticed that there was a chip on the rim of the cup and stared at it perplexed wondering why she had chosen that particular cup to drink from? She stood up, poured the tea into the sink and placed the cup carefully in the bin.

"There," she said out loud as if she had performed a feat of astronomical proportions.

Pat shook her head, trying to take charge of the chaotic thoughts swirling around in her head and sat back down.

Flies buzzed around her and she felt as if the noise was going to make her go mad. All I want is a bit of peace and quiet, Pat thought. Silence, was it too much to ask for?

She looked at the bottle of pills sat on the table in front of her.

She had been to the doctor's the day before and he had prescribed them for her. Pat had picked them up from the chemist and was in two minds whether to take them. Valium, they were called. The doctor said they would help with her nerves. Maybe they were the lifeline she needed.

She had explained to the doctor that she was finding it hard to cope. Was crying a lot and couldn't cope with the kids or the housework. She told him about losing her job and the arguments she was having with her husband. The doctor had dealt with her in a professional manner. He didn't offer her words of comfort or even tell her to pull herself together. He had started writing out the prescription and said, "These might help. Come back If you need anymore."

Pat had taken his prescription, thanked him and walked out feeling no better than she had before she walked in.

Pat hadn't taken the tablets yet. She rarely took pain killers in any form, even for a headache but she knew a lot of women had been prescribed these tablets and she hadn't heard of any horror stories about them. They were being given out like smarties so how could there be anything wrong in taking one or two? Maybe they would help.

Pat filled a glass with water and shook out one of the tablets and quickly swallowed it before she gave it another thought. She sat back down at the table. All was quiet and she could hear the clock in the living room quietly ticking away in the background.

Pat sat thinking. She had no right to feel this way. She should be thinking of her kids, looking after them. She hadn't even taken the Ellie and Sally out on a day out. She always told them she was far too busy. Go out and play, go and find something to do, get out from under my feet but deep down all Pat wanted to do was scream at them, "Leave me alone".

The guilt gnawed at her soul. Fiona and Gary were old enough to look after themselves but she knew that was a lie. She was a crap mother, a crap wife, she felt as if they would all be better off without her. Pat shook her head once more, trying to shake these thoughts from out of her head. They were always there, niggling away, tormenting her. A constant reminder of what a bad mother she was.

The pills weren't working. Surely, she should be feeling something by now? How long before this miracle happened? In an hour would she be back to her old self? Smiling and laughing with the kids, making plans to take them out on a day out? Greeting Harry with a warm smile on her face when he came home from work. Give him a cuddle and a kiss, suggest an early night? Pat laughed at the thought. Harry would definitely think she'd gone mad then.

Pat thought about her job. Although it was a monotonous boring job, she had enjoyed working with her friends. Well, most of them. She had enjoyed the comradeship work offered. It broke up her day, took her away from the house. It gave her some spending money so she could get her hair done, or buy the kids the odd little treat, or some clothes rather than having to ask Harry for it. She'd even managed to put a bit of money aside for Fiona's wedding as well and now Pat had had to dip into it to buy a pair of pumps for Ellie.

Pat couldn't believe how many shoes the kids went through. What on earth did they do to them, it seemed like every week they needed a new pair. But, then again, they grew out of them so quickly as well. That wasn't their fault. Kids had a habit of doing that, growing up when you weren't watching. It felt as if it was only yesterday that it was Danny, Fiona and Gary who had been toddlers. Where had all the time gone?

Pat sighed, she felt as if she was treading water. Every time she felt as if she was coming up for air the wind would be taken out of her sails once more. Pat could be watching the tele, or cleaning up and suddenly it felt as if she'd been punched in the stomach. She would hear Harry coming in and her stomach would clench in agony, waiting for the next argument to commence.

The other day she had watched in disbelief when during an argument he had begun to open up all the windows in the house and then the vestibule door so that everyone in the street could hear what they were arguing about.

"What are you doing?" Pat had asked incredulously, hardly believing her eyes.

"I want all the neighbours to know what I have to put up with. If you want to argue with me, we might as well let them all listen in. Show them what a marvelous wife I've got?"

"Have you gone stark raving mad, why on earth would you want the neighbours listening in on all our business?" But it had quietened Pat down. It had worked, she'd shut up and he'd sat in his armchair with a big smirk on his face.

Pat didn't know who was in the wrong. Maybe it was her. Why did she argue back with him? Why didn't she just let him have his own way? If he came in and wanted to take his frustrations out on her, why didn't she just let him.? What harm was he doing really? He was a hard worker, why couldn't she just agree with him? It would make life easier. Maybe she was a bad wife, always contradicting him and trying to have the last word.

Then Pat remembered how he spoke to Gary, how he treated him and she felt her blood boil. The way he refused to pay for Fiona's wedding on principle. Principle, my arse, Pat thought, he was just a tight bastard. He only wanted to spend any spare money he had on himself.

Pat even doubted that it was because Harry didn't like Simon. Simon had never been rude to Harry or disrespectful. He held down a good job. Treated Fiona well. Pat suspected Harry just didn't want the expense of a wedding because whatever he said he'll have no choice but to help out in the end whether he liked it or not.

Pat grimaced, there I go again. Why do I always think the worst of him. Maybe he does have Fiona's best interest at heart. Maybe Harry sees something in Simon that I can't. Pat didn't know what to think anymore. She was all off kilter. She didn't know if it was all her fault or whether she was more at fault for putting up with it. Aren't I just as bad arguing with him in front of the kids all the time? What type of mother am I?

Then Pat remembered what had happened a couple of days ago. She had been tidying up whilst Harry was out at work and Pat had noticed that one of Harry's suit jackets was hanging up on a peg on the back of the living room door. She had tutted to herself, as it should be in the wardrobe not left hanging there with all the other coats. She had taken it down so she could take it upstairs and hang it up in its rightful place, their bedroom wardrobe. That had been her only intention.

Pat told herself she had not been rooting through his pockets but whilst she was putting it on a coat hanger, she had noticed a bulge in the inside pocket. To Pat's astonishment she had put her hand in and found a hundred pounds inside. Pat had been shocked when she saw it. How could he go out with that amount of money in his pocket when she was struggling to make ends meet?

Pat had waited until Harry came home from work and asked quietly, "I've hung that jacket in the wardrobe if you're looking for it."

Harry had looked at her in surprise and then said, "Oh, thanks."

"I thought you might be looking for it."

"Not particularly," Harry had said.

"It's just that I found some money in the pocket."

Pat wondered why she hadn't just kept the money? Pat realised, later on, that if she hadn't have mentioned it, he wouldn't have noticed it was gone but at the time she was too frightened in case it was some kind of trap he had set for her.

Harry had looked up, his eyes narrowing, "Money? How much?"

Pat had thrown the rolled-up money on his lap. "That much."

Harry had looked down at it and put it in his trouser pocket. "Thanks," he'd said.

"Thanks? Is that all you've got to say? How can you forget you've left a hundred pounds in your pocket?"

Harry had exploded. He knew how much money he had, he thought he had put it away. How dare she question him. Pat knew it was useless. There was no talking to him. It was during this particular row that Harry in his wisdom, had decided to open up all the windows.

Pat looked down at the glass of water, shimmering on the kitchen table. The flies buzzed all around her and the clock ticked. Pat looked down from above and pleaded with the woman to wake up but she just sat there staring at a glass of water with the same sad, worn out, expression on her face.

CHAPTER 15

Coz I Love You

Slade

Ellie was playing in the street, she felt tired and lethargic. Although she liked the hot sunny days sometimes the heat sapped her energy and she and her friends would sit listlessly in the shade too exhausted to do anything. Eventually Ellie had grown too bored doing nothing so she had offered Sally a game of football but it had been too hot to play properly so they had ended up kicking a ball ineffectually to one another to pass the time.

Ellie then noticed that their mum was walking towards them, weighed down with bags of shopping in both hands.

Ellie and Sally ran up to help her. "We'll carry some of that for you, mum".

Ellie and Sally struggled to take one of the bags out their mum's hands and a loaf of bread fell on the floor.

"Clear off will you, you're more of a hindrance, than a help," Pat shouted and Ellie and Sally jumped back in surprise.

"We were only trying to help," Ellie shouted after her, but her mum ignored her.

"What's up with mum lately?" Sally asked, "She looks sad all the time now,"

"I know and she said she's taken some time off work and that's not like her."

"I know," Sally said, "If she is off, you'd think she would take us out somewhere, but she just sits in the kitchen drinking tea and sighing to herself."

They contemplated this for a while until Ellie said, "I'm fed up hanging round here."

"Me too," Sally agreed.

"We could go in the den?" Ellie said but it was only a half-hearted suggestion.

Sally whispered, "It scares me in there, Ellie. Last time I went in there with Billy I could hear all sorts of noises."

"It's probably pigeons in the attic," Ellie said as that's what her dad told her if she heard noises in the night and was frightened.

"Didn't sound like it was coming from the loft," Sally said.

"It could be haunted," Ellie said.

"Don't say that" Sally whispered, "or I'm never going back in there."

Ellie contemplated what they could do next. There were so many places to go to. She wished the summer would last for ever, it felt it already had. She didn't know why all the adults were moaning about it. It was on the tele every night and the newspaper headlines said things like, *"Whew! What a Scorcher'* but what was wrong with that? All you ever heard was: Drought. Save Water. Share Baths. Ellie didn't care, she had always shared baths with Sally anyway. Ellie thought everyone was making a big fuss about nothing.

Her dad certainly wasn't happy with the situation either, but this didn't surprise Ellie in the least. Her dad liked to shout, and this gave him the perfect opportunity to do so. He was always going on about water rates, whatever they were but her dad seemed obsessed with them.

According to her dad it was all the Government's fault. It seemed to Ellie that her dad was glad there was no water, otherwise what else would he have to shout about?

It wasn't just her dad though, everyone seemed to be obsessed about the weather and it wasn't just in the summer. In the winter it was too cold, there was too much snow, the roads were treacherous. Now when it was gorgeous, and the sun was out, and it hadn't rained for ages they were all moaning about the lack of water. Next, they'll be moaning about the leaves in autumn or the daffodils in spring.

Suddenly Sally shouted, "Here's Dennis the Menace."

Ellie looked up to see the bedraggled figure of Dennis walking down the street. Dennis lived in their neighbourhood and everyone knew him. The children were always glad to see him as sometimes he would sing and dance for them. Dennis always wore a brown suit, which was too large for him and a shirt and for some reason large hob nailed boots, which looked incongruous compared to the suit. His one redeeming feature was he always wore a smile. Ellie and Sally ran towards him and Billy appeared by their side as if from thin air.

"Sing us a song Dennis," they all shouted.

Dennis came to a stop in front of them and started to sing 'When I'm cleaning windows' and began to dance as Ellie and her friends formed a circle around him. They weren't concerned that Dennis sang the wrong words, they were just happy to see him.

Her dad told Ellie Dennis was a 'character' and whatever that was Ellie agreed. After Dennis sang a few more songs, he bowed and began to walk away. Ellie, Sally and Billy skipped beside him until they reached the end of the street.

"Where you going, Dennis?" They asked but he just shook his head and put his head to one side as if he was deep in thought.

"I'm off to the Himalayas, to find Big Foot," he said at last.

"Big Foot, Dennis, then what you going to do?" They giggled as they waited for his reply.

"I was thinking I was going to shoot him and wear his fur as a coat as I've been told it's going to be awfully cold this winter but then I thought that's not very nice, so I thought I'd just make friends with him."

"You could bring him home to live with you," Sally exclaimed, and they all laughed.

"I could," he said, "but we don't have the room at my sisters, and I've heard he has very bad table manners so I don't think my sister would approve."

They all giggled, and Dennis smiled at them and then his eyes became vacant and he walked away.

"I think Dennis is funny," Sally said.

"So do I," said Ellie. "Is he a bit," Ellie circled the side of her temple with her finger and they all nodded seriously.

"He's been like that ever since he saved a young woman from drowning, and the propellor of a boat hit him on the head and that's why everyone looks after him," Billy said solemnly.

"I know he's a hero really." Ellie said.

"Maybe he really is going the Himalayas," Sally said, and they all started laughing.

"Maybe we should follow him," Billy said half seriously.

"No, he's probably only going down the pub."

"Yeah," said Ellie, "I definitely think there a few Big Foot's in The Queens."

"Yeah," said Billy, "and your dad's one of them."

After Ellie and Sally stopped chasing Billy, they watched Dennis in the distance as other children began to run beside him asking him to sing but he ignored them as if he really was on a mission and really was going to find Big Foot.

CHAPTER 16
'Save water, Bath with a Friend'
3 July 1976

Ellie and Sally arrived home starving. Pat was in the kitchen and said she would make them some soup. They ate it quickly, dunking thick bread in the soup as they told their mum all about Dennis the Menace.

"Ah he's a simple old soul," Pat said but she seemed distracted and in a world of her own.

Finishing their soup, Ellie said, "Well we can't sit round here all day we've got to see a man about a dog."

Ellie laughed as this is what their dad said sometimes when he was going the pub and he was in a good mood but their mum simply smiled and started washing their dishes.

"Go on, get going the pair of you, I've got work to do."

Ellie and Sally got up slowly both looking at their mum in concern but decided to go out anyway. Once outside the street looked different somehow.

Ellie looked at Sally and asked, "Is it going dark or is it just me?"

They both looked up into the sky and Ellie was amazed to see how dark the sky was.

"Maybe it's going to rain," Ellie asked puzzled.

It was then that she noticed a dark cloud in the sky seemed to be moving and not only had it blocked out the sun but it seemed to be coming towards them. Ellie and Sally stared in disbelief as the dark cloud descended on them. It was like a horror movie.

Suddenly Ellie realised there were ladybirds everywhere. Ellie batted them away with her hand but soon her mum came running out of the house and started to shout at them to come in. Ellie and Sally ran to their mum who ushered them in the house closing the front door behind them.

"Shut all the windows," Pat screamed.

Ellie and Sally ran up the stairs. After her initial shock Ellie calmed down once she realised that the great black swirling cloud was only ladybirds. It was still a bit frightening to see the sky swarming with the tiny insects and to see them bashing against their windows as if they were desperate to come inside but Ellie knew they were harmless.

By the time Ellie and Sally reached upstairs a few ladybirds were in the bedrooms. Ellie and Sally quickly closed all the windows and watched with fascination as the windowpanes slowly turned black. There weren't just a few ladybirds there were thousands. If it had been ants or wasps or bees Ellie would have been petrified but ladybirds were so pretty, she couldn't see the harm in them. What shocked her was the fact that there were so many of them, she wondered where they had all come from.

All of the windows were covered with ladybirds, with so little light penetrating the windows, the house had taken on a peculiar aspect. It was spooky almost and Ellie, although not admitting it to Sally, didn't like it upstairs so ran back downstairs to her mum who looked as shocked as she felt. Sally stayed upstairs with her nose pressed up against their bedroom window and only came down when her mum shouted her to.

"Where have they come from mum? Why do they want to get in our house?" Ellie asked.

"I don't know. It's strange, isn't it?" Pat said as bewildered as her children.

"They're everywhere," Sally shouted trying to peer through the living room window.

They heard the front door opening and Fiona rushed in.

"My god," Fiona cried, "they're everywhere."

They all stared at Fiona, her long blond hair was crawling with the tiny black and red creatures. Fiona was running around the room swiping at her head.

"Stand still, will you," Pat ordered and started to pick them out of her daughter's hair. "Come on help me you two."

"It was horrible. I was at the top of Borough Road when suddenly they came out of nowhere. I could barely see where I was going so, I just started running," Fiona explained still swiping at her hair and brushing herself down.

Ellie and Sally joined their mum trying to pick the ladybirds out of Fiona's hair. Ellie felt like one of those monkeys you see on the tele picking fleas off from one another and thought it was hilarious.

"Found another one!" Sally shouted.

It became a game to see if there were any still any left in Fiona's hair. Eventually they could find no more. The windows started to clear and soon sunlight was streaming in through the windows once more. They all went outside and there were quite a lot of the ladybirds lying dead in the street. Other people began to emerge from their houses, all rushing to tell their own tales.

"This summer's mad," Billy exclaimed rushing over.

"I know it was like something out of a horror film," Ellie said.

They both stared up and down the street and then at the clear blue sky. The ladybirds had vanished, but the heat persisted and still there was no sign of any rain. It was only later when Ellie heard that the ladybirds had come looking for water it made sense. Supposedly the ladybirds had been attracted to the seaside and because they lived by the Mersey, the ladybirds had flown here looking for water. Ellie couldn't blame them as water seemed to be a commodity in short supply these days.

There was even a man called the Minister of Drought, whatever that was, and he was the one who said everyone should share baths and put bricks in the cistern of your toilet to conserve water.

When Harry came in later, he had his own story to tell but he soon became disgruntled by the conversation.

"It doesn't make sense to me," he said. "They couldn't run a piss up in a brewery if you ask me. Bad management that's all it is."

"Stop using that type of language in front of the kids," Pat said half-heartedly from the kitchen knowing Harry would take no notice of her.

"What's the country coming to when bloody ladybirds are coming here looking for water, even my own kids can't even have a bath on their own."

"It does them no harm," Pat said.

"Look at them, they're bloody roasting. I wouldn't mind but the amount I pay in water rates, it's a disgrace."

So, maybe it shouldn't have come as a surprise to Ellie when a couple of days later Sally ran past her with her swimming costume on. Ellie stared after her sister who was running through the kitchen and into the back yard. Then she noticed her dad in the kitchen threading a hose from the tap through the kitchen window.

"What you doing dad?" Ellie asked.

"Going to cool you two ragamuffins down. Go on hurry up, go and get your cossie on," Harry said.

"Why, where're we going?"

"Nowhere."

Ellie looked at her mum quizzically who raised her eyes to the ceiling.

"He's got another idiotic idea into his head," Pat said.

"Oh, get away woman. The kids are boiling. A good hose down will do them the world of good!" Harry added, "Best make the most of it while the water's actually on."

Ellie looked at her dad shocked beyond words. Everyone knew

you couldn't use hoses. This was what all the news reports were about. Ellie was astounded but Sally, who had obviously gotten used to the idea, had a big smile on her face.

"Come on Ellie, it will be great! I'm sweltering."

"They're not going to tell me what I can and can't do!" Harry shouted.

"Oh no God forbid anyone told you what to do!" Pat said. "Hose pipes are banned for a reason not just to annoy you."

"Look my kids are roasting. I don't care what those politicians say. I pay my water rates, more than they probably do."

Ellie was now beginning to get a gist of the idea. Her dad was going to hose them down in the backyard similar to what he did when he gave Benny a wash.

"Oh, mum please. I'm roasting."

"As if it's got anything to do with me what that man does. Just make sure none of the neighbours see you and make sure you don't tell anyone."

Soon they were in the back yard with Benny, who wasn't too happy about it, all getting a good soak. It felt wonderful. It was the coolest Ellie had felt in a long time. She liked breaking the rules and she was glad her dad was always annoyed at politicians and wouldn't do what he was supposed to do either.

Ellie thought it was a shame the ladybirds hadn't chosen to come to their house today, they would have been made up.

CHAPTER 17
You Just Might See Me Cry
Our Kid

Ellie woke up and wondered what was wrong. The house felt quiet. She looked over at Sally and could see she was still sleeping. She threw a teddy bear at her and Sally opened her eyes.

"You getting up?"

Sally looked at her confused, her eyes were sleepy and Ellie could tell she hadn't woken up properly yet. Ellie slid from under the covers and made her way downstairs. The house felt strange. Usually, her mum was pottering around the kitchen making their breakfast or Fiona was getting ready for work, usually moaning at them for being in her way or in the bathroom or any number of excuses she needed as to why she was yet again late for work. Even Gary who was normally slouched on the coach with an early morning vacant expression on his face was preferable than the stillness of the room unoccupied.

Benny sensed it too. He would normally be mooching in the kitchen waiting for his breakfast or curled on the mat but instead he was standing behind Ellie as if he was in alien territory too. Ellie inspected the living room and kitchen and could see the tell-tale signs of Fiona's preparations for work. A hairbrush lay abandoned on the side board, shoes had been pulled out from the cupboard beneath the bureau and left for their mum to tidy up and a plate had been left in the sink with a half-eaten piece of toast semi submerged in water. Obviously, Fiona had already left for work but where was her mum?

Ellie realised that it was later than she thought and she had actually slept in. Normally their mum woke them up so this was unusual in its self. Ellie climbed the stairs. Her mum wouldn't have gone out without telling them but she never slept in either so Ellie was really perturbed by her mum's absence. Ellie hoped with all her heart that her mum was in bed.

When she opened the bedroom door, she could see her mum still tucked up in bed fast asleep and the relief that she felt was overwhelming. Ellie's world had a set of norms that had to be adhered to and one of them was that her mum was right where she should be when she woke up but although it was odd for her mum to sleep in at least she was in the house and Ellie knew where she was, was tangible proof that everything in Ellie's world was how it should be.

"Mum?" Pat stirred. Ellie went over to her, "Mum, I'm hungry. How come you're not up?"

"Oh, go away Ellie, I'm tired."

"But mum I want my breakfast."

Sally came in, "What's up with mum?"

"I'm tired and I've got a headache. Come on you're big girls now, go and make yourself some toast. I'll be down later."

"It's not fair," Ellie said.

"Oh, don't be silly, Ellie it's not the end of the world if I have a lay in."

Ellie and Sally went downstairs. The house still felt empty and cold even though yet again it was a beautiful day outside.

"Why's mum lying in bed?" Sally asked her.

"I don't know she said she's tired."

Ellie remembered that her mum had lost her job but that didn't mean she could lay in bed all day. They weren't allowed to. It just wasn't right as far as Ellie was concerned.

"I don't like mum not being here," Sally said.

"Oh, don't be a big baby, Sally." Sally put head down ashamed but Ellie felt exactly the same but didn't want Sally to know that.

They turned the tele on and the programme 'Why don't You?' was on but apart from the music at the beginning of the show Ellie didn't much like it. It always featured posh kids who had a miniature railway specially built in their fifty acres of back garden or kids who liked to go scuba diving in Bermuda or something. It didn't relate to Ellie or the world she knew.

Ellie and Sally made toast and burnt it but it was okay once they put some jam on it and they each made a cup of tea for themselves. After eating their toast and drinking their tea they began to relax and realised it was quite good to have the run of the downstairs with no one else telling them to behave themselves. Fluffy was lying next to Benny on the floor. Fluffy was a large black and white tomcat, with a beautiful furry coat which made him look loveable and angelic, but it was a clever disguise. Fluffy was ferocious. More often than not whilst Ellie and Sally were innocently tickling his tummy Fluffy would suddenly pounce on them. They suffered many an assault trying to pet him but this did not stop them from tormenting the poor thing and suddenly Ellie had an idea.

"Why don't we dress Fluffy up in some dolls clothes?"

Sally started to giggle, "Yeah that sounds good."

They crept upstairs now not wanting to wake their mum up and rummaged around for the dolls clothes that was stuffed at the bottom of their wardrobe. They found a pink lace dress and a bonnet and ran downstairs laughing. Fluffy was hard to catch but eventually they cornered him and a few scratches later he was dressed in his new clothes and the bonnet was perched on his head.

Once released from their grip Ellie and Sally roared with laughter as Fluffy ran round the room trying to tear the clothes from his back. Ellie and Sally chased after him and Benny started barking and chasing Fluffy too.

"What the hell are you doing?"

Ellie and Sally stopped in their tracks and looked towards the living room door where their mum had suddenly appeared.

"What's all the noise about? All I ask if for one lousy lay in and you have to start making all this racket. Get dressed and go out to play. I've had a belly full of the both of you."

"We weren't making that much noise. We were only laughing at the cat."

Fluffy looked up at Pat.

"So, Fluffy dressed himself this morning, did he?" Pat asked but did not smile.

Ellie and Sally giggled, "Yeah mum he did."

"Go and get ready and get that dress off the poor cat. I'm going back to bed and if you're not out of this house in five minutes I won't be responsible for my actions."

Ellie and Sally undressed Fluffy and skulked upstairs pulling on their own clothes.

"What's up with her?" Sally asked.

"Don't know but she's horrible," Ellie said. "Let's go and knock for Billy and Karen, we'll go down the prom. Nobody wants us round here."

***

Ellie, Sally, Billy and Karen, with Benny in tow went down the beach. They had seen Gavin hanging around outside his house so went the other way and started to run when they heard him calling after them. They reached the prom and were made up to see that the tide was out, a mist hung over the Mersey. The only sounds to be heard were the seagulls' squalls competing with the lapping of the waves. They noticed the odd person walking along the prom but there was no one on the beach. They ran down the slimy brick steps to the sand and pulled their shoes off deciding to paddle. They screamed when they saw a washed-up jelly fish and Billy poked at it with a stick.

"Don't be cruel," Ellie said but they all went over and inspected it. They all agreed it must be dead.

They were tempted to have a swim but had forgotten to put their cossies on so couldn't. In the end they decided to dig a big hole, Billy sat in it and they covered him with sand. It was sometime later when they realised, they were starving. They agreed to go home and once they'd had something to eat, they'd meet back up and come back to the prom. It was getting warmer and the sun was climbing in the sky and the prom was cooler than playing in the street.

When Ellie and Sally arrived home, they were surprised to see that their front door was closed. Their front door was never closed. They knocked loudly on it but there was no answer. Ellie and Sally grew alarmed. Their mum must have gone out and locked the door by accident. They ran up to Borough Road where all the shops were but there was no sign of their mum. They tried knocking once more at their front door but there was still no answer.

Billy and Karen came out after their dinner and Ellie and Sally told them of their predicament.

"I'm starving," Sally said.

"I've got some money so you can buy some chips if you want?" Karen offered and Ellie thought she was the best friend in the world but then she felt sad with the thought of her moving away.

They all went to the chippy and once they had eaten her and Sally felt better so decided to go on another adventure. When they returned home later their front door was still closed but as they were knocking on the door and shouting through the letter box their dad appeared behind them.

"Dad, we're locked out," they explained when they saw him.

"Don't be daft," he said.

"We are honest. Mum's gone out and locked the door. She didn't even tell us where she was going."

Harry looked angry as he took his keys out of his pocket and opened the door. He marched in and looked around the living room. All was quiet. Elle and Sally looked at one another their eyes as big as saucers with the knowledge that there was going to be trouble.

"Isn't Gary in?" Harry asked surveying the living room.

"No," they both answered, "We were knocking for ages, and nobody answered."

"Bet he's in bed the bone idle get," Harry ran up the stairs but Gary wasn't in his bedroom.

"Harry is that you?" They heard their mum's voice.

She had been upstairs all the time.

They heard their dad go into their parent's bedroom. Ellie and Sally looked at each other in alarm, appreciating that this wasn't going to end well.

"What the hell are you playing at woman? The kids have been hanging round the street on their own. What on earth have you been doing and why's the front door locked? They couldn't even get into their own home. Don't tell me you've been lying in bed all day?"

They could only hear their mum mumbling but could hear very clearly every word their dad said.

Then they heard their mum say, "Someone must have shut it by accident. I didn't hear a thing."

"You'd think now you're not working you'd have more time to look after the kids. Look at the state of you."

They couldn't hear their mum's muffled response but it didn't matter as their dad interrupted whatever she was saying.

"You must have heard them? They were knocking the front door down. I can't believe you've been lying in your pit all day while your kids run wild. Have you seen what they're wearing? Did you even get up with them today?"

Ellie and Sally looked at each other, Ellie looked at Sally and thought, thinking about it she does look silly. Sally had a red dress on that was far too small for her, her oldest pair of jeans and was wearing a pair of red wellies. Ellie thought her own outfit of corduroy brown pants and an old t-shirt of Fiona's looked lovely. The argument upstairs was heating up. They could now hear their mum retaliating. Ellie and Sally decided to go out and play.

That night when they were tucked up in bed their mum came in to give them a kiss goodnight. Ellie thought, she looked different. She gave them both big hugs and then sat on the end of Ellie's bed and she noticed her mum was crying.

"Don't cry, mum," Ellie said. Sally slipped out of her own bed and hugged their Mum.

"I'm sorry kids. I just feel so tired all of the time."

"It's okay, mum," Sally said and for some reason Ellie and Sally started to cry too.

"Come on don't be silly, you two, I'm alright. I'm just being silly, ignore me."

"But you shouldn't cry mum. Me and Sally were alright. We only wanted a butty and then we would have gone out again and you could have carried on sleeping."

For some reason this made their mum cry even more.

The trouble was though when they woke up the next day and although their mum was up, made their breakfast and made sure they looked respectable, as she put it, she still went back to bed again. This time though the door wasn't shut. Gary had been told off for closing the door the day before, so it didn't happen again but still they didn't see much of their mum over the next couple of days.

CHAPTER 18
Somebody to Love
Queen

Ellie was playing in the street when she noticed Benny was running down the street towards two women and a couple of kids and Ellie wondered who they were. If Benny knew them, she must know them too. As they approached, she realised it was her nan and aunty Lynne with their cousins Sonia and Wendy. Ellie dashed up to meet them. It wasn't often they visited because they lived 'over the water' in Liverpool so it was really exciting to see them.

"Hiya Nan," Ellie shouted as her and Sally ran up to meet them. "Hiya, aunty Lynne."

Aunty Lynne looked like a younger version of their mum but aunty Lynne looked like a hippy and they'd seen pictures of their mum when she was younger and their mum looked more like a Hollywood film star. Aunty Lynne had a scarf wrapped in her long dark hair and a tasselled multi coloured top on, bell bottom jeans and sandals. Ellie thought she looked cool. Their nan wasn't like their grandmother, she was younger and smiled more and people took more notice of her.

Ellie then looked at her cousins weighing them up because she didn't know them that well and had only met them a hand full of times. They were younger than her but they smiled at her and said 'hiya' and they seemed alright. Ellie and Sally skipped into the house with their nan and aunty and their two cousins straddling behind.

"Where's your mum, love?" Their nan asked.

"She's in bed, nan," Ellie said.

"She's got a headache," said Sally.

"Oh?" Ellie noticed her nan and aunty exchanging looks.

"Pat love, you ok?" Her nan shouted upstairs.

They heard some noise coming from the bedroom.

"I'll go up and see her," their aunty Lynne said.

"Why don't you all go and play out?" Their two cousins hesitated, "Ellie and Sally will look after you, go on."

"It's okay we'll look after you. You're our cousins, we'll show you round."

"Don't go far?" Their nan warned.

"We won't," they all shouted.

Ellie and Sally took their cousins outside, proud to show them off. They introduced them to everyone and soon they were playing hide and seek. Ellie thought her cousins were great. Ellie didn't know how long they had been playing but she decided to go in and have a drink of water.

Her mum, nan and aunty were in the parlour. The parlour was only used for best. It had a fitted carpet, blue velvety flowered wall paper and a mock leather couch with orange cushions and Ellie thought it looked dead posh. As Ellie passed the half open door she stopped to listen to their conversation.

"You've got to get a grip Pat. You can't just take to your bed and leave the kids running wild." Ellie could hear her nan talking.

"They're not running wild," Pat said quietly.

"Look Pat I know you've had that trouble at work but it's not the end of the world."

"It's not just that mam, I'm sick and tired of it all," Pat said. "I'm worn out. The Doctor gave me these pills and they just knock me out. He said they're good for me nerves."

"Well, they won't be good for your nerves if something happens to one of the kids."

"Oh, they're alright. They're good kids, they can look after themselves."

"Pat, they're only kids you can't just leave them fending for themselves," it was Ellie's aunty Lynne who was speaking now.

"And Harry's not happy about it." Ellie's nan interrupted.

"He's not happy about a lot of things, mam. He's never in, he couldn't care less."

"Well, he does care. They're his kids too, y'know. He's worried sick."

"Sure, he is. He's not worried. He's more interested in his mates than his own family."

"That's not true. He phoned me last night and said you'd taken to your bed."

"Oh, I wondered why you were over."

"Don't be like that."
"God, you'd think I'd committed the worse sin in the world. I'm worn out I just need a bloody rest."

"Yes, I could understand that if it was a one off but it's becoming a habit, isn't it? You've been lying in your bed all week from what I've heard." Ellie's nan paused, "Look Pat you've got to sort yourself out. What do you think would have happened to you lot if I would have taken to my bed? And, I had ten of you remember. Do you think your dad would have been happy? He would've killed me if he caught me sleeping in the middle of the day."

"Mum it's the pills."

"Stop taking them, then."

"They help me."

"Oh my god it's like talking to a brick wall. Lynne, you try talking some sense into her."

"Mam, stop having a go, you can see she looks ill. How are you, Pat?" Aunty Lynne sounded more sympathetic.

"Ellie, what are you doing there?" Aunty Lynne had seen Ellie hovering in the doorway.

"Nothing."

"Well, go and do nothing outside." Ellie was surprised to hear her mum laugh.

"That's it, girl," Ellie heard her aunty Lynne say to her mum, "nothing's ever as bad as it seems. Come on let's get you tarted up. We'll soon have you as right as rain."

Ellie walked out into the street wondering why her mum was taking pills, but she soon forgot it when she saw her dad come round the corner with her grandad, uncle Tony, uncle Paul and aunty Renie. Uncle Paul was married to Lynne and uncle Tony was her Mum's brother and aunty Renie was another one of Ellie's aunties. Ellie loved it when her mum's family came over. They always ended up having what, everyone called, a Do.

"Found him in The Queens, told you we would." Uncle Tony shouted as they walked through the front door.

"Why doesn't that surprise me," Ellie heard her mum say but Ellie's nan shushed her.

"Where's my favourite girl," Grandad shouted as he hugged Pat.

Ellie felt as if a weight, she hadn't known was there, had been lifted from her shoulders. After Ellie and Sally had been made a fuss of by their grandad, aunty Renie and uncle Tony they were told to play out once again. It was cool playing with her cousins and all her friends seemed to like them too. Later on, when they went in music was playing and they could hear laughter coming from the parlour.

They looked in and her mum was dancing with her aunty Lynne and aunty Renie. The men were laughing and cheering them on and trying to get their nan up to dance too. They called them in when they saw the children peering in and soon, they were all dancing.

Sometime later Fiona and Simon came home and joined in too. Then Gary came in and uncle Tony handed him a beer and their dad didn't say anything and just laughed. Then they called in Francis and Tommy their next-door neighbours in and soon a full-blown party was under way.

Ellie couldn't remember being taken up to bed. The next morning, she woke up with the sun shining through her bedroom window and the radio playing downstairs. She was half hoping her cousins would still be there but they weren't but she didn't mind because she'd see them again and everything would be alright.

When Ellie and Sally went downstairs their mum was in the kitchen.

"Right, you two, what about chucky eggs and soldiers for breakfast?" Pat said smiling at them.

"Oh, Yes, please mum," Ellie said.

"I love chucky eggs and soldiers," Sally shouted, and their mum laughed.

Ellie and Sally looked at each other and smiled, it was good to have their mum back.

CHAPTER 19
Kung Foo Fighting
Carl Douglas

The holidays seemed to go on endlessly. Ellie and Sally rose early, and when their dad was at home he would shout, 'The sun's cracking the flags out there' and they would open their eyes with the sun streaming through their bedroom window and jump up excitedly knowing it was going to be yet another beautiful day.

Their mum was back to pottering around the kitchen and life seemed to have gotten back into a familiar pattern which made Ellie feel happy. She still noticed that her mum looked sad sometimes but on the whole things seemed to be back to normal.

The radio would be on as there wasn't much on the tele first thing in the morning, and they would eat contentedly while their mum and dad bickered in the background. They hardly heard it, it was a background noise, they were accustomed to it and would probably only notice it if it stopped. Most days Fiona would be running around getting ready for work and hogging the bathroom. If their dad was in, he would usually be shouting up the stairs, telling Gary to get his lazy backside out of bed.

That day they had made plans to go to Central Park to play. Central Park was a large park with a lake, swings, a rose garden and numerous football pitches and grassed areas to play on. There were trees to climb and nooks and crannies to explore. They would take a football, play on the swings, have a picnic and see what else they could get up to. It was a bit of a walk, but they had decided between themselves yesterday that they hadn't been there for a while and it would make for a change of scenery.

Their mum was always too busy to take them anywhere. She was either shopping or cooking or cleaning. Their mum never seemed to stop. Even in the night when they went to bed, Ellie would hear the creak of the clothesline as her mum hung out washing in the backyard. It was a noise that Ellie liked to hear, it made her feel safe tucked up in bed, comforting as she drifted off to sleep.

They had asked their mum earlier if you could make them some butties that they could take with them and she had given them money to buy lemonade for when they were thirsty. It was still early, and they weren't planning to go to the park until later on, so Ellie and Sally went out to play in the street. The street was empty except for Benny who was laying in his favourite position in the middle of the road.

Ellie often wondered why he chose to lay there as he was forced to move if cars came up or down the road. To Benny the cars were a huge imposition which he took personally. He would look up lazily at the car as if he had never seen such a contraption before in his life. He would sigh to himself at the indignity of it all, move and once the car passed by resume his original position and fall back to sleep.

They stood making plans for the day and waiting for their friends to come out when Ellie and Sally saw their grandmother coming down the road. Ellie after seeing her nan only recently marvelled at how different her nan was to her grandmother. Ellie loved them both but in different ways and she wouldn't swap her grandmother for the world as she was funny in her own special way.

Ellie as always was fascinated by what grandmother was wearing. Today her grandmother was in a light blue skirt, blouse, shoes and matching bag. Her hat was something to behold, light blue of course with an adornment of flowers, it was tilted at a jaunty angle on a mop of fluffy white hair.

Ellie's grandmother's skin was feathery, and it reminded Ellie of rice paper with a pink hue on her cheeks and mouth. Her lips were always wet and dewy with just a hint of lipstick. To Ellie she was what a grandma should be. Old and respectable and maybe just a little bit eccentric. Ellie thought her mum was mean when she said their grandmother was 'as mad as a hatter' and although Ellie conceded that maybe her mum did have a point, particularly today with the creation her grandmother had perched on her head, her mum still shouldn't say this out loud.

Ellie forgot all about this though as her and Sally ran up to greet her safe in the knowledge that they would not have to accompany her into their house.

"Hello Eleanor," Grandmother said, smiling at them regally. "Hello Sally," they watched as their grandmother tucked her hand in her handbag and pulled out some sweets.

"Here you go, now what do you say?"

"Thank you, grandma," they said in unionism.

"Is your mum in?" She asked smiling at them.

"Yes grandma."

"Not in bed?"

"No, grandma, she's got over her headaches now," Sally said and smiled.

"Well, that's good news."

Ellie watched as their grandmother walked in through their front door and was glad, they were playing out as there could have been a repeat performance of a couple of weeks ago and they never would have been able to go to the park.

All this was forgotten in an instant when a police car turned into their road, this was an event in itself and they stopped in their tracks to see where it was going. They held their breath as the police car stopped in the middle of the road, waiting for Benny to move and it was only then that the police car could proceed. Ellie and Sally smiled to themselves as Benny once more settled back into his favourite position.

They looked to see where the police car was going and then gasped as it pulled up right in front of their house. Ellie watched in horror as two policemen emerged and pulled their Gary out of the back of the car.

"Oh no, what's he been up to now?" Sally said turning to Ellie.

"Who knows," Ellie said, "but it doesn't look good."

Sally said, "All I can say is thank god me dad's not in."

The two sisters both looked at each other wisely and nodded their heads in agreement. They slowly began to walk back towards their house, trying to look nonchalant as they were joined by more and more children. Ellie couldn't think for the life of her where they had suddenly appeared from, as apart from her and her friends the street had been deserted a few minutes ago.

"What're the Police doing with your Gary?" Someone in the crowd asked Ellie.

Ellie felt her cheeks burn with shame as it dawned on her that Gary could have committed some awful crime and everyone and their dog was going to find out about it but at the same time it was still exciting to know it involved her and her family.

"I don't know," Ellie said as she watched with amazement as her brother stumbled and fell down on the pavement. The Policemen were then forced to lift him up.

"Get off me." Gary said and it was then that Ellie realised he was drunk.

"Come on Gary get a grip will you or you'll end up in the cells."

"Yeah, I'd like to see you try it."

Gary for all his posturing looked puny compared to the two policemen either side of him but even they were finding it difficult trying to keep him up right. Ellie had the impression that if they left him to his own devices he would fall down where he stood and wouldn't be able to get back up again.

"Is this where you live then is it, Gary?"

"Yes, it is," Sally shouted.

Sally had emerged from the crowd and pointed at their house. Not to be left out Ellie followed the policemen as they took her brother inside. Pat though must have heard all the commotion as she was already walking down the hall to see what was going on before the Policemen could even knock at the door. Ellie noticed her grandmother hovering in the background and knew this did not bode well.

"Oh my God, Gary what have you done?" Pat asked.

"Hi, I take it your Gary's mum?" One of the Policemen said.

"Yes, that's right Officer. Mrs. Thomas."

"I'm afraid we have just found your son stumbling along Borough Road drunk and disorderly. Do you know how he managed to get himself into this state at 10 o'clock in the morning?"

"I don't know Officer," Ellie noticed her mum looked confused, angry and upset all at the same time and wondered which one would take precedence in the end.

"Most kids his age should be coming back after a paper round not sprawling along the street rotten stinking drunk," one of the Policemen said sternly.

The Policeman looked at their mum and then he looked down at Gary. Gary looked back up at him and smiled lopsidedly, Gary turned slowly back to his mum.

"Hi mum," Gary said.

"Don't you hi mum me, Gary, coming home in this state, you have a bloody nerve."

Pat stared at Gary intently and it was then Gary took the opportunity to hiccup. Everyone watched as Gary slowly put his hand to his mouth as if he had some semblance of manners and mouthed 'sorry' to his audience sheepishly. He hiccupped once more just for good measure, but this time failed to apologise.

Pat at last managed to say, "Oh my god Officer I know you're right. I can't believe it. I've never seen him in this state before."

"So, he's not in the habit of getting drunk then Mrs. Thomas?"

"No, Officer, I can assure you of that. He's normally such a good lad."

Ellie did not know how her mum could lie so brazenly to the policemen but given the circumstances Ellie conceded her mum had no other option as she obviously didn't want to make matters worse.

"Well, he's certainly had a skin full and at this time of the morning as well. Where did you think he was?"

Ellie thought mum's a quick thinker as almost immediately Pat said, "He told me he was staying at a friend's house Officer. I never thought for one minute he would get himself into this state."

The Policemen stared at their mum long and hard but at last he said, "Well on this occasion we decided to bring him home but if this happens again, we won't be so lenient."

"Thank you, Officer. I don't know what must have gotten into him."

"Well, we'll turn a blind eye this time but as I say if it happens again..."

"Of course, Officer but honestly it won't happen again, he's normally such a sensible lad. All I can do is thank you for bringing him home."

"Well, we thought it was best under the circumstances."

"Wasn't he drunk at Brian's funeral the other month?" Grandmother asked.

Sally and Ellie started giggling and Ellie whispered to Sally, "And when nan came over."

Thankfully their mum hadn't heard Ellie but gave their grandmother a withering glance.

Their mum must have decided the best policy was to ignore their grandmother and continued to speak as if she had not been interrupted, "Officer, I promise you it won't happen again. I'll make sure of that."

"I think he's a disgrace, Pat." Their grandmother said.

"Yes, I am," Gary said with pride, "I'm a fuckin' disgrace."

"There is no need for language like that, Gary," their grandmother said.

"What," Gary said warming to his subject, "Did I fuckin' swear?"

"Now, now Gary any more of that and we'll take you in," one of the Police Officers said firmly.

Their mum interceded, "I'm really sorry Officer if you could just put him on the settee I'll take over. No need to stay any longer than necessary."

"Well, I think he should be taught a lesson," their grandmother interrupted, "he should know better at his age and how has he got into that state this early in the morning?"

"I don't know grandma, but we can talk about that later," Pat said.

"Yeah grandma," Gary sneered, "keep your nose out."

"Gary! You stop that this instance," Ellie could tell her mum was trying to keep her patience but even Ellie could tell she was finding it difficult.

"Gary you are a very naughty boy and when your father comes in, I'll be telling him exactly the kind of language you've been using."

"He can fuck off too," Gary said as he began to sink slowly to the floor.

"Oh, can I?" Ellie had not seen the arrival of her dad but to everyone's surprise, there he was standing at the front door. "What's going on here?" He said after weighing up the situation.

"It's nothing Harry," Pat said, "He's just had too much to drink."

"Oh, is that all."

"He's been swearing at me, Harry," their grandmother intervened.

"Oh, has he? Right Officers if you want to arrest him feel free."

The policemen exchanged glances, "Look sir there's no need for that. He's just a bit worse for worse, if you can assure us, you'll keep him in till he's sobers up I don't think we need to take this any further."

"That's the trouble with this country," Harry said eyeing up the police officers, "No one wants to take any responsibility. A night in the cells would do him some good but you know best." Harry raised his eyebrows and the police officer looked away. "Right put him down Officers I'll deal with this."

"Look Mr. Thomas if you want us to arrest him then we will. We thought it was best if we let his parents deal with him considering his age but yes, you're quite right whatever you think best," the Policeman said staring at Harry.

"No, officers my husband doesn't mean it. We'll sober Gary up and believe you and me he won't hear the last of this." Pat appealed to the policemen, wringing her hands. "We can deal with this, I promise."

"Okay then Mrs. Thomas." The policeman looked at Harry, "Mr. Thomas, we'll leave you to it."

The policeman left the house. Constable Stephens turned to his colleague, Constable Jones and said, "God help him. I think a night in the cells would have been safer."

They both laughed as they got back into their car.

Pat walked the Policemen to the door and was relieved to see them driving away. She turned back to Gary who was now on his knees looking up at them. Pat prayed that Harry would take this calmly but she didn't bank on it.

"Right lad, get up," Harry said.

"No."

Harry dragged Gary up and Gary started to wrestle with him but quite ineffectually.

"Get off him Harry, can't you see how drunk he is?" Pat appeal went unanswered but she persevered. "Just get him upstairs. We can deal with him properly when he's sobered up."

"Sober up? I'll give him sober up. Where the hell has he been to get into this state? Didn't he come in last night?"

"No, he was staying with his mates."

"Well, that's the bloody problem isn't it, he's allowed to run wild."

Ellie was amazed that although Gary and her dad continued to struggle up and down the hallway her parents still found time to argue with one another.

"Typical isn't it. The trouble with him is he thinks he can get away with murder."

"And, I suppose that's my fault, is it?" Pat yelled trying to get between her husband and son.

"Well, it's not mine," Harry shouted as at last he managed to get Gary into a head lock.

"Get off him, Harry you're going to hurt him," Pat screamed.

"That's your trouble, woman, you're too soft. Look at the state of him, do you think this is normal?"

Ellie was further amazed when her grandmother decided to join in.

"I think Harry's right you know Pat. He does seem to be out of control."

Their grandmother shouted from the living room, where she had retreated to once Harry and Gary's tussle began.

"Ma, keep out of it," Harry said.

"Don't you talk to me in that manner Harry. Maybe that's the trouble, he takes after you."

"Yeah, daddy maybe I'm a chip off the old block," Gary said between grunts.

Gary somehow managed a quick manoeuvre and was suddenly free from Harry's grasp and stood swaying where he stood. Harry stood before him.

"Don't you talk to your father like that, young man," their grandmother shouted back.

Ellie wondered at the ease their grandmother had of switching sides and realised that she had even managed to work her way back into the hall and was pointing a finger in Gary's face.

"You shouldn't talk to your father in that manner, Gary, you're very disrespectful and you should know better."

"Grandma, get out of the way. You might get hurt," Pat urged.

"I am just trying to point out to him Pat. He shouldn't speak to his father like that."

Harry lunged once more at his son.

"Get off me ya bastard," Gary shouted from the melee.

"I'll knock you out in a minute, y'little shit," Harry shouted.

Their grandmother turned to Pat, "Pat I'm afraid it might do Gary some good, he needs to be taught a lesson. Look at him swearing and drinking, he needs taking in hand."

"Grandmother I know but at this moment in time it's not helping. You're just making matters worse."

"I am only saying Pat that sometimes a bit of tough love works wonders."

Ellie's grandmother and Pat were having this debate whilst side stepping Gary and Harry as once more they stumbled around the hall.

"Grandma, what would hitting achieve, he's too drunk to even notice and anyway," Pat said exasperated but, in an undertone, "It's a pity you didn't do that to your Darling Harry when you had the chance."

"What was that, Pat?" Ellie grandmother asked.

"Oh nothing, grandma," Pat said.

"Pat, I must say. Harry's right, you're too soft with him. I've told Harry that before, haven't I Harry?"

Harry wasn't listening to his mother. He was too busy tussling with his son in the small confines of their hall and trying not to knock into his elderly mother to take too much notice of what was being said.

Harry had managed to get Gary back into a head lock. Gary had his arms wrapped round his dad's waist and was trying to pull him over.

"Don't hit him Harry, he's drunk. He doesn't know what he's doing," Pat pleaded.

"Hit him dad," Sally shouted from where her and Ellie stood in the vestibule, Sally always liked a good fight, Ellie thought, as long as it didn't involve herself.

Ellie decided to remain neutral under the circumstances until she had weighed up the odds.

"Just get him up to bed and we'll deal with him later."

"Don't put off tomorrow what you can do today," grandmother shouted.

"Oh my god," Pat said, "this is madness."

"Only if you don't stand firm, Pat," grandmother said.

"Grandma we can discuss the why fore's later. Harry will kill him if we don't stop him."

"Oh, I'm sure he won't Pat. Gary just needs chastising."

Finally, it came. Harry punched Gary and knocked him to the floor. Gary lay prone, his nose began to bleed, and he looked up at his dad.

"What did you do that for?" Gary asked.

"Get to bed Gary before he does you an injury," Pat said and somehow, she managed to pick him up off the floor single handily and push him onto the stairs.

Harry went to hit him again, but Pat grabbed Harry's arm. Eventually Gary stumbled up the stairs and then they heard him as he crashed into his bedroom and flopped onto his bed. Calm descended as they all looked at one another.

"Well, I don't know, Harry," their grandmother said, "why did you hit the poor lad? I've seen you in much worse states."

Ellie and Sally decided to retreat. They saw the look on their dad's face as he turned his attention to his wife. They had also seen the look on their mum's face and knew yet another argument was about to ensue. Sally and Ellie went back out into the street. The crowd of children had thinned out but there were a few still hanging around, Billy amongst them.

"Your dad hit your Gary then?" Billy asked.

"Yeah." Sally said matter of factly.

"He's mad, your Gary," Carl added.

"Yeah, but our dad's madder," Sally said.

"Yeah," Billy agreed.

They all nodded sagely.

"Are we going the park or what?" Billy asked.

"Of course," Ellie said.

They summoned the troops and headed for the park with Benny following close at their heels. The argument and the drunken antics of their brother quickly forgotten. It wasn't until later in the evening when Ellie and Sally had come home from the park, with dirty faces and grass stains on their clothes, and were sitting down eating their tea when they heard a shout from Gary upstairs.

"Mum, what's all this blood on me pillow?"

Pat shook her head, "What did I tell you he can't remember a bloody thing."

CHAPTER 20
You Don't Have to Go
The Chi-Lites

Ellie was upset. Karen and her family had moved away a week ago. The street was quiet for a Saturday and there was a strange quality to the air, maybe because there was not a whisper of a breeze. Ellie declined Sally's earlier invitation to play out with her and was skulking on the front door step of their house. Benny was next to her, lolling in the sun with his tongue hanging out and breathing heavily. The tarmac on the road was bubbling in the heat and a hazy mist hung heavy in the air.

There were a few kids playing at the top of the road, but other than that the street was empty. She looked up when Mr Robinson, who lived across the street, came out of his house and waved over to Ellie.

"Hi, Ellie, not like you to be sitting all on your own." Ellie smiled politely not knowing what else to say. Mr Robinson asked, "No, Sally today?"

"She's out playing."

"You didn't want to go with her then?"

"Couldn't be bothered, it's too hot."

"You're not wrong there. Look even Benny's too hot to move."

He laughed and Benny looked up at Mr. Robinson and half-heartedly wagged his tail at him. Benny did not go over to greet him as he would do normally as Mr. Robinson was right, it was far too hot to move.

"Oh well, you behave yourself, Ellie." Mr. Robinson said as he briskly walked away.

Ellie liked Mr. Robinson. Ellie's Mum had told them that his son had been knocked over in this street years ago and died. Mr. and

Mrs. Robinson had not had any more children and Ellie's Mum said it was a shame. He was always really nice to the children in the street, although he didn't like cheeky ones. He especially didn't like Gavin Farrell, so Ellie thought Mr. Robinson must have a pretty good judge of character.

She watched Mr. Robinson go down the street and was wondering whether she should go and look for their Sally when she saw a lorry turning the corner. It ambled along and pulled to a halt outside where Karen used to live.

Two men got out and started to unload equipment from the back of their van. Ellie knew what they were doing. They were bricking up Karen's home. Ellie looked at them in dismay as they carried on with their work oblivious to Ellie's presence.

Ellie watched as the windows and the front door of her friend's former home was systematically bricked up, unsurprisingly Ellie didn't think it was another opportunity to make another den. Ellie stared at it glumly, missing her friends even more as each new brick was laid and feeling in the pit of her stomach that it just wasn't right. Things were changing and she didn't welcome it one little bit.

Ellie walked back into her house, kicking at the floor as she went to go in the parlour. Ellie jumped when she noticed her dad was in there, sitting reading the newspaper. Ellie noticed that her dad was in his jeans and a vest with his slippers on, his usual attire if he wasn't going out.

Harry's belly swelled under his vest, Ellie was amazed how big and round her dad's belly was. When her dad was in a funny mood, he would slap his belly and shout, *this is all muscle* or *It's well paid for* but he didn't seem to be in a funny mood today as he looked up at her and frowned. Ellie thought just my luck, she hadn't known her dad was in. If she had she would have gone right in the living room where her mum was. It was too late now. He had caught her and her dad didn't like her sitting in when she should be playing out.

"Hi, dad," Ellie said smiling sweetly at him.

"Hi, Ellie, what are you doing in on a day like this?"

"Nothing I'm just bored that's all."

"Well, you wouldn't be bored if you were outside playing."

"I've got no one to play with."

"Don't be silly. Go and call for Billy or see what Sally's up to."

"I wanted to play with Karen."

"You'll have to get on a bus to do that now, love."

"I know. It's not fair. Why did they have to move so far away?"

"Because the friggin' Council want to knock down a perfectly good neighbourhood."

Harry set the paper down next to him and Ellie could tell that he had forgotten about her playing out so she decided to use it to her advantage.

"They shouldn't be allowed dad."

"I know they shouldn't but everyone's just rolling over."

"Are you going to roll over dad?"

"Not on your Nellie."

Ellie was warming to this theme. At least her dad didn't want to move not like her mum.

"Mum said our house is a shit hole."

"I've warned you about using language like that."

"Sorry dad but I'm only repeating what mum said."

"Well don't." Ellie's dad looked at her sternly and then asked, "So, when did she say that?"

Ellie sighed with relief as normally her dad would play blue murder if he caught her swearing, so she decided it was best if she kept talking, "Yesterday. She was talking to Francis next door."

"Oh, was she, indeed?"

"Yeah, and she said the whole street should be knocked down."

"Is that right, is it?"

"Yeah, and I don't want our house to be knocked down, dad."

"Don't worry Ellie, over my dead body will that happen."

"But mum wants to move."

"Well, it's not up to her." Her dad looked angry, "Take no notice of your mother Ellie, she doesn't know what she's talking about. I've spent good money on this house. Put a bathroom and everything in and if she or that lousy council think I'll move out after the money I've spent doing this place up they can go and whistle."

"So, we are staying dad?"

"Of course, we are."

"Good because I don't want to move to Leasowe, its miles away and I'd have to change schools and everything."

Ellie had been giving this some serious thought.

"Don't worry love we're not moving anywhere and as for your mother I'm going to have a word with her. Going round behind my back like that and talking to all and sundry, bloody typical."

"I know dad," Ellie tried to continue but her dad interrupted her.

"Anyway, didn't I tell you to go and play out?"

"But I want to talk to you, dad."

"Hard luck, you're not staying in on a beautiful day like this."

"But dad."

"No 'But dad' to me. Go on clear off."

"There's nothing to do."

"Of course, there is. When I was your age, my mother couldn't keep me in."

Ellie stared at her dad but he had picked up the newspaper once more and was reading it. She pulled tongues at him knowing he wasn't looking at her.

She jumped when he said, "Did you hear me?"

Ellie begrudgingly said, "Yes."

"So, what are you waiting for?"

"You to go out," Ellie mumbled.

"What did you say?"

"Nothing."

There was no point arguing with her dad so Ellie reluctantly went back outside and did not see Harry smile to himself as she left.

CHAPTER 21
I Wanna Stay with You
Gallagher & Lyle

It had been another beautiful day. Ellie, Sally and Billy had had a really good day. They had been climbing backyard walls and exploring empty properties. Everyday there seemed to be more and more empty houses and with less people around their neighbourhood they had been able to root around more.

This morning, they had found a large yard which they'd never seen before. It had been built in the middle of interconnecting alley ways and they couldn't understand how they'd never noticed it before. For that reason, it seemed mysterious to them and they convinced each other there must be strange things going on to be secreted away in such a manner.

They had decided to investigate and had climbed the wall to see what was inside. All was quiet so they dropped down into its yard but suddenly a man had appeared from nowhere, and shouted at them, telling them to clear off.

They scurried back up the wall and after Billy shouted a few choice words in return they retreated but were determined to revisit. There was definitely something strange going on and they were determined to find out what. He wouldn't be there all the time they reasoned.

They ran down a series of entries until they were back in their street. Their hearts were beating fast, but they were exhilarated that they had managed not to be caught. Their faces were streaked with dirt and their hair a tangled mess.

"That was a close one," Billy said.

Ellie looked down and noticed that she had ripped her jeans, but she didn't care, they were old, and her mum never fussed over old clothes. Ellie then looked at Sally who never seemed to become as dirty as Ellie and Ellie wondered, not for the first time, how she managed it. Ellie didn't think she'd had a good time if she wasn't covered in dirt after playing out. She didn't bother looking at Billy, his clothes were always worn and dirty, he always looked the same whether he'd been playing out or not.

They decided to play hide and seek when suddenly their attention was drawn to the top of their street. They looked up to see Fiona arguing with Simon at the top of the road. Sally and Billy came out of hiding and they all looked down the road to see what was going on.

They heard Fiona shout, "Leave me alone Simon."

"What's your Fiona up to?" Billy asked.

"I don't know, arguing with Simon as usual, I suppose."

Ellie could see Fiona and Simon gesticulating wildly at one another.

"Get lost," Fiona shouted and began to walk down the street leaving Simon open mouthed where he stood.

"I will then. I'm not running after you Fiona," he shouted after her.

"I don't want you to. I just want you to leave me alone."

Fiona began to march towards them with a determined look on her face. Ellie watched as Simon went to follow her and then stopped as if he had decided against it.

"I mean it Fiona. I'm not following you."

Fiona continued to walk. Simon stared after her and then retreated. Ellie watched as he turned the corner of the road and disappeared. She watched as Fiona turned her head slightly and stared in disbelief when she saw Simon was no longer there. Fiona looked shocked and then started to run towards their house. She rushed past Ellie, Sally and Billy. Ellie was surprised to see that Fiona was crying her eyes out. Ellie followed her. It seemed to Ellie that if it was not one thing it was another.

"Where you going?" Billy asked.

"To see what's happening," Ellie said.

Sally said, "I wouldn't bother they'll be talking tomorrow."

Ellie hunched her shoulders in reply but followed anyway.

Ellie heard Fiona shout, "Mum. Where are you?" as she rushed through their front door.

"I'm here," Pat shouted from the living room. "What's up sweetheart?"

Ellie was not far behind and just about caught the vestibule door as Fiona charged through it.

"I've just had a big row with Simon and I've told him to get lost."

Fiona had already thrown herself into Pat's arms and was sobbing loudly. Ellie raised her eyes to the ceiling. Fiona was so dramatic.

"Oh, come on it's not the end of the world. Why all the tears?"

"He's a pig mum, he's been moaning at me about the price of the wedding and he doesn't want to get married in a church and he said I was nothing but a spoilt brat."

Fiona's crying grew worse and Pat patted her on the back.

"Don't cry I'm sure it's not as bad as all that."

Pat looked at Ellie over Fiona's shoulder and raised her eyes to the ceiling. Ellie smiled.

"I'm not marrying him. I mean it, he's not talking to me like that."

Ellie thought, good riddance to bad rubbish.

"Oh, hush hon don't be silly you've just had a little tiff that's all," Ellie watched as her mum tried to calm Fiona down.

"No, mum it's not just that he's been off with me for a while now. I don't even think he loves me."

"Of course, he does," Pat said.

"He doesn't Mum and I can't stand him anyway." Fiona's sobbing grew louder.

Gary who was sitting watching the tele said, "Do you want me to beat him up Fi, I've never been able to stand him."

"Shut up Gary don't be so stupid," Pat said.

In between sobs Fiona said, "You couldn't fight your way out of a wet paper bag so just stay out of it."

Ellie thought that's not nice seeing's as Gary was only sticking up for you.

Gary said, "That's gratitude for you," and stood up, "I'm going out can't be bothered with all this."

As Gary left, he walked past Harry who was just coming in from work.

"What's going on?" Harry said surveying the scene before him.

"I've finished with Simon that's what," Fiona said looking up from Pat's shoulder.

Harry didn't seem impressed.

"Oh, is that all?"

"What do you mean is that all? I'm supposed to be getting married and he's been treating me awfully."

"Well, I always said he was a waste of space, so you've had a lucky escape."

Harry sat down in his favourite armchair and picked up the paper and began to read it.

"Mum, tell him to shut up."

"Harry behave yourself. You're not helping."

"What do you mean I'm not helping?" Harry continued to read his paper but looked up briefly to say, "She shouldn't be getting married in the first place. It's a bloody stupid idea but yet again my word counts for nothing in this house."

"Harry I'm not arguing with you. Could you just keep your opinions to yourself for once?"

Harry flung the paper down, "Don't you talk to me in that manner."

Harry stood up and was now facing his wife. Pat moved Fiona to one side and stood facing Harry. Ellie thought they look like a couple of gunfighters at the OK Carrol.

"Shut up, dad, for god's sake." Fiona shouted.

"Yes, Harry shut up." Pat shouted. "Our daughter's upset it's not always about you."

Ellie was speechless, no one ever told their dad to shut up and her dad looked speechless too.

Harry found his voice at last and said in a quieter tone, which to Ellie's ears at least was somehow worse, "I've been telling you for months that Fiona shouldn't be getting married."

"I know you have but can we leave that till later," Pat said.

Ellie's noticed her mum's tone was quieter too, but she was still standing firm.

"Under the circumstances I think it's the perfect time to talk about it."

"No, it's not."

Ellie watched as suddenly her dad exploded. Ellie shrank back, when he was like this, he scared Ellie.

"Don't tell me what I can and can't say. This is still my house, isn't it? I still pay the bills, don't I?"

"No one's saying it's not your house," Ellie realised her mum was shouting too, "But I live here too, and I know what's best for my daughter."

"And, I don't, is that what you're saying?"

"Stop twisting everything. Just leave me to it."

Ellie watched as her dad stared at her mum his eyes blazing but then he looked away. He took a deep breath and as quickly as it surfaced his anger evaporated.

Harry said in a more measured tone, "Typical isn't it. We find out he's upsetting her like this and I'm still in the wrong. I can't bloody win. I wouldn't mind but you've been encouraging all this."

Pat eyed her husband up and down. Her face held a look of utter contempt.

"Encouraged it? I have never said Fiona should be getting married but the way you were going on about it she was determined to go through with it just to spite you. There're more ways to skin a cat you know?"

Harry took a step closer to his wife, their eyes once more boring into one another. A boiling kettle all of a sudden popped into Ellie's head and she thought, that's what my dad's like, always letting off steam.

"The way I go about it? Are you saying I should sit idly by whilst my daughter throws her life away?"

"I'm not throwing my life away," Fiona wailed.

"Shut up, Fiona," Pat and Harry shouted simultaneously, and Fiona started to cry in earnest once more.

Ellie's parents ignored Fiona and continued to stare at one another. The animosity between the two was tangible and it suddenly dawned on Ellie how much her parents disliked one another. It was like watching a duel in a Western. They were both eyeing each other up as if they were sworn enemies but Ellie realised that her parents weren't cowboys and they certainly weren't at the OK Carrol. They're my parents and I'm sick and tired of all the arguing, too, Ellie thought.

Ellie felt like crying. She looked at Fiona and noticed she had mascara streaming down her face and her eyes were all red and puffy. Ellie realised that maybe it wasn't a good time for her parents to pick a fight with one another. Ellie crept towards Fiona and put her arm around her.

"Are you okay Fiona." Fiona looked down at her and tried to smile.

"Don't worry about me, Ellie. I'm just being stupid." Fiona wiped her eyes and sniffed.

"Simon's stupid not you," Ellie said.

Fiona laughed despite herself and said, "Oh Ellie, you make me laugh."

Pat stood on the other side of Fiona and although she still had her arm round her daughter's shoulder her attention was focused solely on her husband. *How I loathe that man*, Pat thought. She stared at his red face, twisted with anger. She knew she should ignore him and concentrate on Fiona, but she couldn't help reacting to him. He always made the situation ten times worse and it always had to be about him. Why couldn't he just stay out of it and let her look after Fiona and set things right?

"You go against me every chance you get," Harry shouted.

"No, I don't. When?"

"This house for a start?"

"What about this house?"

"It's a shit house according to you and should be knocked down."

"Who told you that?"

"You were heard talking to Francis."

"Oh, was I?" Ellie squirmed as her mum's eyes fell on her.

Ellie remembered her conversation with her dad from a few days ago and wanted to make a sharp exit but she kept her arm around Fiona's waist frightened to let go.

"Oh my god, I can't believe this." Fiona leapt away from both her mum and sister, "I'm upset and all you two care about is arguing.

You're selfish the pair of you. You don't care about us." Fiona looked at Ellie and shouted at her parents, "Do you think it's nice for Ellie to watch all this? She's petrified."

"Don't be so stupid, Fiona. Ellie's alright," Harry said.

"What would you know? All you two care about is getting one up on one another."

"Fiona love calm down. We're sorry, we'll shut up." Pat pleaded with her daughter, but Fiona ignored her.

"This house is a shit hole father," Fiona continued, "and it would be worth taking Simon back just to get out of it but whether I marry Simon or not I can't live here a moment longer."

Fiona ran from the room and Ellie could hear her running up the stairs to her bedroom. The slamming of the bedroom door was a given.

"See what you've done now," Harry said to his wife.

"What I've done? You're like a bull in a China shop."

Ellie decided that maybe it was best if she left her parents to it. She slipped out of the room as they continued to shout at one another. They had forgotten about Fiona. They had forgotten about her. Fiona was right all they cared about was arguing with each other.

Ellie felt sad. Nothing seemed to be going right lately. Everything was upside down and although she loved her dad, she didn't like him shouting at her mum. Ellie felt pulled between her parents. She wished they would get on, but Ellie couldn't remember a time when her mum and dad actually talked let alone were nice to each other. It seemed to Ellie as if the only way her parents communicated was by arguing.

She used to think it was normal but lately Ellie had started to realise that not all parents fought all the time. Karen's mum and dad weren't always arguing. She had even seen Karen's mum and dad cuddling and when they lived in their road, Karen's mum would go to the front door to kiss her husband goodbye. Her mum and dad never cuddled or kissed.

Ellie looked up and down the road and saw Billy whizzing up and down at the far end of the street on his bike with Sally on the back. Ellie ran back into the house to drag her bike out of the hall. She cycled up to Billy and Sally and asked them if they wanted to go on a bike ride. Sally jumped off the back of Billy's bike so she could get her bike from the house.

"I'm coming," Gavin Farrell shouted, and they all groaned as they realised, he was already on his bike and was cycling towards them at full pelt.

Soon, with Benny hot on their heels, they were all riding out of the road. Ellie could feel the wind in her hair as she stood up on her pedals to go faster. She was soon leading the way and could hear the excited laughter of her friends behind her, as they rushed to keep up with her. Ellie raced on leaving her worries and cares far behind her.

CHAPTER 22

50 Ways to Leave Your Lover
Paul Simon

Pat came in from shopping, she was exhausted. Pat placed two shopping bags on the kitchen table and started to pull out the contents. She looked around her small shabby kitchen, it had a larder, the obligatory sink, oven, fridge and kitchen table. She barely had space to move but from here she cooked, washed and cleaned. She usually sat in the kitchen to get a bit of peace. It was her domain. The walls were whitewashed, the tiles on the floor coming up in places and the window looked out on to a small back yard.

God, Pat thought, little did I imagine when I was younger this is where I'd end up. It wasn't so much as the penny pinching or even the state of the house, she could live with that, but it was the pure monotony of life. A marriage which had gone stale and without a job she felt there was nothing left to look forward to anymore.

Pat pulled herself together and reminded herself she had five lovely children. She smiled to herself when she thought of them. She thought of Danny away at sea and hoped he was alright. He was her rock and she missed him terribly. Danny had always understood her.

Pat knew he had joined the merchant navy to get away from home. Even though Harry respected him in a way he had never respected Gary their relationship was still strained at times. Harry had to be the boss and Danny was too pig headed to stand for it. He went away to sea at the age of sixteen and Pat didn't blame him, but it was an added anxiety to her life. She prayed for him every night.

Pat looked back to the contents of her bag which now lay strewn across the table. She would have liked a salad but Harry would only complain that it was 'rabbit food' so it was going to be meat, potatoes and veg. Pat knew it was too warm for a hot meal, her clothes were sticking to her, but it would avoid an argument with Harry. She wanted to go out tonight without a row so decided it was best not thinking about it.

On her way in she had spoken to Ellie and Sally in the street as she had been suspicious when she noticed they were hanging round a bricked-up house, which only the day previously she had noticed had a huge hole where the front door once was. Pat had only seen this by accident when she had heard a loud bang and had peered over the wooden fence to see where the noise was coming from. It was only then that she noticed the knocked-out bricks but now seeing Ellie and Sally hanging round there she hoped they weren't going in there and maybe it had been her own children she had heard.

Pat sighed feeling guiltily, it was impossible to keep her eyes on them all the time, but other than keeping them under lock and key what other choice did she have but let them play out. Of course, they would get up to mischief but all she could hope for was they came home in one piece and touch wood, up until now they had.

Pat had said to them, "You two better not go in there. It could be full of rats and God knows what so don't even think about it." Pat stared at them hoping to put the fear of God in them and so added for good measure, "You hear me?"

"Yes mum, we won't. Benny had gone in there but we shouted for him and he's out now." Sally explained and Benny wagged his tail at her.

"Good, make sure you two don't."

Pat was sure her advice was falling on deaf ears but with her two shopping bags weighing her down, she decided to leave them to it. Walking in she heard music being played in the parlour. She called into Gary who she presumed was in there and who was supposedly keeping an eye on Ellie and Sally while she was out shopping, to let him know she was home. Pat heard a grunt in reply so was happy that at least he had had stayed in and done as he was told for once.

Pat could hear the music from the parlour drifting in and began to hum to herself but inevitably she started to worry. She worried about Danny away at sea. She worried about Gary and Fiona. She worried about the house being compulsory purchased. She worried about Ellie and Sally and how it was affecting them. She wished she could talk to Harry about it all but he was the one person she could not discuss it with. Harry had his head in the sand. When the letter had arrived from the Council, he had torn it up. He had not consulted her or asked how she felt about it, he had simply torn it up and said they weren't moving anywhere.

Pat thought the women in her group know more about her anxieties than her own husband. Months ago, they had told her to put her name on the council's housing list and Pat had ignored them. They were right. She was as bad as Harry. Pat decided she would do it first thing tomorrow morning. She couldn't carry on like this as if nothing was happening. Pat began to peel the potatoes. Harry seemed to think they could stay here come what may. Well, maybe he should she thought and she and the kids should move out. It was a radical thought for Pat, and she smiled to herself for daring to think the unthinkable.

Fiona came in. She looked fed up. Pat could kill that, Simon. He hadn't showed hide nor hair here since Fiona had sent her engagement ring back. Pat knew Fiona was upset but believed her pride was hurt more than anything else. As far as Pat was concerned Fiona was far too immature to be getting married. Fiona just liked the thought of a big white fairy tale marriage. Sending the ring back after a little tiff said it all as far as Pat was concerned.

"What's for tea Mum," Fiona asked as she put her bag down.

Pat looked up at her daughter and smiled for whatever strain

Fiona was under she always looked lovely. She should be a model or an actress, Pat thought. That was what Pat aspired to be when she was younger and dared to dream of such things, but nothing came of it. Maybe I should have encouraged my daughter more Pat thought, not to be a model or an actress but to try harder at school. Pat realised now that education was far more important. Pat watched as Fiona helped herself to a glass of water, she looks so much like me when I was her age except for the hair of course. Fiona, Gary and Sally all had blond hair like their father. Pat was dark haired, and Danny and Ellie had followed suit. Her children were a mixed bunch, Pat thought, all so different. She wondered what would become of them all.

"Mum?" Fiona said drawing Pat away from her thoughts. "I just said, what's for tea?"

"Pork chops," Pat said knowing her daughter wouldn't be happy.

"Oh, mum I'm not eating that it's too hot."

"You'll have to as there's nothing else in."

Fiona didn't answer her, she was leaning against the kitchen door sipping her water and watching her mum as she worked.

"You going anywhere tonight, love?" Pat asked looking up at her.

"No."

"You need to get yourself out. Doing you no good mooching around here all the time."

"Danny Taylor asked me out, but I told him where to go."

Pat laughed, "He's always had a thing for you."

"He's got another thing coming, wouldn't touch him with a barge pole."

"So, have you heard anything from Simon?" Pat knew it was a touchy subject, but she had to ask.

"No and I don't want to."

"Maybe it's for the best."

"Here we go," Fiona said.

Fiona straightened up and went to go back into the living room. It was rare these days Pat had a chance to talk to her daughter earnestly, so she decided to try another tact.

"So, what is it that you want?" Pat had been thinking of all the opportunities out there for her daughter and decided it was high time Fiona broadened her horizons. Fiona sighed but didn't answer. Pat said, "I was thinking you're a bright girl. Why don't you go to college?"

Fiona stopped and stared at her mum incredulously. Pat tried to keep the conversation light, but she could already tell Fiona was becoming agitated.

"Mum I've got a job why would I want to go to college?"

"To get a better job."

"I don't want a better job."

"All I'm saying is now that you've called off the wedding maybe it's a good time to alter your plans and think of yourself for a change."

"I am thinking of myself."

"What by staying in every night?"

"Well, I'm not staying in on Saturday night." Fiona smiled, "I've agreed to go out with someone. He's a sales rep at work and he's got more prospects than stupid Simon Worthington."

Pat shook her head, "Bloody hell Fiona. I was talking about bettering yourself not finding another man. You don't just find your worth through men, you know."

"Did I say I did. I'm only going on a date."

Fiona looked pleased with herself, and Pat knew she should be happy that at least Fiona wasn't sitting in but continued to press her point while she had the chance.

"It doesn't sound like that when you're talking about his

prospects." Pat said exasperated at her daughter, "What I am trying to say is that you need to find out what you want from life. There's more to this world than being just a wife and mother you know. You've got your whole life ahead of you, you could be anything you want to be."

"Oh god mother you sound like one of those feminists. I *want* to be a wife and a mother."

"I'm not saying you can't be, but you could build a future for yourself now and think of that at a later date."

"Mother you're living in cloud cuckoo land. I'm only going on a date I'm not about to walk down the aisle." Fiona laughed, "well not yet anyway."

"It's like talking to a brick wall. I only want you to have a good think about your future. I just want better for you that's all."

"You're getting on my nerves now mother."

Fiona was walking away, as far she was concerned the conversation was over.

Pat tried a different tact, "I don't want us to fall out. I Know you think I don't know what I'm talking about but I'm not your enemy."

"Doesn't sound like it." Fiona had turned back to talk to Pat.

"Don't listen to me then but mark my words you'll remember these words one day and you'll know I was right and that I only had your best interests at heart."

Fiona sighed, "Mum, I know you mean well but I've got to find my own way in this world."

"I know you do but believe me marriage isn't the be all and end all of everything and now that you and Simon have ended maybe it's a good time to reconsider your options."

"I know you've said that but one day I will meet the right person and get married and have kids. That's what I want to do and what's wrong with that?"

"Nothing's wrong with that as long as you don't think it's a walk in the park because before you know it, you'll be worn down by life, worn down by your husband, or by your children or by the sheer drudgery of life and it will be too late by then to change your mind or think of yourself." Pat continued as Fiona hadn't interrupted her and Pat hoped that maybe Fiona was listening to her for a change, maybe she was getting through. "You can always choose a path just for yourself. It's whether you have the courage to take it that's all I'm trying to say."

"Mum where's this all coming from? I think those tablets have messed with your head." Fiona laughed and Pat felt like she'd been slapped across the face.

"Don't start ridiculing me, Fiona."

"I'm sorry mum but you're just going on."

"I'm sorry about that but I thought I could talk some sense into you."

"My dad's right. Those stupid meetings you're going to are putting stupid ideas into your head."

At first Pat was lost for words. For years she had been the backbone of this family. Putting everyone first and now to hear her own daughter talk to her in that manner she realised that not one of them respected her. She was just 'her in doors'. She had no identity.

Pat found her voice at last and shouted, "Don't you be siding with your father. There's more to me than just being a wife and mother you know."

"No, there isn't. Me Dad treats you like a door mat and you just put up with it. I can't believe you have the cheek to stand there and tell me how to live my life."

Pat was shocked. Fiona had a sharp tongue on her, but she had never spoken to her in that manner before. Pat took a sharp intake of breath and then deflated. Fiona was right. She was one to talk. How could she expect her daughter to choose another path when she set such a terrible example?

"You're right Fiona but I'm telling you now, I'm going to stand on my own two feet from now on and so should you, do it now while you're still young, while you still have the strength." Pat could hear her own voice breaking but was determined to have her say, "You only have one life, grab it with both hands, take it for yourself, not to please anybody else, they don't care about you as much as I do, I am the only one who will ever have your back believe me and you."

Pat started to cry and Fiona stared at her in surprise. It was the first time she'd seen her mother break down and she felt awful. Fiona put her arms around her mum.

"Mum, I'm sorry. You've done a great job with us, and you should go to your meetings. I don't blame you, but you shouldn't have to put up with the way we treat you, especially me father. I'm just saying take a bit of your own medicine. You're still young too, you don't have to put up with his behaviour."

"I know I don't," Pat sobbed. "I watched my own father beat up my mother over the slightest thing and swore blind I wouldn't let a man treat me like that."

"I never knew that," Fiona said alarmed at this new revelation.

"There's a lot you don't know," Pat said. Pat felt like a damn had been broken and continued, "The irony is I thought your father was wonderful because he didn't hit me, and I was grateful and thought he must be a gentleman because of it but he's just as bad. He's worn me down and I don't know what to do about it."

"Leave him mum. He's never going to change. We'll be alright. God, in a few years we'll all have left home and you'll just be left with him."

Pat laughed, "That's a frightening prospect."

Pat and Fiona stood embracing each other but an idea was beginning to germinate inside of Pat, and she thought to herself, maybe I should heed my own words, maybe I owe that much to myself at least.

Pat undid her arms from around Fiona and said, "Oh take no notice of me love. I'm just being silly."

"No, you're not. I'm a cow."

Pat laughed, wiping away her tears, "Go and get those two in for me love, tea will be ready soon."

"You sure you're alright?" Fiona hesitated.

"Of course, I am." Pat turned away.

As Fiona went to walk out, she turned back to her mum and said, "Maybe you are right mum. Maybe I should think of what I want do with my life but if I do you have to promise me that you will too."

Pat smiled, "Okay then. It's a deal."

"What you two gassing about?" They both looked up as Harry walked in.

"Oh, the usual father. Boys." Fiona winked at her mum and they both laughed as Harry looked at them puzzled.

"What's for tea?" Harry said changing the subject.

"Salad," Pat said.

"I'm not eating bloody rabbit food."

Before he could continue Pat said, "I'm only joking. Chops."

"Thank God for that," Harry said, "Nearly had a heart attack then."

"Chance would be a fine thing," Pat muttered to herself as Harry sat down and turned the television on.

CHAPTER 23

Now is the Time

Jimmy James & The Vagabonds

Sally and Ellie were playing in the street when they noticed a group of women coming down the street. Ellie recognised Joan and Lisa at the front and realised that the rest of the women were from Biltons. They were all shouting and laughing and Ellie ran up to them.

"What's going on?" Ellie asked.

"Is your mum in?" Lisa asked.

"Yes," Ellie answered. "Shall I go and get her?"

"You better had," Lisa said laughing, "or she'll miss out on all of the fun."

Ellie dashed down the street and into the kitchen where her mum was standing at the sink.

Pat looked up shocked, "What's up?" Pat screeched, thinking there had been some kind of an accident.

"Nothing, it's just Joan and Lisa and a bunch of women are all on the front waiting for you."

"Get away," Pat laughed thinking Ellie was playing a trick on her.

"They are mum, honest," Ellie grabbed her mum's hand and dragged her out of the kitchen.

When they went outside, there was a big cheer as Pat walked out.

Pat was shocked. "My god what are you lot doing here?"

Pat was confused, why weren't they at work?

"Pat, we've walked out," Lisa shouted, and another loud cheer went up from all the women gathered around.

"I don't understand," Pat said, "What's happened?"

"Well Debbie finally admitted to what happened and then young Sonia Duncan and Donna Ingram came forward and said he'd done the same to them."

"Dirty bastard," Sandra Tweadle shouted, "Wish he'd tried it on with me I know what I would have done to him."

"God help him," someone said and they all laughed at the thought of it.

"Anyway, we've had a load of meetings with the union, and with these women coming forward to collaborate what you've said all along the union have had to take us seriously. So, it's all above board and we are now officially on strike."

"My God," Pat said, "I can't believe it."

"It's about bloody time, if you ask me," Paula said.

"Yes," Joan added, "And we're not going back until you get your job back. That's non-negotiable."

Pat felt tears running down her face, "I don't want you all to put your jobs on the line for me. You can't do that."

"Pat," Lisa said, "It's not just about you. We're not putting up with that sort of behaviour in the workplace and on top of that they can't sack a decent woman like yourself for challenging his behaviour."

"Too right they can't," Sandra Tweadle said.

"Three cheers for Pat. Hip Hip Hooray," Lisa suddenly shouted.

The women all shouted back, "Hip Hip Hooray. Hip Hip Hooray"

Ellie looked on in wonder as all the women began to hug each other, all laughing and crying at the same time.

"Come on we're taking you the pub," Lisa shouted, "No arguing."

"Can we come," Ellie and Sally shouted.

"Yes, why not, better than leaving you here causing mischief," Pat said.

Pat ran in and came back out carrying her handbag. Ellie and Sally couldn't believe their ears, it seemed too good to be true.

"We let the wheels down on Turnip Heads car," Ellie shouted overcome by all the excitement to think what she way saying.

"What?" Pat said and they explained what had happened a few days ago. The women all began laughing and Pat said, "You shouldn't encourage them," and Ellie was surprised she didn't get the telling off she had expected.

"They're a chip off the old block," One woman shouted and before Ellie and Sally knew what was happening, they were lifted onto the shoulders of the women and carried down the street.

"I did too," Billy shouted but no one heard him.

Billy didn't know what was going on, but it looked exciting, so he followed them too with Benny at his side.

The women turned into Borough Road and began to sing as they marched along: -

One, Two, Three, Four,
We want Turnip Head out the Door.
Five, Six, Seven, Eight,
Won't go back till he's out the Gate.

Ellie and Sally felt as if they had died and gone to heaven.

Meanwhile, in a pub not too far away Harry was enjoying a quiet pint.

"Harry," a man rushed in, "have you heard about Biltons?"

"Why what's happened?"

"They've all gone on strike in support of your Pat."

"They've done what," Harry could hardly believe his ears.

"Your Pat, my god I bet you're proud aren't you, sticking up for young Debbie Walters like that."

Harry looked at him dumb struck, he coughed, "Yes course I am. I always told her to stick up for the underdog."

"It's about time someone stuck up for the young girls in that place, by the sound of it he's been having a field day for years."

Harry suddenly felt very angry, "I'm going to punch his bloody lights out."

"You'll have to get in the queue then, Harry," the man said patting Harry on the back. "Let me buy you a drink."

Not long after another man rushed in, "Come on what you sitting here for? Biltons are having a meeting about the strike down The Dale, drink up will you, they need your support."

It didn't take long before the pub emptied. The Landlord shouted after them, "Tell them they can have the next meeting in here." He added as an afterthought. "I'll make them all some sandwiches," but it was too late, there was no one left to hear him. There was a strike to organise.

CHAPTER 24

I Am Woman

Helen Reddy

Pat walked along Borough Road arm in arm with her friends. She couldn't stop laughing every time she looked up to see Ellie and Sally on Steph and Lisa's shoulders. Ellie and Sally were squealing with laughter and we're singing along with the women.

Pat felt swept along by it all. It didn't seem real. I suppose, she reminded herself, that she had nothing to lose as she'd already lost her job but it still worried her to think of all these people willing to risk their jobs by striking. She'd never imagined she would have received this amount of support. Her heart kept on beating faster every time she thought about it, so she tried to concentrate on what was going on around her instead.

Borough Road was packed full of people. It was the main high street in their district, locally called The Village as it was filled with shops of one description or another. A lot of the people stopped and stared after them, shocked to see all the women swarming along the road. People she recognised tried to grab her attention, but Pat couldn't stop to talk, Pat was being pulled along by her friends.

The women were shouting an explanation to anyone who cared to listen, "Biltons have gone out on strike."

They reached The Dale, a pub chosen because it had a large room at the back where they could hold the meeting. The women flooded into the room and towards the bar. Ellie, Sally and Billy, Pat didn't know where Billy had come from, had been supplied with lemonade and crisps. Pat told them they would have to wait outside as some of the discussions would not be suitable for children's ears. Pat listened to their protests but no amount of remonstrations were going to change her mind.

"Don't worry I'll buy you some more lemonade later, but this is for adults only. If you get bored, you can always leave." Pat laughed at the look on their faces.

Pat walked back into the room, someone had bought her a drink and she sat down. The talk and the laughter died down and everyone looked at Pat expectantly.

"My God," Pat said, "I didn't expect this. So, what's gone on?"

Everyone started to talk at once until at last Lisa shouted, "Come on we'll have to do this properly or no one will be heard. Should I Chair the meeting?"

"Woo, get you," Sandra Tweadle shouted.

"Well, someone else can do it if they want but it's the only way we're going to be able to hear what everyone has to say."

Sandra Tweadle shouted, "I was only messing. You just sounded so official."

Lisa smiled at Sandra knowing she meant no harm but continued, "Okay then. I'll start shall I as someone has to tell Pat what's gone on."

"Go on then," Sandra Tweadle roared, "You've got the floor."

"Thanks Sandra," everyone laughed. "So, Pat, Debbie's finally admitted to what happened and after that Sonia Duncan, remember her the one with the red hair?"

"Yes, I remember her," Pat replied.

"Well, she came forward when she heard and then a Donna Ingram came forward too. They said they'd both had similar experiences with Kinnear and either left or been forced to leave as a result."

"Yes," Steph interrupted, "and what makes this so important is they all tell virtually the same story, so they can't all be making it up, so it gives more credence to what you said, Pat."

"And," Lisa added, "it makes a mockery of Kinnear's version of events."

"So, we have a pattern of behaviour," Pat said.

"Yes, and the overriding theme," Lisa continued, "is that they left just to get away from him and they kept quiet because they either felt embarrassed, or they didn't want their husbands or boyfriends to know. Donna said she just kept out of his way, but he made working at Biltons such a misery that she had no other option to leave in the end."

Paula interrupted, "Sonia said she literally got the sack when she refused his advances and Kinnear made up some cock and bull story about her time keeping and that the standard of her work wasn't up to scratch."

"So, he's had a history of this all along?" Pat asked.

"Yes, it seems so," Joan said quietly.

"There's probably loads we don't know about," Paula said.

Lisa continued, "It also looks like he had a type. Young…"

"Obviously," Pat said.

"Quiet, shy. Basically, the type of girl who isn't going to kick up a fuss."

Helen Smith, a colleague of Pat's said, "I can't believe it. I tell you what I'm not going back unless they get that man out of there. I'm telling you that for nothing."

"We should go the police," Sylvia Wright, a woman who worked in the packing room with Lisa, shouted.

The noise level rose once more until at last Lisa shouted, "Yes we should go the police, but we don't think we'd get very far, and the women involved don't want to, they said it's not like he raped them or anything."

"Look the only thing we can do is strike for unfair dismissal for Pat but tell the management we want him out. We can only do this through industrial action," Steph shouted.

"I agree," said Paula. "Striking is our only option."

Lisa continued, "So we've been in talks with the union about you being unfairly dismissed Pat but once the other women came forward it put it all into perspective as to why you got the sack, if you know what I mean?"

"Yes of course," Pat replied.

"That's why it's taken us so long for them to listen to us, the wankers," Lisa said losing her professional edge in an instant.

Paula picked up where Lisa had left off, "It just goes beyond the grain that he sacked you with no warning and sent you packing in such a manner. I mean that alone is enough to call a strike and the unions agreed but we have also demanded that Kinnear is looked into. We have said we won't be going back unless a thorough and proper investigation takes place. We want his conduct looked into as it will back up your claim for unfair dismissal. The two go hand in hand really."

Pat sat quietly taking it all in.

Joan said, "We didn't want to give you any false hope Pat until we knew the union were taking it seriously, but we haven't been idle, I can tell you."

Pat felt like crying. There she'd been thinking she was coping with this all alone and all of these women had been working in the background trying to help her.

"I can't thank you enough," Pat said.

"Now don't be getting all soppy on us Pat Thomas," Steph said hugging her.

Paula said, "We told you we had your back."

"My God," Pat replied, "I think you're all bloody marvellous."

Suddenly the doors swung open, and a group of men entered.

"Right, ladies I hope you haven't left us out of your discussions?" Neil Dawson asked as the men gathered around the women.

"No, we've only just got here," Lisa answered.

"What the men are involved too?" Pat asked bewildered, she thought it was only the women who had downed tooled.

"Of course, we have, we're not letting you get sacked because of a fuckin' toe rag like that," Neil said. "What do you take us for?"

Pat shook her head. It was all becoming too much to take in. "Thanks," she said and stood up and gave Neil a hug.

"Alright Pat, no need for any of this," Neil said becoming embarrassed.

"Oh, piss off will you Neil, you love it," Sandra squealed.

Neil ignored Sandra and sat down. "Hi, Pat, it's good to see you but would you mind telling us exactly what happened between you and Kinnear, then?"

"Kinnear, Fuckin' Turnip Head you mean," Sandra Tweadle shouted.

"Who the fuck is Turnip Head when he's at home?" Neil asked.

"Bob Kinnear," Joan shouted, "otherwise known as Turnip Head."

"More like Dick Head," Steph shouted.

Neil started to laugh, "He does look like a fuckin' turnip doesn't he."

Pat began to repeat what happened on the day she was sacked for the men's benefit.

"Despicable," Neil said, he stood up, "I'm getting a drink anyone want anything?"

"I can't believe nothings been said earlier," Albert, Steph's husband said. "Steph only told me last night that he was trying it on with her when she first started. Fuckin' driving lessons, I'll give him driving lessons. I'm going to knock his fuckin' head off."

Everyone stared at Albert, he was a big man, and no one questioned that he wasn't more than capable of inflicting a lot of damage on anyone who upset him, but no one wanted him to get too riled up or hell would break loose.

"Look, Albert," Pat said at last raising her voice, "that won't help matters. He'll only get the police on you and then where will we you be? We have to do this officially, it's the only way we can stop him in his tracks. It's no good using violence, he'll still be working there, and you'll be in a police cell."

Steph said, "Yes use your head for once why don't you. This strike is official. We've put our demands on the table and we'll make them listen. You go and do that and everything we're fighting for will be undermined, surely you can see that?"

Albert grunted in reply and sat down looking morose.

"No, I agree with Big Al, I don't know why we're sitting here," another man, John Curtis said. "he'll soon get the message if we deal with him. Fuck all this striking business."

The clamour of voices rose to a crescendo everyone arguing their point.

"Shut up the lot of you," Pat stood up. "This isn't about you men proving how tough you are. This is about stopping this man from continuing to assault young innocent girls. What will beating him up achieve? You'll all lose your jobs and he'll still be in there, carrying on as usual. We've got to use our heads not our fists."

"Yes," Lisa cried. "Listen to Pat will you. We've got to go through the proper channels, or he'll carry on doing this and no one will be able to stop him."

"Here, here," was shouted.

The door opened once more, and another crowd of people walked in. Pat looked up and saw Harry amongst them. She stared at him dumb founded, he was the last person she expected to see in here.

"Hey, Harry glad you could join us," Albert shouted over to him. "I can't believe what's been going on. I bet you wanted to kill him when you heard?"

"Too right I did," Pat stared at him and couldn't believe her ears. She couldn't believe he had the cheek to look her right in the eye when he said it too. "I just didn't know what our Pat could do about it but if you all stand behind her maybe they'll have to listen and then maybe she'll get her job back."

Pat watched as Harry puffed his chest out.

"Glad to see you're behind her," Albert said.

"A hundred percent," Harry said.

"The cheek of the man," Pat muttered to Joan, "he's been calling me all the names under the sun for the past three weeks."

"Typical," Joan whispered back, "he always was all mouth and no trousers."

"Couldn't have put it better, Joan."

Pat and Joan chuckled together as they watched Harry going the bar to get a round in.

"So," Pat said turning to the men, "All I can say is thanks for your support."

Lisa began to explain how the other women had come forward. Everyone listened. No one interrupted and Pat could tell by the look on the men's faces that they were taking these allegations seriously. It was a major milestone having the men on board, and Pat knew it would make them a lot stronger if all the workforce was united.

The discussion continued until at last Joan, of all people, said in a very decisive tone, "So are we all in agreement, until Pat gets her job back and Kinnear is shown the door we don't go back?"

"Yes," everyone shouted.

"Right then let's get organised," Pat said. "Anyone got a pen or paper?"

Pat, Joan, Steph, Lisa and Paula fell about laughing. "No, said Steph but I've got an eyeliner."

No one else present knew what was so funny and looked at the women in confusion.

"What's so funny?" Albert asked.

"Oh, nothing," said Steph, "you wouldn't understand."

Soon a pen and paper were found, and the meeting started in earnest.

Outside Ellie, Sally and Billy had finished their lemonade.

"I'm going back in for some more," Ellie said.

She returned with more lemonade and crisps. They were sitting on a bench outside with the sun beating down on them. Benny was tucked under the table fast asleep.

"This is great," Billy said.

"I know," Ellie said, "but you want to hear the language out of them all. My mum was mortified when she saw me and couldn't get me out quick enough."

"Are they swearing?" Sally asked.

"Swearing and shouting, I've never heard the like." Ellie said, "Turnip Head's not going to know what's hit him when that lot get hold of him."

CHAPTER 25
Get Up Stand Up
The Wailers (with Bob Marley)

The sun was beating down and the women and men gathered outside Biltons were dressed in loose summer clothing, but it was still too hot standing outside in the heat. After the first day a makeshift awning of sheets had been erected, propped up with pieces of wood and hung on the fence surrounding their workplace. This had at least provided some kind of protection, but this had caused consternation with the Biltons management who had insisted they take it down. This request had been met with short shrift.

"Fuck off," was the general consensus when Dean, the Biltons security guard had approached them half-heartedly and tried to broach the subject. "Scab," was shouted at him as he scurried back into the factory.

"Snively nosed bastard," Sandra Tweadle said, "Never liked him."

"Who would," shouted Lisa, "He's so far up Turnip Heads arse, you can't tell where one begins and the other ends." Everyone laughed.

The comradeship was palpable, even in the baking hot sun they could have a laugh. Ice creams were distributed, people stopped by with cold drinks and cars and trucks beeped their horns as they passed. They all knew they weren't there for fun, but there was no harm in enjoying themselves at the same time. Most of the strikers were worried about money and getting the sack but a chord had been struck in each and every one of them and they knew they had to maintain this fight at all costs or fall together as one.

Pat beamed with pride as she listened to their jokes and the songs which erupted from nowhere when they began to feel a bit jaded. She had never felt this sense of belonging before, and it gave her a great deal of satisfaction when she looked at her co-workers, who had all stood up for her.

"Don't worry," Joan said as she noticed a frown crossing Pat's brow, "we're not going to give up until you're re-instated. Each and every one of us have had enough of him and he's not going to get away with it anymore."

Steph who was standing close by overheard Joan's comment, "Too right he's not."

"I don't know Steph, I don't want anyone to lose their job over me," Pat said.

"Don't be daft will ya, Pat," Lisa shouted, "Sorry to disillusion you love but this isn't just about you, you know. This about that fat bastard in there, behaviour. He's not getting away with touching up the young girls any longer. I'm afraid this strike has taken on of its a life of its own and there's nothing you can say or do to stop it. So, stop worrying, do you hear me." Lisa rubbed the top of Pat's head and Pat shook her off laughing.

"Okay girls, I get the message loud and clear," Pat conceded, her worries drifting off in the mid-day sun.

Paula always the first to start singing, began to sing, "We shall overcome, we shall overcome," and on cue everyone joined in.

Pat looked up and could see Turnip Head standing at the window, with Tina Brown at his side.

"There he is," Pat shouted, "the scum bag."

Pat felt her face grow hot, she'd never shouted insults at anyone else other than Harry before and it felt wrong, but the words had come out of her mouth, along with her anger and she had been unable to stop herself.

"Yeah, get out here and face us, you bastard," Sandra Tweadle shouted. "I'd love you to try it on with me."

Steph whispered to Pat, "She'd probably be grateful."

Pat burst out laughing but said, "Seph don't be so awful, solidarity and all that."

The women had become far more vocal than the men in their company, and some of the women's language was far worse than the men had realised. As one of the men, Dan Nichols had said in the pub the night before, "They'd make a docker blush, I mean it," and the men gathered around him had laughed. "I'm not joking," he'd said raising his glass to his lips before taking a long, much needed, drink. "God help Turnip Head if they ever get hold of him. They'd string him up, I'm telling ya."

The strike continued, soon it was week two with no negotiations in sight. The Unions had argued their case, the management had held firm. There seemed to be a stale mate but still the strike continued. Some of the strikers decided to bring their dogs along and one wit had stuck a cardboard emblem on to his dog's collar which read, "If you think I'm ugly, you should see my owner!"

On a Friday afternoon, drinks were consumed, and it was a Friday afternoon, week two, when one of the union reps, Sid Ashton, put in an appearance. Sid approached Pat as she stood taking a sip of cider.

"Hi, Pat," Sid said, and everyone peered over.

"Hi, Sid to what do we owe this pleasure?" Pat asked, straight faced.

Pat wasn't happy with Sid Ashton and his lack of appearance at the picket line had been noted and commented on.

"Hi, Pat, yes sorry I haven't been over much, but we've been working flat out on your behalf believe it or not and that's why I've come over to have a word."

"Oh right," Pat said raising her eyebrows at his words. "So, go on then. What is it?"

Sid smiled, "Well the thing is me and the lads have been talking and we wondered if you wouldn't mind coming over to the Liverpool branch meeting next week to talk to some of our comrades over there? We think it would give a greater understanding to what the real core issues are over here."

Pat stared at him. "You want me to come over there to explain that we're on strike because we didn't like the fact that a dirty old man has been putting his hand up young girl's skirts? What part of that is so difficult to understand?"

Sid gulped, "Pat we know that but we thought if you came over and you explained it to them, it would humanise it. It would be better if they heard it directly from you, first hand so to speak."

"Why what have they been saying? That we're a load of hysterical woman who are making a big deal over a bit of slap and tickle?"

"Now come on Pat, you're putting words in my mouth now."

"It's not just women here you know Sid, there's men here too."

There were shouts of 'here, here' from the men.

Sid took a deep breath and looked around at the crowd, "You're getting me all wrong, we know this is a serious issue we just thought if Pat was to come over, she could make them understand what's at stake here."

Pat sighed, "I thought they were on our side, now I realise there as bad as that shower in there?" Pat pointed over to Biltons.

"No there not, Pat, they do understand but it's just that you're a very articulate woman and yes some of the men are dinosaurs and that's why it would do them good to hear it direct from the horse's mouth, so to speak."

Pat stared at Sid and Sid stared back. "Why me? There's plenty of people here who could do a better job than I could."

"Well, obviously there is," Sid looked around at the people gathered, and took on a conciliatory tone, "but we've heard you talking Pat and you make sense, you don't beat around the bush, and anyway it was agreed by a unanimous decision, that the best person for the job was you.".

"You haven't got me mixed up with someone else have you, Sid," Pat said looking around at her friends and laughing.

"Don't be soft, of course we haven't."

Pat stood quietly as the true weight of Sid's words finally dawned on her, at last she said, "Oh come on Sid, behave yourself, I wouldn't know what to say."

"Of course, you would. Me and the lad's think you'd do a much better job trying to persuade our comrades on how important this strike is, than we've been able to do."

Lisa intervened, "That's a brilliant idea, Sid. Pat, of course you've got to do it, you must. We need to be heard and you're the person to do it."

This was met with shouts of encouragement, "Go on Pat... you can do it."

"Don't you lot start," Pat said looking around and shaking her head.

Pat looked at Sid and asked, "Just a talk then?"

"Well, more of a speech if I'm honest."

"A speech, it just keeps getting better and better."

"Come on Pat, we can't shut you up normally," Sid said laughing.

"Pat, we'll help you. We'll all put our heads together and write a speech that will stick a fuckin' firework up their arses. My god we've been talking about this for long enough, this is a brilliant opportunity," Lisa said smiling at Pat.

"Oh, I don't know, talking in front of a load of people. I'd feel so embarrassed."

"Embarrassed my arse," Lisa said, "This isn't the time for embarrassment. This is the time for action."

Joan suddenly appeared and put her arm around Pat, "I for one have every faith in you, Pat. You're the one who brought all this to the fore. It has to be you. You do understand that don't you?"

Pat felt tears sting her eyes but laughed them away, "Oh get lost will you. Ganging up on me."

"So, you're going to do it then?" Sid asked.

Pat took a deep breath, "Of course I bloody am, just try and stop me."

Cheers erupted and Pat took a deep breath, and thought, bloody hell what have I let myself in for.

CHAPTER 26

I'd Really Love to See you Tonight
England Dan & John Ford Coley

It was a Friday night. Ellie and Sally had just finished their tea. Pat was getting ready in the bathroom. Pat was going to the meeting tonight over in Liverpool and it had caused a lot of consternation in the Thomas household. Ellie and Sally didn't want their mum to go out and neither did Harry. Pat tried to ignore the fact that Harry still hadn't come home from work. She had asked him specifically to come home after work to look after Ellie and Sally and she knew for a fact he would be doing this on purpose just to upset her.

Pat continued to get ready, her hand shaking as she put on her eye shadow. She was nervous about tonight, the thought of having to speak to a room full of people made her stomach turn over every time she thought about it and now on top of everything else Harry, not coming home, was only making matters worse.

Harry had certainly changed his tune since the meeting in The Dale. Behind me one hundred percent, as if, Pat thought. Why couldn't he understand how important this was to her? Not only for her, for everyone who was on strike as well. Pat realised Harry felt threatened by her new found status. He wanted her to remain at home. Working for pin money was okay as long as she didn't get above her station. Oh, sod him, Pat muttered to herself she was not going to allow herself to be brow beaten anymore.

Pat came out of the bathroom and looked at Ellie and Sally sitting on the settee watching the tele. They seemed alright. Fiona too was sat watching the tele and Gary was in the parlour listening to records with a couple of his mates. She knew Ellie and Sally would be okay with Fiona and Gary but she wished

Harry would come in so she could go out without worrying. Pat had made his tea and now it sat in the oven waiting for him.

Pat turned to Fiona and said, "So, Fiona will you be alright looking after Ellie and Sally for a couple of hours?"

"Yes of course, mum. I told you I would, anyway Gary's in as well so it's not like I'm on my own."

"Well, as long as you're sure?" Fiona pulled a face and continued to watch the programme on the tele.

Pat walked over to the oven and turned it off.

"Tell your dad, his teas in the oven and he'll need to reheat it when he gets in."

"Yeah, okay mum," Fiona said.

"You look nice, mum," Ellie said.

Pat had been the hairdressers to have her hair set and she was wearing make-up. Pat was wearing a black dress and high heels. Her mum looked so much better than she normally did. Ellie thought, her mum should dress like that more often.

"Thanks love," Pat smiled. "Right, there's money by the meter in case the leccy or gas goes but I've only just put some in so it should be alright. Your dad should be in soon anyway." Pat said to Fiona. "Fiona, whatever you do, make sure they don't go out the street and if your dad doesn't come in you make sure they're in for nine."

"Ah, Mum," Sally wailed, "that's dead early. Billy's allowed to stay out till ten."

"You're not Billy, though are you," Pat said, and Sally knew it was pointless arguing.

They watched as their mum checked her make up in the mirror above the fire and Ellie and Sally watched in fascination at their mum, who looked so different. Ellie and Sally's programme they had been watching on the tele had ended and they decided it was time to play out but they hung back watching their mum putting her keys and make up in her bag.

They knew their mum was going to a meeting over in Liverpool and it was supposed to be a big deal as their mum was going to make a speech and everything. They had heard her practising it when their dad was out. They had giggled as she'd sounded so serious and at certain points, she raised her voice to make a point. Ellie and Sally had clapped at the end, even though they didn't understand half of it, but to them it sounded good.

As far as Ellie was concerned the only downside was their mum was going to leave them, it wouldn't be the same if their mum wasn't where they expected her to be. Ellie wished her mum would stay in and watch the tele with them like she usually did on a Friday night. She usually bought them lemonade and crisps as a treat and they all cuddled together on the settee. It felt wrong their routine had been upset but Ellie was trying to put a brave face on.

Ellie had heard her mum talking to Fiona about the meeting earlier. Fiona had said, 'Just because he doesn't want you to go, don't let him ruin it for you'. It had been an ongoing debate all week, every time their mum mentioned the meeting to their dad, he became cross. Ellie was confused, her dad had tried to convince them all that their mum was wrong for going to this meeting but at the same time Ellie knew it was important to her mum also and didn't know why her dad had to go on about it so much.

Ellie thought her mum looked really nice and was looking forward to this meeting even if she kept on saying how nervous she was. So, Ellie had decided she wasn't going to ask her mum 'Not to go out' as it wouldn't be fair. Ellie had even said to Sally, when Sally had raised her concerns, that most nights they hardly saw their mum until it was time to go in so what was the difference? But still Ellie thought it would feel odd that their mum wouldn't be in the house if they needed her. Ellie told herself not to be a big baby, she knew she was being ridiculous.

When eventually Pat left the house Ellie and Sally walked her to the top of the road and waved to her as she walked towards the Ferry.

They both shouted, "Good luck, mum."

Pat shouted back, "Behave yourselves, I'll be fine."

Once their mum was out of sight Ellie quickly forgot about her concerns, especially when a game of hide and seek began but then Ellie realised that there were fewer kids playing out. Ellie went back to the matter which was really troubling her and that was she could no longer ignore the fact that her street would soon be knocked down. A lot of families had moved away, more houses were being bricked up and their street had taken on a different aspect. Windows had been smashed and slates, which had fallen from the roofs lay broken in the middle of the road. Ellie couldn't put her finger on it, but their street seemed forlorn and abandoned. Ellie knew it wouldn't be long before they had to move too but she pushed that to the back of her mind.

Sally must have been feeling the same because she was sitting on the pavement despondently, so Ellie sat next to her. They sat quietly together both lost in their own thoughts. Suddenly their attention was drawn to a red sports car coming down their road. Ellie and Sally looked at it as if it was from another planet. They were even more amazed when it pulled up outside their house. A tall dark-haired man climbed out of the car and walked to their front door. They watched in fascination as Fiona answered the front door. No longer was she wearing her oldest pair of pyjamas, the ones she had been slobbing around the house in all day. Now Fiona was resplendent in a trouser suit and strappy wedged sandals. Her hair had been washed and curled and her makeup was applied immaculately.

Ellie watched as Fiona casually leaned against the front door frame and giggled as she talked to this strange man. Ellie and Sally stood up and sidled up, as they couldn't hear what was being said, from where they had been sitting.

"Oh, Brendan, I can't go out looking like this. I look awful." Were the first words Ellie heard. The man, who was about to say something in return stopped as he saw Ellie and Sally approach. Fiona bristled and said, "Get lost you two."

"Are these two your sisters?" The man asked smiling at them, Ellie stared at him suspiciously.

"Yes, they are. Look at the state of them. They're like little urchins."

The man laughed, "No, they're really cute."

Fiona snorted, "Cute those two, you must be joking."

"Who's he?" Ellie asked Fiona.

"None of your business," Fiona said.

"Bet Simon would like to know." Ellie and Sally laughed.

Fiona looked them in the eye, and said, "Clear off or you're coming in." The words cut like a knife and Ellie and Sally backed off to the other side of the road, watching their sister out of the corner of their eyes.

"I wonder who he is?" Sally whispered.

"Don't know but I don't like him."

"He's got to be better than Simon."

"Do you think?"

"Yeah, he might give us a ride in his car."

Ellie began to warm to the idea as she said, "He's better looking than Simon, isn't he?"

"That's not hard," Sally said, and they both laughed.

It was all becoming a bit boring and eventually Ellie and Sally found better things to do but suddenly they heard their names being called. They looked up shocked to see Fiona sitting in the sports car next to the dark-haired man. She was now wearing sunglasses and the roof of the car had been pulled down. She looked like a film star and Ellie and Sally both stared open mouthed.

"You'll be alright until me dad gets in, won't you?"

"Yeah, but where are you going?" Ellie asked.

"If you don't know you can't tell," Fiona and the man laughed. "Gary's in if you need anything and dad will be in soon. Don't go out of the street." Fiona warned as the car took off, leaving Ellie and Sally watching it as it skidded round the top of their road.

"Looks like Simon's history," Ellie said.

"Yeah," Sally agreed and they went off bemused at their sister's sudden change of mood.

It wasn't until Billy was called in that Ellie and Sally realised it must be late. Their front door stood open, but their house was ominously dark. Ellie and Sally walked in and realised there was no music drifting out from the parlour. They looked in. Gary wasn't there. They went into the living room and had to turn the light on. No one was there. Ellie and Sally stared at each other frightened.

"Where is everyone?" Sally asked.

"I don't know."

They checked upstairs but knew no one was in. They went

outside and looked up and down their deserted street. All the front doors were closed.

"Dad'll be in soon," Ellie said trying to convince herself more than anything else.

"Where do you think Gary is?" Sally asked.

"Who knows, he didn't even tell us he was going out."

"Me dad'll kill him if he's not in soon," Ellie said sagely.

"I'm frightened," Sally said. Ellie felt frightened too.

They decided to knock at Billy's in the hope that his mum would let them stay with them until someone came home so they nervously walked up to Billy's house. Notoriously Billy's mum never let anyone in their home. It was totally off limits and that's because their mum said it was a 'midden'. They knocked tentatively on the door and eventually it opened.

Billy's Mum Carole stared at them. "What do you two want?"

She never was one to stand on ceremony.

"No one's in. Our Gary's gone out and he didn't even tell us where he was going and me dad hasn't come in." Ellie explained.

"So, what's that got to do with me?" She looked down at them and as far as Ellie was concerned, she had a smug look on her face.

"We just thought…"

"You thought what?" Carole asked.

"Erm, well," Ellie didn't want to ask now if they could wait inside. "Nothing, it's okay."

"Where's your mum?"

"She's gone to a meeting in Liverpool," Sally piped in.

"Alright for some," Carole said and then as an afterthought she added, "Your dad'll be in when the pubs close," and with no further ado closed the front door.

Ellie and Sally looked forlornly at each other. They went back to their house and stood on the front step looking up and down the road for their dad or their Gary to come home. When a drunken man staggered down the road they ran inside and locked the front door. Sally began to cry, and Ellie was also close to tears.

They sat in the front room and turned the tele on but it didn't help them. The house was strange without at least one of their parents being there, even scarier with Fiona or Gary not being in either. Although Ellie would have assumed, she would love to have had the house all to themselves now that they did it felt silent and cold. It seemed as if any number of things could happen to them, and no one was there to protect them. Eventually the national anthem came on the tele and there was nothing left to watch.

"Do you think this house is haunted," Sally asked staring around their familiar living room.

"I don't know. It might be," Ellie said even though the thought had never occurred to her before.

"I don't want to go to bed until someone gets in," Sally said.

"No, me neither."

"What if someone breaks in?"

Their imagination was on over drive and before long they were talking of not only ghosts but of burglars or bad men. Bad men who would know they were on their own and would come in and take them away and no one would know where they were.

"I'm going to get a hammer out of me dad's tool box," Ellie announced and they went in search of it.

They sat on the settee with the hammer in between them dozing off intermittently until a sound sometimes as innocuous as the clock striking would make them jump with fright. Suddenly they were startled to hear the noise of the front door opening and footsteps coming along the hall. Ellie jumped up; the hammer clutched tightly in her hand. They watched as the living room door opened and to their relief their dad stood staring at them.

"What the hell are you two doing up?" His voice sounded slurred and he smelt of beer.

"No one's in," Ellie said the tears at last falling.

Harry's voice reverberated round the room, "What do you mean, no ones in? Where's your mother?"

CHAPTER 27

Fox on the Run

Sweet

"First and foremost, I would like to thank you all for coming here tonight and to thank you all for showing your support to everyone at Biltons." Pat pauses as everyone claps.

Pat looks out at the expectant faces and sees Lisa, Joan, Steph and Paula all smiling at her. She sees Joan put her thumb in the air as Lisa mouths, 'You can do it girl'. Her brother Tony is also there, and she smiles over at him, glad to have his support.

Pat looks at her notes and takes a deep breath, she can feel sweat pooling between her shoulder blades and notices her hands are trembling. Pat's mind suddenly goes blank, and she wonders why she is up on this podium and why she even had the nerve to think that she could do this. The room goes quiet, and Pat can hear people shuffling in their seats and a few coughs as rows of faces stare up at her. Pat gulps, fighting for breath and then she remembers why she is here. She thinks of little Debbie Walters crying in the toilets.

Pat looks up, smiles and finds strength from the fact that she is not here for herself, but she is here representing all the young women groped by that man over the years. Pat, with her voice loud and clear, begins.

"I'm here tonight, in the hope I can go some way to explain why we at Biltons believe we had no other alternative but to strike and that is because we have found out to our disgust that the manager, who shall remain nameless,"

"Otherwise known as Turnip Head," Lisa shouts and Pat tries to keep a straight face as everyone begins to laugh.

"Who shall remain nameless has systematically, over a number of years, been groping or should I say assaulting young women who have had the misfortune of working at Biltons. When I called this man out, I was sacked. It is as simple as that. Now, you all may think that the strike is to have me reinstated but it's not. The strike may have started out because of that but when the facts became clear everyone at Biltons made the unanimous decision that we would not go back to work until the owners of Biltons carry out a thorough and proper investigation into this man's behaviour.

The fact they have refused to do so has put us in a terrible position. Until an investigation takes place my colleagues are refusing to return to work and even if they offered me my job back tomorrow, I wouldn't go back either. This is what we are fighting for, do I have your support?"

There are murmurings amongst the crowd, but not the applause Pat was hoping for. Pat knew it was a difficult subject and they'd talked about how they could explain their stance without antagonizing some of their audience. Pat knew a lot of the men had chauvinistic attitudes and many probably thought this was all a bit of a storm in a teacup. Pat and her friends had debated for a long time how they could overcome these prejudices and Pat knew it was going to be an uphill battle, but she knew she had to give it a go so carried on regardless.

"The simple truth of the matter is the management at Biltons will not listen to us. By standing by this man, they are disrespecting each and every one of their staff and that is why we feel until they listen to our concerns, we have no other alternative but to continue with industrial action. It is the only action we have at our disposal. It is the only way to make them sit up and listen.

Obviously, on a personal level I am both proud and humbled by the stance my colleagues have taken not only on my behalf but on behalf of all the young girls who have had to put up with this man's behaviour over the years."

"Too right," Lisa shouts.

Pat takes the opportunity to catch her breath before continuing, "So yes, the reason I was sacked was because I dared to take this man to task for assaulting a young girl. A young girl who is barely out of school. The fact that I was sacked for doing so did not surprise me in the least. Maybe it should have done. Maybe we all should be shocked to find that I can be sacked because I don't like a dirty old man putting his hand up a young girl's skirt?"

"Dirty bastard," someone shouts and Pat nods before continuing.

"We always had our suspicions at Biltons about this man."

Someone shouts, "Bob Kinnear," which is followed by jeers and boos.

Pat waits for the noise to die down before continuing, "As I say, we always had our suspicions that this man was an unsavory character."

"You can say that again," Steph shouts out and there is laughter before Pat can continue. "But what shocked us the most is when these allegations were brought to the management at Biltons attention they refused to take these allegations seriously and refused to listen to our concerns.

The stance that the management at Biltons have taken in supporting that man's behaviour is deplorable and that is why I am here tonight to ask you to support us because to be honest we need all the help we can get. They're determined to ignore what's happening but it's up to us to make them see him for what he is because otherwise he'll carry on doing this and it is up to us to stop him."

Pat feels the atmosphere changing with notes of disapproval

becoming louder. Pat raises her voice, carried away by the reception she is receiving and is surprised to find that she is enjoying herself. It's good to be up here, she realises, to articulate how she feels but most of all it feels good to be listened to. Pat takes another deep breath, "Some people would say that the unions don't care. That they are simply a bureaucratic institution whose only concern is improving wages for its male members and that they are not concerned with the interest of women, but if you give us your support tonight you will prove that the union is here for all of its members, not just for men but for women also."

"Here, here," someone shouts.

Pat continues, "I also want to take this opportunity to encourage men in the union to become a part of the fight and recognize what some women have to put up with in the workplace. The looks, the remarks, the badgering for sexual favours, comments on our appearance, the sheer degradation of it all is bad enough but what we should not have to put up with is the forced physical contact by one person onto another person.

For far too long this man has violated young girls who have had the misfortune of working at Biltons. He has used his position of power for his own perverse pleasure. This is not about me getting my job back, this is about Biltons respecting their employees and getting rid of that man from our place of work.

Because we at Biltons don't want young women to feel ashamed because of that man's actions. We don't want young women to be sacked because they wouldn't comply with that man's wishes."

Pat pauses to take another deep breath and lowers her voice, "We have to take a stand, this is not just a bit of slap and tickle, harmless fun in the workplace, this is a gross violation, and we are not going to ignore this type of behaviour anymore. Now this is out in the open we're not going to allow it to be hidden away again."

Pat pauses for effect, "I ask you ladies and gentlemen, or should I say comrades, do we continue to ignore this type of behaviour? Or do we stand up, all of us, men and women together, and say enough is enough?"

Paula shouts, "Enough is enough."

There are loud cheers but Pat notices that some of the men are smirking and nudging one another.

"You may think it's funny." Pat glares at the men, "Maybe some men here think the young girl was simply being hysterical, maybe you think I'm being hysterical. Maybe you think this man has the right to touch up his staff?" The men look away embarrassed, "But I for one say he doesn't. I was sacked for daring to question this man's authority, but I would do it again and I'll keep on doing it until men like that are stopped."

"You tell 'em, Pat," Lisa shouts.

"I have a husband and children and yet at a drop of a hat..."

"Or his trousers," some wit chips in.

Pat continues undeterred, "Yes, if you like, at the drop of that man's trousers, my livelihood is taken away from me. Why because I dare to stick up to a bully. Because that's what he is. A bully hiding behind his position and a dirty little bully at that."

There's a shout of, "Too right he is."

Pat once again appeals to her audience, reveling in the atmosphere, almost pinching herself that she's had the nerve to address all of these people, people who are not only willing to listen to her but who are also reacting to her words. "All we're asking for is a bit of respect at work. I ask for young women to be able to work without being molested. We have to combat these outdated attitudes that a woman, or in this case a girl, 'Must have been asking for it' or 'her skirt was too short, so what did she expect?'

"I for one am no longer going to stand by and turn a blind eye. This could have been your wife, your daughter, your sister and no one should have to go to work and put up with that kind of behaviour, because by God I certainly don't go to work for the good of my health. Do you? We go to work to put bread on the table for our families, to put a roof over our heads but what a young woman, certainly doesn't go to work for, is to be molested by a dirty old man and I for one am not going to stand for it any longer. Are you?"

There are loud cries of, "No..."

"So, I ask each and every one of you to support us in our strike. Give us back our dignity."

Lisa shouts, "Give Pat back her job."

Which is repeated as a cry and taken up by the crowd.

"No." Pat shouts, "Give women back their dignity."

"We're behind you, Pat," someone shouts.

People begin to clap which develops into a crescendo. Pat shouts, "Thank you everyone. Thank you all for coming here and listening to me. It's times like this when your trust in human nature is restored."
When Pat walks off the stage she is surrounded by people who want to talk to her. The crowd retires to the bar. It's a long night, full of good wishes and good advice.

It's only later when Pat sees the time that she realises it's time to go home. Her brother Tony, says, "You might as well stay at ours Pat. No use going home now."
"But what about the kids?" Pat asks.

"Harry, Fiona and Gary are at home, aren't they?" Pat nods. "Well then that's settled. They'll be fine."

Pat pushes her fears to one side. Of course, they'll be fine. It won't hurt Harry to stay in with his own kids for one night and besides there's too many people to talk to. There's so much help to ask for, what harm will it do if she stays out for one night? Pat looks around at the crowded room, her spirits are high, she feels as if anything is possible. Maybe the strike can be won after all.

CHAPTER 28
She's Gone
Hall & Oates

"That bloody meeting. I told her not to go and now look what's happened." Harry bellowed and then he asked, "So, where's Fiona and Gary?"

"We don't know. Fiona went out with a fella in a sports car, and we don't know where Gary is." Ellie said.

Harry looked at his children dumbstruck. It was not often he was lost for words. Ellie and Sally both started to cry as if they were somehow to blame for the situation. It was bad enough being left on their own but now their dad was angry and all hell would break lose now.

"It's not our fault, dad," Sally said.

"We didn't want to stay in on our own," Ellie added.

"I can't believe this," Harry said.

In the end Harry carried Ellie and Sally to bed and tucked them in. They were both fast asleep before he had closed the bedroom door.

The next morning, they were woken by shouting downstairs.

"Me mum said you were coming in."

"I don't care what your mother said, not only did you leave your two sisters alone but you went gallivanting off with someone in a sports car or so I've been told."

"I wasn't gallivanting, I was on a date."

"A date? You were getting married to Simon this time last week."

"I'm going out with Brendan now."

"Brendan, who the bloody hell is Brendan when he's at home?" Harry's voice was getting louder as Ellie and Sally exchanged glances. "And, what time did you roll in last night?"

"It wasn't late."

"Not late, I wasn't in till 1 o'clock and you still weren't in. So, it must have been a bloody long date."

"We were talking."

"Must have been a hell of a conversation."

"Don't you be insinuating things, father, you always think the worst."

"The worst, the bloody worst. The worst thing, and don't you forget it, is you left your little sisters on their own."

"I didn't Gary was in."

"Gary? He can't even look after himself let alone Ellie and Sally."

"Is that my fault? I'm not their nurse maid. Just because I'm a girl I don't see why it should all be down to me."

"It's not because you're a girl it's because you're older than Gary and you should have more sense than to leave him in charge."

"I didn't know he would go out."

"Well, he did go out, didn't he and so did you. What so you could go out with Brendan, whoever he is and get a ride in a bloody sports car."

"It wasn't like that."

"So, what was it like then?"

Ellie and Sally waited for Fiona's response, up until now it seemed as if she didn't have a leg to stand on.

"Mum said you were coming in. Isn't it your fault too?"

Ellie raised her eyebrows and Sally smiled, seemed as if Fiona had come back fighting.

"Don't you be questioning me in that manner," Harry roared.

"Well, it's not fair. I'm getting all the blame and you didn't come in either."

"I'm your father."

"And, they're your children."

Ellie and Sally were intrigued to hear their dad's response but suddenly they heard their Mum's voice.

"What the hell are you two shouting and arguing about? I could hear you from the top of the street."

"It's me dad, mum," Fiona said, relieved to see her mum. "He's blaming me for going out and leaving Ellie and Sally on their own but when I went out Gary said he was staying in and I thought me dad was coming home anyway. So, I don't know why I'm getting all the blame?"

"What Ellie and Sally were left on their own? I go out for one bloody night and not one of you can be left to look after them properly?"

Ellie was shocked, her mum's voice was actually louder than their dad's. Ellie was impressed because this took some doing.

Her dad was not to be beaten though and he raised his voice and shouted, "You have the cheek to stand bawling and yelling at me while you leave your own children running around the streets on their own while you go to some lousy meeting?"

"I told you I was going out. I asked you point blank to come home after work and you said you would be in before nine o'clock."

"I can't remember that," Harry's voice had quietened somewhat.

"I haven't stopped going on about it all week."

Ellie could remember the conversation herself, she mouthed to Sally, "She did too, I remember she said it to him every single night."

"Yeah, me dad told her not to go on about it," Sally whispered back.

They returned their attention back to the argument downstairs.

"I thought you were coming in. I wouldn't have gone out otherwise," Fiona interceded and Ellie felt like saying, 'Game, set and match' but their dad was not going to be beaten that easily.

"I had to work late. I was under the impression that neither you or Gary would leave your two younger sisters on their own."

"I didn't," Fiona said simply. "Gary did."

"I'm going to kill him," Pat said.

"Not if I see him first," Harry said.

They heard Fiona coming up the stairs. When she opened the bedroom door, she was smiling to herself.

"Gary isn't half going to get it," she said to them.

They smiled conspiratorially to one another.

Ellie and Sally were eating their breakfast and watching Swap Shop when Gary came in.

They looked up at him as Pat came in from the kitchen.

"And where may I ask have you been?"

"Out." Gary said sitting on the settee.

"Out where?" Harry asked quietly from his favourite armchair.

"With me mates."

"What all night?"

"No, I was up early."

"Oh, was you now?" Harry asked.

"Yeah. Why?"

"Why?" Pat screamed, "Because you left Ellie and Sally on their own and you've been out all night."

"No, I didn't Fiona was in."

"No, she wasn't and well you know it," Harry said.

"She was, she was talking to some fella on the front doorstep and I told her I was going out."

"She said you were still in when she went out," Pat said.

"No, I wasn't. She saw me going out."

"Not according to her," Pat said.

"We'll see about this. Fiona." Harry shouted up the stairs where Fiona had retired to.

Fiona didn't respond and it wasn't until Harry bellowed up the stairs that Ellie and Sally could hear Fiona making her way down the stairs.
Fion entered the living room and looked askance at her parents. Then she spotted Gary.

"Oh, there you are," Fiona said sarcastically.

"Fiona you were in when I went out. I'm sick and tired of always getting the blame and you get off Scot free," Gary was glaring at Fiona.

"You were in. You were in the parlour."

"No, I wasn't. I walked past you when you were talking to lover boy on the step and told you I was going out."

"No, I told you I was going out and you said you would be back in a minute."

"Yeah, but I didn't know that you wouldn't wait until I got back."

"And, I didn't know you wouldn't be back."

"Oh, this just gets better and better." Harry said. "So, between the two of you, you decided you had far better things to do than look after your kid sisters?"

Harry jumped up from his chair. His face was red and he glared at Fiona and Gary, who looked like two rabbits caught in headlights, but before anyone else had a chance to speak Pat turned to Harry and asked, "And, you what's your excuse?"

"What do you mean? My excuse. I'm not answerable to you."

"I know that. You're a law unto yourself. You're okay blaming everyone else but you know what," Pat said staring at her husband, "you know who's fault this really is? Yours."

"What? Mine?" Harry asked angrily.

"Yes. I asked you to stay in for one night of your life and you couldn't manage it could you? And, don't give me that," Pat paused choosing her words carefully, "baloney that you had to work late. I bet you went the pub. That's where you were, weren't you? Admit it."

"That's not the point. These two went out and left Ellie and Sally on their own."

"Yes, but you promised me you would be in. You know how important that meeting was to me. It seems to me you did it on purpose."

"On purpose, don't be so bloody ridiculous"

"Ridiculous, other men might actually want to support their wife. My god other men might have actually wanted to see their wife give a speech but oh no not you."

"Don't be so stupid, I told you I had to work."

"Why can't you just be honest for once in your life? You don't care how much that meeting meant to me and you can't be bothered looking after your own children. Let's face it you preferred to go the pub. What is it, did you have to make a point because for once in my life other people wanted to hear my opinion, hear what I have to say? Does it stick in your throat that much?"

"Don't turn the tables on me."

"Why not. You're looking for someone to blame. Why not yourself for a change? Take some responsibility."

"I take some responsibility? You said you were going to that meeting, but you didn't say you would be out all night."

"There were no taxis, so I stayed over at our Tony's. My god you roll in whenever you want, I thought it would make a nice change if it was me for once."

"So, this is what it comes down to does it? You stayed out all night on purpose?"

Fiona, Gary, Ellie and Sally were merely spectators now. This was between their parents. Suddenly Ellie felt an over whelming anger envelop her.

"Stop it," Ellie shouted, "stop being nasty to each other. Why can't you be nice to each other for more than five minutes. All you ever do is argue and fight."

Pat and Harry were shocked into silence.

"Ellie don't get upset, you know what we're like, we don't mean it," Pat said trying to soothe her daughter.

"Yes, you do, you hate each other. You tell us to play nicely but all you do is shout at one another."

Pat looked at Ellie, she felt ashamed, "You know what Harry, Ellie's right. We can't go on like this anymore. It's not fair on us and it's certainly not fair on the kids."

"Oh, don't be so daft, Ellie's just being silly," Harry said shaking his head.

"No, I'm not," Ellie shouted.

"Okay Ellie that's enough of that," Harry said to her sharply.

"Out of the mouths of babes hey," Pat said quietly.

"Ellie can keep her opinions to herself. I'll not be told by a ten-year-old what I can or can't do."

"Don't be so bloody daft Harry, she's just upset that's all."

"I don't care if she's upset, I'm bloody upset. I'm upset that two young children are left all night in on their own and somehow, and for the life of me I don't know how it happened, I'm getting the bloody blame."

"Oh, for Christ's sake," Pat said. "Can't we for once talk about this in a rational manner?"

"What I can't even speak my own mind in my own house anymore?"

"Yes, you do nothing but speak your mind but let's face it we are all to blame. Let's just accept that we all messed up and make sure it never happens again."

"All I know is," Harry shouted raising his voice, "I work bloody hard and if I want to have a few pints with my mates after work I bloody well will. As far as I was concerned these two selfish bastards should not have left their two little sisters in on their own and you woman shouldn't have stayed out all night."

"Yes, I agree but you have to accept some of the responsibility too." Pat's tone was measured, and she was trying hard not to react to her husband's anger.

"Look, if any of you don't like living in my house, under my rules, you know what you can do about it."

"That's a really mature approach," Pat said sarcastically but Harry wasn't listening.

"I mean it, it comes to something when I can't even open my mouth in my own house," Harry turned to Pat as if he had found his second wind, "And, as for you, all I know is you'd better buck your ideas up and start concentrating on your children."

"There's no talking to you is there," Pat shook her head, "I don't know why I bother. Sometimes I wish I could just walk out that door and keep on going."

"Go on then, I'd like to see how far you get." Harry started to laugh, "You wouldn't last five minutes, so just behave yourself, and start acting with a bit more decorum. Call yourself a mother gallivanting off all over the place?"

"But, it's alright for you to do it?"

"As a matter of fact, it is. I work hard, I pay the bills so I'll do what I bloody well want and I tell you what if you ever go off all night like that again you won't be getting back in through that front door."

Pat's voice rose and she screamed in her husband's face, "My god it is like talking to a moron, I feel as if I'm going mad. Why can't you just try and for once see someone else's point of view? Why do you have to be so pig headed?"

With that Ellie watched as her Mum ran from the living room and up the stairs. Ellie realised she was crying. The house fell silent.

"What's up with her?" Harry asked.

"If you don't know now, father, you never will." Fiona said as she too ran from the room, following her mum up the stairs.

"I don't know what's got into that woman." Harry said slumping back on to his armchair.

"I'm going out," Gary said.

"Yeah, clear off you waste of space." Harry called after the retreating figure of Gary.

The house had gone silent. Ellie looked at her dad. He looked defeated and Ellie felt sorry for him.

"Dad, you alright?" Ellie asked.

"No, I'm not. I can't believe how I'm spoken to in my own house." Ellie and Sally stared at him. He suddenly turned on them, his voice a nasty snarl, "Get out my sight the pair of you." Ellie and Sally backed away. "Get out, I mean it."

Ellie and Sally needed no more persuasion and followed in Gary's wake.

CHAPTER 29

You Sexy Thing

Hot Chocolate

It was a quiet afternoon and the air was still. Benny lolled in the middle of the road, softly panting as the sun beat down on him. Ellie sat on the front doorstep, half-heartedly reading one of her favourite books, James and the Giant Peach. Ellie wondered what it would be like to fly high in the clouds.

Ellie looked up at the sky imagining being in a giant peach, held up by seagulls as they flew through the air. Then she forgot her day dream and looked up and down the street at the increasing number of houses which were now bricked up. It made her feel sad that the street had taken on this neglected aspect and her neighbours were slowly but surely leaving. Sally was at her friends in the next street and Ellie had decided not to accompany her as she didn't like it when Sally was with this particular friend, as Sally showed off and it got on Ellie's nerves.

Pat was in the house, tidying up and sorting out washing. Pat had been at Biltons most of the week and the only reason she was at home was because the woman took it in shifts so they could fit in the strike alongside their house work. Pat had been home but she hadn't stopped to have a break and now she was brushing the living room floor and had shooed Ellie away when she had offered to help.

"Go out and play, Ellie," Pat had said but Ellie was too hot and bothered to play and had decided to read instead.

Ellie sat listlessly on the step only glancing at her favourite book every now and then until suddenly she noticed three women turning the corner at the top of the street. As they approached Ellie realised it was Lisa, Joan, Steph and Paula, her mum's friends.

Ellie stood up to greet them as they must be coming to see her mum. I wonder why they're not outside Biltons, Ellie wondered as they headed towards her. They stopped in front of Ellie and smiled at her.

"Hi, Ellie is your mum in?" Lisa asked with a big smile on her face.

"Yes," Ellie said, "I'll just go and get her." Ellie ran into her house and shouted to her mum, "Mum, Lisa wants you and she's with Joan and the others. They want to talk to you."

Ellie knew something was going on. The women looked far too happy, even though they joked a lot they had all been worried about the strike, Ellie could see it on their faces, hidden behind the bravado. Ellie wondered why were they so happy all of a sudden.

Pat propped the brush against the wall and walked out to the front door closely followed by Ellie.

"Hey, yous," Pat said as she greeted her three friends who stood outside, still with beaming smiles on their faces. "How come you're not on the picket line?"

"Because, Pat, we're here to tell you that you've got your job back. That's if you want it?"

"What?" Pat said staring at the women in disbelief.

"You heard. They've crumpled. We all reckon it was that speech you gave the other night. We think you made a real impression on the big wigs from the union because they all turned up today, had a meeting with the Big Boss and the next thing we knew, old Turnip Head was seen packing up and leaving, with his tail between his legs. Then the next thing I knew, I was called into the office and was asked to come and get you."

"Get lost," Pat said shaking her head, and looking at her friends as if they'd gone mad. "I wonder what they want?"

"They're going to offer you your job back," Joan said.

"I don't know about that. I think I've caused enough trouble."

"Don't be daft," Steph said, "It wasn't your fault what happened. We all know whose fault it was."

"I know but all the same," Pat looked at her friends quizzically. "I just wanted him to stop his behaviour. This wasn't about me."

"Of course, it was about you. For the first time they've actually listened to what a woman had to say. You did that Pat, no one else."

"I just wanted him to keep his hands to himself."

"We know that love," Joan said, "but buck your ideas up, let's go and see what they have to say."

"I can't believe it," Pat said as the news slowly started to sink in. "But did they actually say I've got my job back?" Pat asked.

"They're not going to ask Joan to come and get you if they're not, are they?" Steph said.

Lisa interrupted, "They didn't say as much but Sid Ashton from the union gave me the nod and said they're going to offer you your job back, but they need to speak to you first. They know quite well we're not going back until your re-instated."

"I can't believe it," Pat said lost for words once more.

"Well, you'd better believe it. We've won, Pat, we did it. We stuck together and we only bloody well won."

Ellie looked on in wonder as Pat grabbed hold of all her friends and the four women hugged one another amid, squeals of laughter.

"I'd better get ready," Pat said disentangling herself from her friends and running a hand through her hair. "Come in, while I get ready. "

Pat ushered Lisa, Joan, Steph and Paula into the parlour. The four women sat down, talking excitedly amongst themselves as Pat rushed up the stairs to change.

"Would you like a cup of tea," Ellie asked, for once remembering her manners.

"No, love, don't you worry about us."

Lisa smiled at Ellie, "See Ellie, let this be a lesson to you, anyone bullies you, you stand up for yourself. You hear me, don't let anyone push you around. Take a leaf out of your mother's book, because if you end up anything like her you won't go far wrong."

Ellie beamed with pride. She had always known her mum was brilliant, but it was good to hear other people say so as well.

Ten minutes later Ellie watched as her mum walked up the street with her four friends. She could hear the howls of laughter as they marched with their arms wrapped round one another. Ellie was made up. She couldn't wait to tell everyone. She decided to go round to Sally's friends and let Sally know, then she would have to let Billy know. Her friends were going to be made up when she told them.

Before they left her mum's friends had pressed money into Ellie's hand and told her to 'treat herself, and patted her on the head, and called her 'their little comrade in arms', whatever that meant. Ellie decided she would share her windfall with Sally and all their friends. Ellie ran through the entry which led to the next street with the money firmly clasped in her hand. Ellie thought a celebration was in order, if there was ever a time for a bottle of lemonade and some sweets for everyone it was today.

CHAPTER 30
You'll Never Find Another Love Like Mine
Lou Rawls

It was a Friday night. Ellie and Sally had washed and put on crisp clean pyjamas and were now sitting on the settee watching tele. Ellie and Sally were sat either side of their mum and Ellie felt warm and comfortable. The only light in the room was the flickering of the tv screen. Ellie was slowly eating a chocolate bar and was drinking a glass of Dandelion and Burdock that she would replace carefully onto the coffee table between each sip. Friday was Ellie's favourite night. Their mum always treated them to a chocolate bar and bought either a bottle of Dandelion and Burdock or Cream Soda, Ellie's two favourite pops, but the best thing about it was they were allowed to stay up later than usual and watch television.

Their mum occasionally went into the kitchen and Ellie could hear her mum pouring a drink into a glass. Ellie knew she was drinking alcohol and as the night progressed their mum became more relaxed and would tell them stories about her childhood. Ellie loved these nights she always felt safe and cocooned in a world all of their own. There was only the three of them in.

Harry had had his tea, washed, put on a suit and gone to the pub. Ellie had never known her dad to take her mum out with him and Ellie was glad because if he had then their mum wouldn't be sitting on the couch telling them stories or buying them chocolate and pop.

Gary was out with his friends and Fiona had gone out with a couple of friends also. Ellie had watched her getting ready, slowly applying her make-up, curling her hair and painting her nails. Once she had finished, she had twirled in the living room showing off the new dress she had bought. Then Rose and Debbie, her two closest friends had called round and they had sat in the parlour listening to records. Ellie and Sally had tried to go and sit with them, but Fiona told them to 'sod off' and locked the door.

They could hear music drifting out and loud bursts of laughter, until abruptly they departed with only the smell of their perfume lingering in the air. Ellie couldn't wait to get older so she could dress up and wear make-up and go out drinking with her friends.

For now, though Ellie was contented to be young enough to cuddle up with her mum. During the summer holidays this routine had been all but abandoned but tonight Ellie and Sally had gone in quite meekly when their mum had called them in. They still felt a little raw after being left on their own so needed the comfort only their mum could offer. It was nice to relax in front of the tele, all washed and ready for bed for a change. The thought of sweets and lemonade had also added to the attraction and her mum's stories of her grandad and hobgoblins always kept them enthralled.

It wasn't long before Ellie noticed Sally had drifted off to sleep. Ellie remembered thinking what a baby Sally was that she couldn't manage to stay awake when she too must have fallen asleep as suddenly the living door swung open, and a blast of cool air shook both her and Sally awake.

"What are the kids still doing up at this time?" Harry asked stumbling into the room.

Ellie felt her heart contract. She looked up to see her dad standing in the front room doorway swaying slightly as he surveyed the scene. Ellie knew instinctively that when her dad was in one of these moods it only meant trouble. She looked to see her mum's reaction, but her mum continued watching the tele as if he wasn't there, but Ellie knew her mum was well aware of her husband's presence.

"Did you hear me?" Harry shouted.

Eventually Pat turned to look at her husband, "Yes I'm not in the other room."

"Why are these kids still up? It's past their bedtime."

"Because I said they could stay up until this show's finished."

Ellie felt torn she didn't want to go against her dad but at the same time she felt too frightened to move.

"Get to bed now," Ellie and Sally looked to their mum for support.

"I said they could stay up." Pat said calmly.

"I've told them to get to bed."

"You're not usually in by this time, what had an argument with one of your cronies?" Pat asked serenely.

Ellie watched her mum's face with fascination, at the smile playing at the corner of her mouth, at the innocent look she gave her husband. Ellie sensed the change in her mum, normally she would have told them to go to bed to placate their dad but Ellie realised her mum was in no mood to succumb to her husband this time.

"I didn't know I needed an excuse to come into my own house."

Harry's face was red, and he had a glazed look in his eyes.

"You can do what you want as long as you haven't just come home to cause trouble," Pat said calmly.

Ellie watched her dad staring at their mum, she noticed that his eyes had narrowed and if he did not recognise who she was, and his head was nodding slowly side to side as if he had no control over it.

"Is this trouble, is it?" He shouted. Ellie watched in alarm as her father marched to the back of the television and pulled the cables out of the back of the set. The screen went blank and in the ensuing silence Pat jumped to her feet.

"How dare you come in and do that in front of the kids."

"I'll do what I want in my own home. Now get to bed the two of you."

Harry glared at his family and Sally started to cry. Their mum stood in front of her husband. Ellie peered up from the safety of the settee but had put her arm round Sally who was trying not to cry too loudly. Ellie had never seen her mum look so angry.

"You drunken bastard," Pat shouted at him, her calm persona evaporating in an instance.

Harry ignored Pat and rushed into the kitchen. He began to open and slam cupboard doors.

"Where is it? I know you've been drinking." He said as he searched the cupboards.

"If you're looking for my martini it's in the fridge." Pat joined Harry in the kitchen, she said, "I forgot I had to ask your permission if I wanted to have a drink on a Friday night."

"Drinking in front of your children, you should be ashamed of yourself. And, you have the cheek to call me a drunken bastard? What does that make you?" He had found the bottle of martini in the fridge where Pat had left it and held it aloft in the air.

"Put that down," Pat said and went to grab the bottle.

Ellie and Sally watched as their dad pushed their mum to one side and unscrewed the bottle. He began to pour the martini down the sink. Sally had stopped crying too shocked by the commotion to continue, and now she joined Ellie to peer over the back of the settee. They watched their parents in fascination as if it was a continuation of the television drama, they had just been watching on the tele.

"How dare you," Pat screamed.

Pat felt as if a damn had burst. She had had enough. Before she knew what she was doing she had picked up a potato peeler, that had been innocently sitting on the side of the sink and swung it ineffectively at her husband. Harry grabbed his wife's hand

and twisted. Pat let out a yelp of pain and the potato peeler clattered to the ground. Pat and Harry glared at each other, both breathing hard.

"You bastard," Pat yelled, "You've broken my finger." Pat was holding her hand and wincing in pain.

"I haven't touched you," Harry said but his voice had lowered, he stood unsteadily on his feet watching his wife. "Drinking in front of your children. What type of mother are you?"

"Me drinking? You hypocrite, coming in here rotten stinking drunk and causing mayhem. How dare you have a go at me. I have a couple of glasses just to relax at the end of the week. I'm not knocking it back like you every night."

"Fine example to set to your children," Harry's voice was slurred.

"You're one to talk," Pat shook her head, "Oh what's the point. I'm not putting up with this anymore."

"Oh, what you going to do? Go to one of your meetings?" Harry asked his voice taking on a sarcastic tone.

"I'll do more than go to bloody meetings. I'll be going to a solicitor. I'll be getting a divorce."

"I've heard that before."

"This time I mean it. I'm not putting up with this anymore. There's more to my life than just being your lackey you know. I'm not just your wife or a mother to your children. I'm a person in my own right and I refuse to be treated like a second-class citizen anymore."

"A second-class citizen my arse. You have an easier life than me I can tell you. I'm out morning, noon and night working for this family. In the freezing cold and I have to put up with you always whingeing about how bad you've got it. You've got a cheek, woman."

"I've never said you don't provide for your family, but you treat me like crap. I've been put on tablets by the doctor, told I'm useless and worthless by you. I hit rock bottom and you still don't care, do you. But you know what, I'm not going to be a victim anymore. I will have a life outside of these four walls and I'll have a life without you."

Harry started to slow clap his wife, "Bravo. Let me present to you the winner for the biggest load of crap I've ever heard, Pat Thomas." He started laughing, he was enjoying himself now.

"Fuck off," Pat said and Ellie was shocked, she had never heard her mum swear before, "Fuck off back to your friends in the pub, go back to your world, I refuse to be part of it anymore. I'm going to divorce you and there is nothing that you can do about it." Pat smiled triumphantly at her husband.

"Yeah sure," Harry said. "You're useless without me. Who else is going to pay the bills, feed the kids, support the lot of you?"

"We'll manage."

"Feel free, be glad to get some peace. You're nothing but a parasite. Feeding off me, that's all you're capable of."

"You can call me all the names under the sun, but I'm not putting up with your bullying anymore. I'm not putting up with you telling me what I should or shouldn't do. Who I should or shouldn't be. I am me. I am not just a distorted reflection of you."

Harry started to laugh, "Get that from one of your bloody books, did you?"

"Yes, I bloody well did, as a matter of fact, you moron."

"I'm the moron who keeps a roof over your head."

"Yes, and I'm the one who keeps this all going so you can come home and feel like the king of the castle every bloody night of the week."

Harry looked lost for words, but eventually he said, "Call yourself a wife, you're a disgrace."

"If I'm that bad then you won't mind living on your own, will you? The Council have offered me a house and I'm going to take it. I've had enough of you. I've had enough of your shouting and screaming making a holy show of us round the district. Telling me where I go wrong while you do as you please. Why on earth I've put up with it for so long is beyond me. I'm going to the solicitors on Monday and I'm leaving you. I'm leaving this pathetic stupid life and taking my children with me."

"Good riddance. Do you think I want you here?" Harry shouted.

"That's good then you won't miss us when we're gone."

Harry stood staring at his wife and then walked back into the living room as if all the air had been taken out of him. He flopped next to Ellie and Sally on the couch and looked at them in alarm, as if he had forgotten they were there.

Pat stared at him and then laughed, "Come on kids let's go to bed and leave your father staring at the tele he broke."

Ellie and Sally ran to their mum.

"Yeah, clear off the lot of you," Harry mumbled to an empty room.

Pat tucked Ellie and Sally in their respective beds and sat on the edge of Ellie's bed. She was quiet and was still nursing her sore finger.

"Are we really going to move to another house, mum?" Ellie asked.

"Yes, we are. I'm sorry it had to come to this, but I can't take it anymore."

For once Ellie didn't try and persuade her mum otherwise. Even she knew that her dad was in the wrong and her mum had had enough.

"The thing is," Pat continued, "is that whether I leave your dad or not we will still have to leave this house, you know. The Council aren't going to change their minds and not knock these houses down so whether we go now or later, we will still have to move. You do understand that don't you, Ellie?"

"Yes," Ellie said quietly.

She didn't understand, she wished everything could stay as it was, but she also knew that would be impossible. She knew her dad was getting angrier and angrier by the minute. She knew how unhappy her mum was, she knew they were moving whether she liked it or not, but she still didn't like it.

"I think you should divorce, dad," Sally said. "I think he's horrible and I think he does treat you like crap, mum."

"First things first, Sally, don't use that word, even though I did it doesn't mean you can and secondly your dad loves you. He loves you all but he's not acting very nicely but that's got nothing to do with you. That's about me and him."

Pat stopped talking. She felt choked up with it all. She looked down at her two little girls and felt like her heart was breaking. They shouldn't be listening to all this at their age. When Pat was a young girl, she had always promised herself she wouldn't be as foolish as her own mother. She would never put her own family through what she had to endure as a child and now here she was, history repeating itself. Not anymore though, she wouldn't do it to them anymore. She would be the person she wanted to be all those years ago. She had to leave. Pat knew that now, there was no other alternative. Tears ran down her face.

"You okay, mum," Ellie asked.

"Are you crying," Sally asked.

"I'm okay sweethearts. We're all going to be okay. I'm going to make sure of that."

Pat wiped away her tears and kissed them drawing them close to her. "Goodnight, you two and don't worry. Everything will seem better in the morning. You just wait and see."

Pat left them and they could hear her going into her bedroom and closing the door.

"Dad's mad," Sally said.

"He's just drunk," Ellie said.

They contemplated their dad's behaviour both seeing it from slightly different points of view but even Ellie found it hard to have any sympathy for him.

"Do you think we'll have to choose who we live with?" Sally asked at last, "because I'm living with mum."

"So am I, but I wouldn't want to go to court and have to choose."

"Neither would I," Sally agreed. "Why, do you think we would have to?"

"I don't know but sometimes parent fight over the children don't they and it can turn nasty."

"I can't see dad fighting over us, Ellie," Sally said. "Maybe for Benny but not us."

Sally was only half joking and Ellie decided to ignore her comment. They contemplated the dilemma.

"I don't think it will come to that, mum wouldn't let it," Ellie said after giving it some careful consideration.

"And, dad wouldn't be able to go the pub if he had to look after us all the time."

"We could always go with him," Ellie said and they both started to giggle at the thought.

"Yeah," Sally said, laughing, "Ellie and Sally can't come to school today as they're both in the pub with their dad."

"Imagine," Ellie said and they both started to laugh but thought it was best not to laugh too loud in case their mum heard them and thought they didn't care.

They both grew quiet as the giggles subsided both lost in their own thoughts, a frown clouding each of their faces as they drifted off to sleep.

CHAPTER 31

Golden Years

David Bowie

Ellie woke up the next morning and to all sense and purposes everything seemed the same. She could hear the radio on downstairs and the sun was once again streaming through the window of her bedroom. The argument of the night before seemed to be a million miles away and Ellie did not give it a moment's thought as she went downstairs. Her mum and dad always argued, and everything would stay exactly as it was.

Sure, enough her mum was in the kitchen and their dad was sitting in his favourite armchair reading the paper. Benny was lying on the mat in front of him and Fluffy was curled up on the settee fast asleep.

"Mum, I'm starving," Ellie shouted to her mum.

"Do you want some toast love," her mum called in. "Yes please," Ellie said and wandered into the kitchen to oversee proceedings.

Her mum had her back to her and was putting bread under the grill. Ellie was about to say something to her but was stopped in her tracks when her mum looked around and she noticed that her eyes were red rimmed and filled with tears.

"You okay mum?" Ellie asked instead.

"Yes hon, I'm fine. Nothing to worry about." Ellie went to her and hugged her. Her mum sniffed and then said, "Come on now don't be daft."

"You're not really divorcing Dad, are you?" She asked looking up at her.

"Ellie, you're too young to worry about all of this."

"No, I'm not. If you are, I just want to know."

"Look hon," her mum said crouching down so they she could

look into Ellie's eyes, "I am yes. I'm going to make an appointment at the solicitors and I'm going to get in touch with the housing and we will be moving out."

"What was that you said," Ellie jumped as she heard her dad's voice. He was standing in the kitchen doorway.

"I have nothing left to say to you," Pat said looking at her husband.

"You're talking a lot of nonsense, woman," Harry said.

"Am I? What do you think was going to happen after the way you carry on?"

"The way I carry on," Harry roared but Ellie noticed her mum didn't flinch she just continued looking at Harry as if she was seeing him for the first time.

"Harry I'm not arguing with you. I'm passed arguing. If you can't understand that your behaviour is ruining this family there's nothing more, I can say to you."

"What about you?" Harry asked but he was no longer shouting.

"What about me? If I'm such a bad wife and mother, you should be glad to see the back of me."

"I never said you were."

Pat laughed, "Well, you have a pretty selective memory that's all I can say as that's all you ever say."

"This is bloody stupid. One silly argument and you're talking about solicitors?"

"It isn't just one argument though is it, Harry? Our whole marriage has been one long argument and I can't take it anymore. Do you think this is fair on the kids having to listen to this all the time? I think it's best if we just call it a day."

"I think you're talking bloody nonsense," Harry looked at his wife and Pat held his gaze. Ellie noticed his face hardening, "Oh the hell with you woman. You're right, do what you want. I'm not going to stop you."

With that Harry resumed his position in the front room and Pat turned the bread over under the grill, when it was toasted Pat calmly took it and began buttering it for Ellie. Ellie sat at the kitchen table eating her toast and drinking a cup of tea her mum handed to her.

CHAPTER 32
Afternoon Delight
Starland Vocal Band

"Are you two ready yet?" Pat shouted up the stairs to Ellie and Sally.

"Coming," Ellie shouted down.

Ellie tried not to think about her mum and dad divorcing as far as she was concerned everything seemed back to normal but she had noticed her mum and Fiona whispering a lot in the kitchen. Their dad had been quieter too. He seemed to be looking at their mum with a puzzled expression on his face. Ellie tried to put it to the back of her mind, she had her new school to think of. That's what she decided to concentrate on, that way Ellie could pretend everything was back to normal.

Ellie was going out shopping today with Sally, her mum and Fiona for her and Sally's new school uniforms. She was even more excited as they were going to go over to Liverpool to buy them and that meant getting on the ferry boat. Ellie loved the ferryboat. She couldn't wait for the day to begin.

Ellie's new uniform was going to be grey and although she was a bit disappointed at the colour, she was still looking forward to buying it. It made her feel older that she would now have an official uniform with its own school tie. At her Primary school they didn't have to wear a uniform but Ellie's mum had always insisted that her and Sally wear one but it wasn't the same as having a proper school uniform. Ellie was also annoyed that although she was going to big school Sally was also coming with them to buy a uniform as well.

Ellie thought the day should be about her but her mum had told her off when she suggested this so she'd kept quiet but secretly resented Sally for butting in on what, really, should have been her day. They were now arguing because Ellie had put on a new pair of jeans recently bought for Sally.

"Mum, Ellie won't take my new jeans off." Sally shouted down to her mum in frustration.

"Ellie take Sally's new jeans off," Pat shouted back.

"No, she's always wearing my stuff, why can't I wear hers?"

"Because they're brand-new Ellie and they're not yours."

Sally smiled smugly at Ellie.

"But mum," Ellie shouted down.

"Ellie if I have to come up there, god help you."

"I'll get you back Sally," Ellie said to her smiling sister.

"You and who's army?" Sally sneered.

Ellie ran after Sally, but Sally dodged behind the bed before she could catch her.

"Mum, Ellie's trying to hit me." Sally shouted to her mum.

"Ellie," their mum shouted and by the tone of her voice Ellie knew this time she meant business.

Ellie took her sister's jeans off and grabbed her own jeans and started to get ready.

"Last time you borrow anything off me, Sally," Ellie warned.

Sally ignored her and put her jeans on. Ellie sniggered as Sally preened in front of the wardrobe mirror.

"They don't suit you anyway, they look better on me."

Ellie was trying to ignore the fact that she had butterflies in her stomach because now it was time to buy her new uniform it meant the holidays were drawing to a close. In just over a week's time, she would be starting her new school. Shopping for her uniform made it more real somehow. Ellie wasn't sure if she was happy or scared.

Gorsedale was a big school and she didn't know whether she would fit in properly. Lots of things were secretly worrying her and although she had been looking forward to her big school now it was here, she felt scared at the changes taking place. Why couldn't things just stay the way that they were? It seemed as if every aspect of Ellie's life was shifting in one way or another.

When they went downstairs Fiona was standing looking in the mirror over the fireplace and applying her makeup. Ellie wondered why their mum had been rushing them along when they all knew they would end up waiting for Fiona anyway. Although Fiona was still seeing Brendan her initial enthusiasm for him had waned. A few times he had called round and Fiona had told them to say she was out. 'He's not really my type,' Fiona said when Pat had asked her about him and she had begun to mope around the house rather than going out with her friends.

In the past Fiona was always too busy to go shopping with them but today Ellie's mum had insisted and told Fiona it 'would do her good to get out of the house for a bit'. Even Ellie had to agree with that, Fiona had been mooching around and Ellie suspected that it was because she was pining for Simon.

Ellie didn't know why her sister was so unhappy. Fiona had dumped Simon not the other way around. Ellie thought Fiona should be glad to see the back of him. Simon had eventually called round and begged Fiona to take him back and Ellie and Sally had peeped out from behind the blinds in the parlour and watched as Fiona refused to go back out with him. They had pulled tongues at him as he walked away and he had glowered at them but not said anything.

A couple of days after the 'Kids left on their Own' incident, as it was now officially referred to by all parties concerned, Simon had again returned to their house.

Ellie and Sally had heard Simon shout, "Who's the guy in the red sport car, Fiona? Didn't take you too long did it."

"Nothing to do with you anymore, Simon," Fiona replied and had slammed the door in his face.

Fiona had said, 'He can go to hell' but had still taken to her bed and had been intermittently crying. More notably so when 'Young Hearts Run Free' by Candi Staton came on the radio. Then Gary had made it worse by saying 'All by Myself' might be a more appropriate and started to sing the song up the stairs to Fiona but then he had been told off by their mum.

Gary, Ellie and Sally thought it was funny and they would all hum it at Fiona when their mum wasn't around. That was all by the by now, as they realised, they had gone too far when Fiona had chased them round the house with the yard brush in her hand threatening to kill them all if she heard them hum that song to her one more time.

"Go on I dare you," she screamed and even Gary looked scared when he was cornered in the back yard and only barely managed to escape by scrambling over the back yard wall.

Fiona was being a nuisance because although the arguments between their parents had ceased Fiona had taken over. If she wasn't arguing with Gary, she had begun finding fault in everything her and Sally did and was forever complaining about them to their mum. It seemed that bad feelings between them all was inevitable part of their lives.

Ellie wished everyone would just get on. Ellie was surprised when Fiona had agreed to come out with them today but now Ellie wished Fiona hadn't because they were still waiting for her to get ready.

At last, Fiona was ready and they all left the house. They headed towards Seacombe Ferry, as it was there that they would catch the ferry which would take them over the Mersey to Liverpool. Ellie and Sally were excited, they loved going on the ferryboat.

They raced ahead and were already asking for the tickets at the ferry terminal as their mum and Fiona arrived. Suddenly they realised that the ferry had already berthed and their mum and Fiona shouted for them to run ahead to catch it.

Ellie and Sally ran down the gangplank shouting to the men to wait but the men ignored them. They started pulling the gangway up but when they saw Fiona they suddenly stopped and waited patiently until Fiona and their mum were safely on board.

Fiona thanked them and one man said, "Anything for you gorgeous" and it was the first time Ellie had seen Fiona smile in days.

Ellie and Sally raced to the top deck so they could look out over the water. Yet again it was a beautiful day and it even made the waters of the Mersey look lovely and blue. Ellie knew looks could be deceptive though, as the weather only masked how grey and filthy it looked on ordinary days.

Seagulls were circling the boat and squawking, and Ellie could smell the brine, as her dad called it, in the air. The ferry boat swung away from Wallasey and the Liverpool skyline replaced the dotted houses and greenery of the Wirral. It felt cooler on the ferry boat, the wind whipped their hair in their faces as they ran along the decks.

Pat and Fiona had made their way up the stairs to the top deck of the ferry boat and sat down on one of the benches. Pat shouted half-heartedly at Ellie and Sally, "Stop running around like lunatics," but knew it was pointless as they were out of sight the minute, she took her eyes off them.

Ellie could see the Liver Building beckoning to them from the other side. It dominated all the other buildings which stood in its midst. Their mum told them it had once been white and that it had been blackened with all the chimney soot over the years, but Ellie found that hard to believe.

Ellie and Sally stood hanging over the railings staring at the buildings along the Liverpool shoreline. Ellie pointed out three tall chimneys to Sally and told her they were called the Three Ugly Sisters. Sally then asked Ellie what the big tall building with lots of clock faces on it was called and Ellie was proud when she remembered that her dad had told her it was called the Docker's Clock and she could tell Sally its name.

There was so much to see but then they remembered that if you went on the lower deck, you could go right to the front of the ferryboat where a flagpole stood and there was a ledge you could stand up on it. Soon Ellie and Sally were clinging to the mast and peering over the side. Their vantage point from here was unrivalled and they were able to lean out with the wind in their hair and marvel as the ferry sliced through the water.

Liverpool grew ever nearer and soon they were bumping against the side of the Pierhead. Ellie and Sally jumped down and watched in fascination as ropes were thrown to the waiting ferrymen, who neatly caught them. The men all worked together trying to tether the boat to the iron bollards set on the side of the quay.

At last, the boat was dragged to its mooring and the ropes howled in protest. Ellie thought it sounded as if they were pain but at last the ferryboat was secured, and was left bobbing up and down with the swell of the tide. A great clattering followed as the gang plank was lowered and Ellie realised their journey had come to an end.

As they disembarked the ferryman who had called Fiona

gorgeous sidled up and asked her if he could take her out on a date but Fiona said No. Pat pulled Fiona away and told the man, 'Not to be so cheeky' but then the man had then said to their mum, 'What about you then?' and their mum had started to laugh and said, 'Chance would be a fine thing'.

"You can't blame a bloke for trying," he shouted after them as they made their way up the gangplank.

"Still got it, hey mum," Fiona said giggling.

"Behave yourself young lady," but they were both laughing as Pat said, "The cheek of the man, I'm old enough to be his mother."

Pat hurried them along ignoring the catcalls of the ferryboat men.

At the top of the gang plank was a hot dog stand and the smell drifted out towards them. There was a queue of people all waiting to be served and Ellie and Sally begged their mum if they could have a hot dog too but their mum said, "No, you don't know where his hands have been' and wouldn't let them have one.

The bus terminal was at the top of the Pier Head and buses seemed to be coming at them from all different directions. There were beeps and shouts and there seemed to be swarms of people all bumping into one another but Pat kept a firm hand on both Ellie and Sally and before Ellie knew what was happening, they had boarded a bus and were on their way.

Once on the bus Ellie and Sally ran upstairs whilst their mum and Fiona sat downstairs. Ellie stared out of the bus window and marvelled at the contrast between Wallasey and Liverpool. Liverpool had large imposing buildings and the streets were packed full of people. The streets were busy with cars and buses and it was so much noisier than it was in Wallasey. All around there was a bustle of excitement and Ellie felt it right in her belly and loved every minute of it.

Soon their mum shouted for them and they were hustled off the bus and informed them that the first stop would be TJ Hughes as Pat said that it sold everything but it didn't because they didn't buy anything from there. Then Ellie and Sally were dragged to other shops until at last they had slowly wound their way down to Church Street. Ellie no longer cared if she ever bought a school uniform in her life as her feet were killing her and she had lost the will to live.

Ellie realised that her mum and Fiona obviously loved shopping because they ohhed and ahhed at all of the clothes and seemed to have lost sight of the fact that they had come over here to buy school uniforms. It all seemed to be about Fiona buying a pair of red Birmingham bags. Large baggy trousers that were all the rage at the moment but every pair they saw were just not good enough for Fiona.

Suddenly they were in a shop trying on school uniforms. Ellie and Sally tried various skirts and jumpers on and at last found the perfect ones. Ellie began to feel it had all been worthwhile but then she realised that Fiona and their mum had no intention of stopping. Ellie felt as if they were possessed, they seemed to have a manic look in their eyes and shopped as if their lives depended on it.

Ellie and Sally gave up, and decided to play games of hide and seek instead and began to hide in the various stores they visited but this only exasperated their mum and Fiona more. Nerves were becoming frayed. Fiona started to shout at Ellie and Sally because they kept running away. Fiona told them that they were nothing but spoilt brats and were just doing it for attention.

It was getting late and some of the shops were already pulling down their shutters and even though Ellie felt as if her legs were falling off her, Fiona still insisted that they should go and have a look round St. John's market.

Ellie looked at her mum with despair and was glad when her mum said it would be closed by now and maybe it was time to go and find something to eat. Ellie felt like crying with relief and Sally stopped mid-sentence from telling Fiona that 'She'd look stupid in those stupid trousers anyway' as calmness once more prevailed as they went in search of a café.

It was a relief to everyone when they eventually all sat down and their food was ordered. Ellie and Sally were laughing and blowing down their straws into their orange juice to make bubbles so were oblivious to most of their mum and Fiona's conversation. It was mainly about Simon but Ellie's ears pricked up when she heard Fiona say, "I know he's my dad mum but I don't think you have any other choice but to divorce him."

"You're not really getting a divorce are you mum?" Ellie asked quietly.

"Ellie, love don't you worry about it," Pat said gently.

"But you're talking about our dad. I don't understand why you would want to divorce him, mum?" Ellie continued.

"Can you really say that with a serious face, Ellie?" Fiona said raising her eyebrows and staring at Ellie pointedly.

"Fiona, stop it," Pat glared at Fiona.

"But I didn't actually think you would get a divorce, mum, not really?" Sally asked concerned too.

"I'm sorry and I know how difficult this is going to be for the pair of you but I've made up my mind." Pat smiled at them and her bottom lip trembled but she continued, "You will still see your dad, it's just that we wouldn't be living in the same house as him and there wouldn't be so much arguing and shouting. It can't be nice for you to hear that all the time."

"I don't care. I don't want you to divorce dad," Ellie said and felt ashamed that she was on the verge of crying as she was too old to cry.

"Mum's really unhappy, Ellie. You're old enough to see that. My god you're going into big school in a couple of weeks, you're not a baby."

Fiona stared at Ellie daring her to contradict.

"I don't like dad," Sally said.

Harry had been particularly nasty the day before when he had shouted at them when they wouldn't come in for their tea. It hadn't ended well and Sally had still not forgiven him for sending them up to their bedroom after they had eaten.

"Well, I do like my dad," Ellie cried turning all her anger and frustration onto Sally, "Just because you don't help dad when he's in the backyard fixing things and don't like to go for walks down the prom when he asks. I do."

"Okay Ellie that's enough, it's not Sally's fault." Pat said but Ellie didn't care even when Sally started to cry.

"You don't cuddle him on the coach when we we're watching tele. You're horrible to our dad."

"No, I'm not," Sally shouted in defence, "but I don't like it when he shouts at mum or turns on us, he's always shouting."

Ellie felt defeated. She knew Sally was right and Ellie wanted her mum to be happy too, but she felt pulled and didn't want to leave their dad on his own.

They sat in silence lost in their own thoughts until Sally, her tears now subsided, asked, "If you did divorce dad, mum, would Benny come to live with us?"

They stared at their mum expectantly because they both knew that if there was one member of the family their dad loved it was Benny.

Pat laughed, "Is that what you're worried about?"

Fiona said, "Typical that stupid dog is the only thing they do care about."

"No, it's not Fiona don't be so silly," Pat turned and looked at her two daughters and thought at least I can solve this one problem and said, "Of course Benny will come and live with us, he's your dog and where ever you go so will he."

Both Sally and Ellie sighed with relief.

"That's a shame," Fiona said but they knew she was only joking.

"Look girls I don't want you to worry, and I don't want you to say anything to your dad as well. Just leave it for the adults to sort out."

"So, whatever happens now I'll still be leaving my house." Ellie said defiantly as the full implications began to dawn on her.

"Oh, shut up Ellie, you sound like me father," Fiona snapped.

"Well, I don't want to leave our house" Ellie said petulantly.

"Sometimes you have to think of other people not just yourself," Fiona said.

"Yeah, Ellie stop being so selfish," Sally butted in.

"Leave her alone you two. Ellie you know quite well the houses are being pulled down whatever your father says, it's going to happen and where ever we live, as long as we're together, it'll be our home."

"Yeah, a home without our dad," Ellie said and turned away.

Ellie sat quietly deep in her own thoughts and was called a sulker but Ellie decided it was best just to ignore them. She could hear them chattering away unconcerned but Ellie wasn't happy. She wasn't happy, not one little bit. She had been looking forward to this summer so much, but everything had changed. Her mum had gone on strike, her house was being knocked down and now her mum and dad were divorcing.

Ellie wished this summer had never happened. She thought back to the day when the ladybirds had come and wished she was a ladybird too. If she was a ladybird, she could have flown away with them and left all of this behind her.

CHAPTER 33
Kiss and Say Goodbye
Manhattans

Ellie realised that the summer holidays were drawing to a close. Her mum had kept her promise and had been to a solicitor and a letter had been sent out to their dad, but he refused to read it. The major event though was Pat had been given a new house by the Council. The only silver lining for Ellie was that it was only around the corner from where they lived so at least they wouldn't be moving too far away.

Billy's family were also moving but they hadn't been given a house yet and Ellie only hoped it was close to them and they could still be friends. More and more houses were being bricked up. Her dad said he wasn't going anywhere.

Everything seemed to have happened so fast. Ellie couldn't believe her summer holidays were drawing to a close, how could so much have happened in such a short space of time. Ellie was actually starting her new school on Monday. Ellie's head was reeling with it all.

Since her parents talk in the kitchen her parents remained relatively calm. Harry did not seem to be taking the divorce very seriously as his only comment had been, 'You should have more sense at your age,' when he received the letter from his wife's solicitor. Ellie's mum had stopped cooking for him. She said he had better get used to it. Ellie's thought her dad was pretending it wasn't happening but even she could see her mum meant business.

Pat had been given her job back. After her meeting with the owners, she arrived home looking pleased.

Pat said to Fiona, "They only offered me the supervisor's position but I told them where they could stick it. I'm not being bought off that easily."

"Mum isn't that cutting your nose off to spite your face?" Fiona asked.

"Oh, I couldn't be doing with it, Fiona. I'd rather just get on with my job than keep an eye on the girls all day."

"So, what's happened to Tina Brown?" Fiona asked.

"She handed in her notice once she heard Kinnear was going. Everyone was going to send her to Coventry anyway. I mean not only had she been sticking up for him but she'd actually spread bare faced lies around in order to protect him so her position was untenable really," Pat said.

"Good riddance, that's what I say," Fiona said. "So, who's the new supervisor?"

"Joan," Pat replied smiling. "Couldn't have gone to a better woman."

"You sure Joan's up for it, I mean she normally doesn't say boo to a goose," Fiona laughed.

"She'll be fine, there's more to little Joan than most people give her credit for, she'll be fair and that's the main thing but what I wanted to tell you is the unions asked me if I want to take over the Shop Steward position and I've agreed."

"Bloody hell, mum, that's good."

"More up my street to tell you the truth, hon. I'm really looking forward to it."

"My God they won't know what's hit them if they try anymore funny business."

"Let's hope they've learnt their lesson but I'll be up for it if they do."

Pat smiled it felt as if a huge weight had been lifted off her shoulders. She felt as if she'd finally managed to gather all the threads of her life together. Pat laughed to herself, maybe I've finally managed to overlock myself back into shape but only time will tell if all the loose ends will stay in place.

Pat felt scared thinking of starting all over again on her own but she knew she'd made the right decision, not only for herself but for her family as well. For far too long she'd put up with Harry's constant bullying and it wasn't good for her and it wasn't good for the kids.

It's about time I stand on my own two feet for a change and take responsibility for myself and the kids. I can't go on just blaming Harry for my own unhappiness I need to take back control. For the first time in years Pat felt as if she could make plans to suit herself and what was best for her children.

She also knew it would do Harry good, both of them had been far too unhappy for far too long. Somewhere along the way they had taken different paths and had both blamed each other for changing. They were so young when they married it was a lifetime ago when they had been completely different people. Pat realised they both deserved better.

"Anyway" Pat brought herself back to the present, "I've told them I'm going to start back next week. I've got too much to do before the move to go back straight away."

For the rest of the week Pat was busy. She had been packing clothes and ear marking items that she would be taking with them. Harry's only input being that he would keep their double bed, whether that was an admission that his wife was leaving him was hard to tell. Pat said, 'Fine, you can have it.'

Pat had taken Ellie and Sally to see their new house after she'd picked up the keys from the Council. It was a three bedroomed house, with an upstairs bathroom and a front and back garden. It was brighter, it was warmer, it was situated just up from the street from where they lived now. It was a few streets away from Ellie's new school. It was perfect Pat said. Ellie hated it.

Of course, Ellie did not want to leave her home but even she accepted the fact that the houses were going to be demolished whether she liked it or not there was not a lot she could do about it. Billy was hanging round the street sulking. He kept looking at her with puppy dog eyes and saying it wasn't fair. Ellie said, 'I'm only down the road' but they both knew it wouldn't be the same.

Even Benny seemed sad and lolled around knowing something wasn't quite right. Benny had taken to following Harry round the house and Harry would sit on his armchair with Benny's head on his lap. Harry would sit stroking Benny absent mindedly as if was him and Benny against the world. Fluffy the cat didn't care. What went on in this household was beneath his contempt.

CHAPTER 34
This is It
Melba Moore

Ellie woke up and looked out the window. She couldn't believe it, the sky looked dull, and the sun was hidden behind clouds. It seemed cooler, the nets fluttered as a breeze blew in through the open bedroom window. Ellie was surprised that it felt good to feel the cold air. Downstairs she could hear the radio and her mum clattering around the kitchen. Sally was fast asleep in the other bed as she didn't start school until the next day, so Ellie crept around as she didn't want Sally waking up and getting in her way as she tried to get ready.

Ellie felt the butterflies in her stomach beginning to dance with the knowledge that, at last, she was about to start middle school. She wasn't exactly frightened but it was still a big day for her, and she hoped her new school was as good as Gary and Danny said it was. She looked at her uniform which was hanging on a hook on her bedroom door, pristine and new.

Pat shouted from downstairs, "Ellie hurry up and get washed or you'll be late for your first day at school."

Ellie ran down the stairs to get a wash and then raced back up the stairs. Ellie put on her new school uniform feeling all spotless and clean and turned to admire herself in the mirror, marvelling at how all brand spanking new it looked. Her new shoes gleamed, and she tapped them together in a childish gesture thinking of Dorothy in the Wizard of Oz.

"Saw you," Sally said sleepily from her bed.

"Oh, go back to sleep will you Sally."

Ellie ran back down the stairs and into the kitchen. Her mum was washing dishes.

"There you are," her mum said, "Let's have a look at you."

Ellie twirled round and took a bow. Pat stood staring at her, and Ellie thought her eyes looked a bit watery.

"Don't you look smart. You'll be the best dressed girl there today," Pat finally said.

Ellie ate her breakfast quickly and then let her Mum fuss over her. She even let her mum brush her hair and pin her hair back with a new hair slide they had bought. Ellie had to admit, once she had a chance to look in the mirror, that it did look quite nice, but she still frowned when her mum said, 'How pretty she looked'.

Sally and Gary had both made an appearance and were now sitting in the living room watching the tele.

"Bye Ellie," Sally said, "good luck." Ellie smiled at her.

"Hope you get bullied," Gary said in a sing song voice and smiled sweetly at her.

"What like you did," Ellie said, laughing.

"As if," Gary said and turned sullenly back to watch the tele.

Pat followed Ellie to the front door and gave her a kiss. "I'm sure you're going to love your new school," Pat said.

"Yeah, can't wait mum," Ellie said smiling trying to ignore the knot that was gnawing at her stomach.

Pat was still waving her goodbye when Ellie reached the top of the road. Pat blew her a kiss and Ellie looked around glad no one was around to witness her mum's behaviour.

When she turned the corner, she heard her name being called and looked round to see Billy chasing after her.

"I thought you said we'd go together," Billy said out of breath.

"Oh, sorry I forgot," Ellie said. "I would have waited for you once I realised."

Ellie had been in a world of her own and had forgotten all about their plans to walk to school together. Ellie smiled at Billy, for once he looked smart, with his new uniform on. Somehow his hair looked neater too, but Ellie didn't think this new look would last that long. They both walked along silently for a while.

"Are you nervous," Ellie asked.

"A bit," Billy admitted.

"I'm sure it'll be alright, really," Ellie said trying to sound braver than she felt.

"Yeah, we'll soon get used to it," Billy muttered. "When you moving?"

Ellie sighed, "Next weekend. I can't believe it. I won't half miss living in this Steet."

"I know, we'll be going in a couple of weeks ourselves."

It was strange, Ellie thought, it only seemed like yesterday when her and Billy were running home from their primary school so happy that it was the summer holidays. Ellie couldn't believe the number of things that had happened since.

They continued to walk along in silence. It wasn't a long walk to Gorsedale, so it didn't take too much time before they neared the school gates. Ellie took a deep breath and looked around apprehensively. The schoolyard was large and full of children charging around and Ellie peered around to see if she could recognise anyone.

Billy said, "I'll see you later."

Billy left her to join a group of his friends and Ellie heard a chorus of hellos.

Hannah Collins, a girl from her old primary school asked, "What was your summer holiday like?"

Ellie thought she could answer sarcastically and say, 'Well my mum and dad are getting a divorce, my mum was involved in a strike and our old house is being knocked down but apart from that, it was brilliant' but instead she decided to skip the intro and just say, "It was brilliant."

Other girls joined them, and everyone began to talk at once, all with stories to tell. Ellie looked around the playground. Ellie didn't like the fact that she was now one of the youngest in the school. Ellie looked at her friends and reassured herself that at least she wasn't the only one. She recognised some of the older kids from her area and others who had been a few years ahead of her at her primary school, so she didn't feel completely out of her depth.

Ellie heard a whistle and everyone in the school yard stood still. A male teacher stood in the middle of the playground. He was old but ramrod straight with a mop of white hair, a thick pair of half-rimmed black glasses hung perilously from the end of his nose.

"That's Barton," someone said.

Ellie suddenly understood that she hadn't been frightened of coming to a new school it was the stories Gary had told her about some of the teachers that had really scared her. There seemed to be an array of gruesome characters that you had to watch out for, but Gary had always reiterated that they were 'alright' really and Gorsey was great, and she'd love it, but Ellie wasn't so sure.

"Right, first of all year ones," Barton shouted, "if you could form an orderly queue, these two reprobates will lead you into the assembly hall."

Ellie looked towards the two reprobates. There were two older girls standing next to Mr. Barton. They looked very prim and proper and as far as Ellie was concerned did not look at all like reprobates. Everyone lined up and they entered the assembly hall, which seemed massive. It had a gleaming polished wooden floor and a huge stage on which a man in a tweed suit stood.

"Now," his voice boomed from the stage, "when you hear the teacher calling out your name go and stand by them." It was then that Ellie noticed that equally sombre teachers were standing in front of the stage. Ellie swallowed nervously as he shouted, "As long as there's no funny business this shouldn't take very long."

Ellie waited patiently until she heard her name being called and then was led to her classroom. Their teacher began to read out their names in alphabetical order and allocated them a seat each. Ellie was placed next to a girl called Shelly Turner and they smiled shyly at one another. She looked nice Ellie thought, she had mid brown hair, a little elfin face and huge brown eyes that seemed too big for her face but in a nice way, Ellie conceded.

"My name is Mrs. Leeson, and I will be your form teacher for the next year. Hopefully we will all get along splendidly but if anyone is silly enough to think I'm a pushover they will be in for a shock," she smiled at them with a smile that didn't quite reach her eyes, "I hope I make myself clear?"

She stared at them until they all said, "Yes Miss Leeson," there was a slight pause and then a voice piped up and said, "Of course Miss Leeson." There were a few muffled giggles.

Miss Leeson who had turned to the board swung round and glared at the boy, "I hope you're not being sarcastic boy?"

"No, of course not, Miss Leeson." He said in a sugary voice.

The voice came from behind her, and Ellie was itching to turn round and see who it was. Ellie wasn't sure if whoever it was had just missed his cue or was deliberately trying to provoke their new teacher.

"What's your name?"

"Matt Williams, Miss Leeson."

Ellie realised it was the way he kept saying *Miss Leeson* that was annoying Miss Leeson.

"Think you're smart, do you boy?"

"No, Miss Leeson."

For some reason Miss Leeson was seething but there was nothing she could admonish Matt Williams for. Miss Leeson stared at him, raised her eyebrows ever so slightly and smiled. I'll have you, the smile said, and Ellie knew that Matt Williams was now in Miss Leeson's bad books.

Ellie sneaked a peak at Matt Williams as Miss. Leeson briefly looked away and to Ellie's surprise, he winked at her. Ellie smothered a giggle but was impressed how he kept his face perfectly serene whilst looking earnestly ahead. He kicked the back of her chair, and she could barely contain her laughter.

"So, you think it's funny too, do you" Miss Leeson exclaimed, "Name?"

Miss Leeson had swung round and was now staring at Ellie.

Ellie stammered her name, "Ellie Thomas, Miss Leeson."

Ellie resisted the urge to say *Leeson* the way Matt had and somehow felt cowardly not doing so but knew it would probably be the straw that broke the camel's back.

"Right Ellie Thomas, I have a way of picking out the bad apples in my class and I can assure you that you really don't want to be one of the bad apples."

Miss Leeson glared at the class watching their faces until her words sunk in.

"So, Matt Williams and Ellie Thomas, you had better watch yourselves if you think you can get one over on me."

Ellie swallowed hard. She was not used to teacher's talking in this manner. Miss Leeson continued to glare at Matt Williams and then looked at Ellie, studiously examining her and Ellie felt all her amusement evaporating. Ellie lowered her eyes and hoped she had passed whatever test Miss Leeson had set.

By home time Ellie and Shelly were firm friends and talked excitedly to one another about everything which had happened during the day. They both agreed that they both liked their new school and thought it was much better than their primary schools. By the end of the week Ellie felt as if she truly belonged to Gorsey. For that was what she would forever call it as no self-respecting member of such an exclusive club would ever dream of giving her new school its official title, only boring teachers or snobs would call it Gorsedale and Ellie certainly didn't fall into either one of those two categories.

CHAPTER 35
Living Thing
The Electric Light Orchestra

Ellie saw a large removal van turning the corner. She knew uncle Tony and uncle Paul were hiring a van for the day and coming over to help. Ellie ran in the house to tell her mum the van had arrived. Ellie didn't think it was strange that her dad was helping them move out. It had been agreed that Pat would have all the furniture from the parlour and Harry would keep the furniture from the living room. Ellie watched as her dad and Gary started lifting the settee into the van. Ellie felt detached from it all. Ellie looked around her old home. It seemed odd she would be sleeping in a new house tonight.

Once all the furniture had been lifted into the van uncle Paul and Gary climbed in the back of the van and pulled down the shutters at the back.

Their uncle Paul shouted, "Steady as she goes," to uncle Tony who was driving.

"Can I go in the back of the van too?" Sally asked but Ellie didn't feel the same level of enthusiasm as her sister.

Ellie wasn't surprised when she heard her father shout, "No, you can't, it's too dangerous."

Ellie went to stand with her mum, Sally and Fiona as Harry jumped into the front of the van next to uncle Tony. Ellie watched as her dad scooped up Fluffy from the front step and held Fluffy him in his arms. The window of the van was open, and Harry called out that he would see them at the house. He didn't seem upset or anything. He was laughing with uncle Tony as if it was all a big joke.

Finally, Ellie watched as the removal van began to move down the road. Suddenly there was a blur of fur as Fluffy hurled himself from Harry's arms and shot out of the window. Ellie and Sally chased after it, but it disappeared up the entry and by time they ran down after it, it was gone. Ellie and Sally went back to the van which was pulled up in the middle of the road.

"Couldn't find it, dad," Ellie shouted.

"It doesn't matter. It'll turn up," Harry said. "Me and the cat seem to be the only ones who want to stay round here."

"I want to stay too," Ellie said earnestly, "but I don't seem to have any choice in the matter."

Harry didn't seem to have heard her and the van moved off. Ellie stood transfixed as it drove away.

"Right, grab these bags," Pat said, "Anything we forget we can always come back for."

They walked together lugging bags with Benny trotting behind. Fiona said they looked like a crowd of vagabonds and she felt ashamed, she continued to complain all the way to their new home.

Ellie said, "You should have asked Brendan if we could use his lovely red sports car."

Fiona gave her a dirty look. When they turned the corner of their new road, they could see the van parked in front of their new home and the furniture was already being removed from it.

As they neared Pat said, "First things first, let's get the kettle on."

Everyone worked together. Harry, uncle Tony, uncle Paul and Gary all carrying the heavy items. There were even laughs along the way. Ellie thought it was odd how her dad was taking it. It made her feel more relaxed, even normal, especially when he called Gary a 'lazy sod' and told him to 'pull his weight.' At last, it started to look like a normal home.

Ellie and Sally were excited putting their bedroom together, although Fiona had the last word on where everything should go. Gary was having the box room and Ellie had to admit that they did have more room and it was a lot nicer.

Harry and uncle Tony disappeared with the van but a few hours later they returned laden with cans of lager. Their nan and grandad, aunty Renie and aunty Lynne arrived. A party was underway. It was great. They were playing records on the radiogram and it seemed like old times. Ellie even thought maybe their dad will decide not to go home and come and live with them.

As the night wore on, he tried getting their mum up to dance but she shooed him away.

Harry said, "What about another five kids, hey, Pat?"

Pat said, "Not on your Nelly."

The next morning Ellie ran down the stairs excited that her dad might still be there, but it was not to be. Her dad had gone home. Ellie's mum was in the kitchen with the kitchen door open and Ellie could smell the sweet scent of flowers wafting in on the warm summer air. She had to admit the kitchen seemed bright and airy with the sun shining through the windows and she could hear birds singing. It seemed a far cry from her old neighbourhood.

"It'll be nice once we get the grass mowed," Pat said as her and Ellie surveyed the garden. "There're some nice plants underneath all that undergrowth. We'll soon have it looking lovely."

"Better than a backyard," Ellie agreed. Her mum smiled and put her arm round her.

Sally came to join them, and Gary came in and started to make some toast for himself.

It was the familiar sounds of her family, the only person missing was her dad, but Ellie hated to admit that the atmosphere did seem more relaxed without him. By now their dad would have started to argue with someone or told someone off. He also didn't like them sitting inside but her mum hadn't even mentioned the fact that they were still in their nighties and were making no moves to get ready.

"Mum," Fiona shouted from upstairs, "turn the immersion on I'm going to have a bath."

"Okay, love," Pat said as they all went back inside.

Ellie could hear Fiona humming from upstairs.

"She must be going out with Brendan," Sally said, and they laughed because they always over accentuated the name Brendan whenever he was mentioned and fluttered their eyelashes at one another.

Brendan had not given up easily and was still appearing and luring Fiona out in his sports car but even Ellie could tell Fiona was no longer impressed. Ellie had decided she liked him, he had even given Ellie and Sally a ride in his car round the block and it had been brilliant.

"Chucky eggs and soldiers, all round?" Pat asked interrupting Ellie's thoughts.

"Yes please," Ellie and Sally shouted as their mum busied herself making their breakfast.

"Can we eat it watching the tele?" Ellie asked hopefully.

"Okay, but don't be getting used to it. There are a few rules we're going to abide by here, you know. I'm not running a holiday camp," Pat said waving her spoon at them.

"You're not going to turn into dad are you, mum?" Sally said laughing.

"I'm going to be worse. Mark my word, I'm going to run a

tight ship here, me hearties," Pat said, adopting a pirate accent. "Them that die will be the lucky ones."

Pat chased them round the kitchen dragging her leg and both Ellie and Sally squealed with laughter.

"Aye, aye captain," Sally said copying their mum's voice and Ellie wished she'd thought of saying that.

Ellie and Sally were eating their chucky eggs and soldiers watching the tele when suddenly Ellie felt guilty. Her poor Dad would be all on his own in their old house all cold and alone while she was eating chucky eggs and soldiers and laughing as if nothing in the world was wrong.

As if reading her thoughts Pat shouted in from the kitchen, "Once you've finished your breakfast go and get ready. You promised your dad you would go around and see him today."

Ellie felt somewhat subdued after that and finished her breakfast deep in thought. When they were washed and dressed, they called to Benny. Benny was lying asleep at the top of the stairs. He yawned and stretched and then slowly came down the stairs to follow them out of the house. As they neared their former home Ellie hoped her dad was alright and he wasn't missing them too much.

They caught sight of Billy playing with Carl and Ian Williams. Ellie and Sally waved over to them but carried onto their house, but they were in for a surprise, the front door was closed. Fluffy was curled up on the front basking in the sun, he briefly looked up at them and then fell back to sleep.

They knocked on the door thinking that they would hear their dad coming to answer it, but he didn't. They looked at the front door in dismay. Billy came over to where they were standing.

"Your dad went out about half an hour ago," Billy said.

"Do you know where he was going?" Ellie asked.

"No, it's not like he's going to tell me, is he?"

"Probably the pub," Ian said joining them and Ellie knew he was probably right.

"He could have waited to see us," Sally said. "We said we'd come round today."

"I know," Ellie agreed, "but he's not going to ruin his routine just for us, is he."

Ellie felt let down. All that worrying about him and he couldn't even be bothered to wait in for them. She looked down at Fluffy.

"Might as well take Fluffy with us," Ellie said.

Fluffy snarled as Ellie picked him up. They began to walk up the street with Fluffy in their arms with Billy, Ian and Carl walking in step with them. Fluffy wriggled in Ellie's arms but Ellie held on tight. Suddenly his paw whipped out and he scratched Ellie. Ellie let out a howl and the cat jumped and was away before they knew what was happening, he had fled.

"Stupid cat," Ellie said rubbing a claw mark on her hand.

Billy laughed, "Even the cat doesn't want to go with you."

"Shut it, Billy," Sally said.

"No, I won't," Billy was still laughing.

"Get lost Billy," Ellie retaliated by pushing him away from them.

"You don't even live here anymore," Billy said as he walked away with Ian and Carl.

"Yeah, and we're glad we don't," Ellie shouted after them.

"Get back to your own street," Ian shouted and the three boys fell about laughing.

Ellie and Sally felt mortified. They didn't live here anymore.

Billy was right. They couldn't even go into their own home because it was all locked and bolted. Ellie felt as if the world had shifted from underneath her and she no longer had any bearings. They walked home both feeling sad.

***

Pat greeted them when they arrived home.

"You were quick."

"Dad wasn't in," Sally said.

"He's locked the door," Ellie added.

Pat said nothing, other than, "That's a shame. Oh well you can go and see him tomorrow after school, Ellie. He hasn't emigrated."

"Yeah, I might do."

"He knew we were coming round," Sally said.

"It must have slipped his mind," Pat said.

"Fluffy scratched me when I tried to bring him home," Ellie showed her mum her war wounds.

"Cats are funny things, very territorial," Pat said as she rubbed Ellie better, "We'll have to get him in a box so he doesn't run away and then keep him in for a bit until he gets used to his new home."

"Maybe I should go in a box too," Ellie snapped, "until I get used to my new home."

Pat laughed, "Yeah put the two of you in one, it would be far less trouble."

Ellie laughed in spite of herself.

"Where's Gary?" Ellie asked.

"Out with his mates," Pat replied, "So no changes there, then and Fiona has gone for a spin in Brendan's sports car."

"Ohhh Brendan," Ellie and Sally said and they all laughed.

Suddenly there was a knock on the front door and they all looked at each other in alarm as if it was an unknown quantity. Pat went to answer it and Ellie and Sally stood behind her in the hall. As the door opened, they realised it was Simon.

"Hello, Simon," Pat greeted him, she did not sound the least bit perturbed by his presence.

"Hi Simon," Ellie and Sally said in a sing song voice, peering at him from behind their mum's back.

They tried not to laugh at how serious and forlorn he looked standing there. Simon smiled back at them, but Ellie thought it looked forced.

"Hello, Mrs Thomas. I heard you'd moved." He held a bunch of flowers in his hand and gave them to Pat. "These are for you, as a housewarming present."

"Thanks, Simon, that's very thoughtful of you. They're beautiful." Pat sniffed them appreciatively.

Simon seemed nervous.

"Is Fiona in?" Simon asked tentatively.

"I'm sorry she's not, love."

"Oh," Simon's face was crestfallen. "Could you tell her I called round and I'd like a word?"

"Of course, I will. I'd invite you in but we're a bit upside down at the moment."

"No, it's okay Mrs. Thomas. I've got things to do anyway."

"Well, take care love," Pat said as she closed the door. She looked at the flowers, "The poor love," she said to Ellie and Sally.

"His scooter doesn't stand a chance against the red sports car," Ellie said.

"Ellie," Pat said sternly but Ellie could see she was trying not to laugh. "You never can tell, young lady, if he plays his cards right Fiona might look beyond the glamour of Brendan's," Pat began fluttering her eyelashes mimicking Ellie and Sally, "gleaming red sports car."

"I doubt it," Sally said laughing.

"I hope not," Ellie said in mock alarm with her eyes wide in horror.

"Simon's not that bad," Pat said, shaking her head at them as she went back into the kitchen.

"Oh yes he is," Ellie and Sally shouted after her pantomime style.

They giggled when Pat shouted back, "Oh no he isn't."

Ellie suddenly felt happy. Maybe it wouldn't be that bad here after all.

CHAPTER 36

You Don't Have to Be a Star (To Be in My Show)
Marilyn McCoo and Billy Davis, Jr.

The summer was a distant memory. Autumn with its golden leaves and shorter days had gone unnoticed as Ellie had been too busy to take heed of the changing season. She had been too busy settling into her new school and making new friends to think of anything else. Ellie loved her new school and her new friends and there were so many things to do that she hardly ever thought of her old home.

Today as Ellie came in from school, Ellie was hoping to get out quickly. She would have her tea, get changed and meet Shelly at the top of the road as they were going to the Boysy, a local youth centre, tonight and she couldn't wait to get out. Ellie was hoping that her mum was having a meeting in the house, so she could get out without too much interference.

Sure, enough as Ellie opened up the front door, she could hear lots of laughter coming from the living room so popped her head round the door.

"Hi Mum," Ellie surveyed the scene. Joan, Lisa, Steph, Paula and Sandra Tweadle were all sitting in the living room. There were also a couple of other women who Ellie didn't recognise. They all looked up at her and smiled.

"Hi Love. You had a good day at school?" Pat asked.

"Yeah, it was okay," Ellie said.

"Your teas in the oven, love," Pat said, "Fishfinger and mash, you're favourite."

"Ah ta mum," Ellie said as she went into the kitchen to fetch her tea out of the oven. "Is there any parsley sauce?"

"Yes, and peas, they're all on there," Pat shouted. "Do you want a hand?"

"No, I'm fine mum," Ellie said taking hold of a tea towel so she could take the hot plate out of the oven.

"Do you have any homework?" Pat asked.

"No, not tonight mum." Ellie said relieved she didn't have any. "I'm going down the boysy tonight, mum." Ellie said as an afterthought.

"I know, love, just make sure you're in by nine and me and you won't fall out."

"I know mum," Ellie said exasperated that her mum had to always reiterate this threat.

Ellie heard a loud burst of laughter coming from the living room but ignored them too intent in eating her tea to give the women another thought. Ellie was used to her mum's meetings by now. Some of the women in her mum's group took turns to host a meeting. There were other women who couldn't hold meetings as their husband's objected to it. Ellie couldn't understand why some men were like that but then remembered how her dad had been and knew he would never have allowed it either.

Ellie ran up the stairs to get changed. Her beloved uniform was now thrown on the floor in her haste to get ready. She could hear the low murmur of voices drifting up the stairs and wondered what they were talking about tonight. Her mum's group interested Ellie but tonight she didn't care, she couldn't wait to get down to the Boysy so wouldn't interrupt them as she sometimes did.

Occasionally, Ellie's mum would allow her to sit amongst them but only if her mum thought the conversation wasn't too controversial and if Ellie made a point, they would all listen to her attentively and speak to her as if she was a grown up.

Ellie had learnt a lot from these women and wondered why last summer she had been so opposed to her mum's meetings. Their talks were really interesting, and she could understand why her mum looked forward to them. Ellie found their comradeship fascinating. When Ellie joined them, she would listen to their conversation enthralled with their insights about the world and life in general.

Her mum seemed different somehow too, not just because she

seemed so much happier, it went beyond that. Her mum had a quiet dignity about her which encouraged everyone who met her to take her seriously and treat her with respect but, it was also because her mum no longer looked harassed and worn out. Her mum dressed better, wore make up and basically just looked after herself more.

Her mum had also started a new job with the union over in Liverpool. Ellie wasn't too sure what it entailed, but it sounded interesting. Every morning Pat would leave the house and catch the ferry boat to work, and her mum had told her it was lot better than working at Biltons. The best thing was though it paid more. Things were still tight, but they weren't poverty stricken like her dad had predicted. Pat managed and Harry helped out too.

What had also surprised Ellie though, was how much their homelife had improved since they'd moved. Their home seemed more orderly now, things had become less chaotic, but the best thing was there were no more arguments. Obviously, there was the general squabbles amongst Ellie and her siblings but nothing that became too nasty or couldn't be worked out.

Ellie felt calmer too. Although she still hated Mrs. Leeson, Ellie enjoyed going to school. Ellie's mum always made sure her, and Sally did their homework on time and would often sit with them if they were finding it hard and help them out. Her mum would also go the library and get her books out if she thought it would help with her and Sally's studies.

Ellie had been amazed to find that in most subjects she was top of her class and wondered how that had happened. Ellie had not considered herself to be particularly bright at her primary school but now she found that she enjoyed most of her subjects, even maths.

Her mum was also going to night school. She was taking her O levels in English and maths and Ellie thought she was mad, but her mum seemed to enjoy it. Her mum said she was going to keep on going to night school until she could go to university. Her mum said she had the backing of her union and if she passed all her exams, she would get an even better job than she had now.

Ellie was very proud of her mum but what made Ellie feel really proud was the fact that her mum had stood up to Turnip Head and called him out for what he was when no one else had.

Surprisingly though Ellie did not miss living with her dad. Gary was a pain, but for all of Gary's faults he was not as hard work as now, Ellie acknowledged, her dad had been. They could shout Gary down or laugh at him and their mum was there to tell him off too. Even Gary had bucked his ideas up and without having their dad putting him down all the time, he seemed a lot happier too.

Once Ellie dressed, she looked in the mirror. She had a new pair of jeans on with an Aaron jumper, her grandmother had knitted for her, but what she was particularly proud of were the ankle boots she was wearing. She'd begged her mum for them for weeks and last weekend her mum had bought them for her. Ellie absolutely loved them. Ellie gave her hair a brush and with a final look in the mirror went back downstairs to kiss her mum goodbye.

Ellie left the women drinking tea and smoking in the living room. They all looked as if they were enjoying themselves, but, Ellie thought, they wouldn't have as much fun as her and Shelly would have at the Boysy. Ellie smiled to herself and hoped Matt would be there tonight and if he was then that really would make her day.

CHAPTER 37
Silly Love Songs
Paul McCartney & Wings

Ellie's days drifted by, she was looking forward to Christmas, had been chosen to be a shepherd in the school play and everything seemed hunky dory. The only cloud on the horizon, as far as Ellie was concerned was Fiona. Brendan, the onetime boyfriend with the sports car had disappeared and had never been seen again but what was really concerning to Ellie though, was the fact that there were the ominous signs of a reappearance of Simon.

Simon at first, knocked round for a chat with Pat. Ellie knew what he was up to but Pat seemed blissfully unaware of his true intentions. Ellie watched from the side lines scornfully and tried to have a word with her mum but Pat laughed at her and said, 'Simon's a lovely lad'.

The writing was well and truly on the wall when Ellie had come home from school the other day and found Fiona fawning over Simon in the kitchen, giggling incessantly at every little remark he made.

Last night though had been the final straw when Ellie had found Fiona preening herself in front of the mirror and trying on numerous dresses in preparation for a date with Simon that very night. No one had noticed Ellie's tuts of derision or her loud sighs of discontentment. Sally was no use as she had even been helping Fiona choose what outfits to wear.

"I'm going out," Ellie said to her mum after her tea hoping her mum would cotton on to her disapproval of the events unfolding.

"Okay, hon," her mum said. "Don't be late."

"I don't know why you're encouraging it," Ellie said finally unable to keep her thoughts to herself.

Her mum looked at her with confusion and asked, "Encourage what?"

"Simon."

"Oh, don't be daft, Ellie," Pat replied.

Ellie retorted in a sing song voice, as she knew what was coming next, "He's a lovely lad."

"Yes, he is, Ellie so stop being sarcastic."

Ellie shook her head and walked out the door realising it was a losing battle. Ellie decided to go and see her dad. It was cold and dark outside and a damp mist hung in the air, obscuring the road in front of her. She shivered and fastened up her coat as she set off at a good pace to warm up. She thought of her dad sitting all on his own in his house. He was still living in their old home and his argument with the Council had escalated. Most of her old neighbourhood had been knocked down but still Harry refused to move.

Harry had told Ellie that the other day he had stopped a bull dozer who he was sure was just about to start knocking his back yard wall down. Harry had told Ellie that he had tried to pull the man out of the cabin of his truck but other workmen had run to their colleague's rescue. Her dad seemed to be enjoying himself and revelled in his ongoing battle.

Pat had said, "It gives him someone else to argue with now that I'm gone' and Ellie thought her mum might have a point. Ellie felt torn though because on the one hand she felt proud of her dad for standing firm but embarrassed on the other hand now that he was living on a demolition site.

It was scary now walking to her dad's. The streets where she had grown up and played were now a wasteland. Although there was a main road Ellie could have walked down to get to her dad's, it took so much longer that Ellie always chose to cut down a narrow lane which took her practically to the top of their old road, but it was deserted and only had the odd streetlamp to light her way. Pat told Ellie repeatedly to take the long way round when visiting her dad but Ellie always ignored her advice.

Ellie realised that with all the shenanigans going on with Fiona tonight her mum hadn't even asked Ellie where she was going let alone told her to take care. She turned down the narrow pathway and picked up her pace. The streets were silent and she felt weary once she realised how quiet and dark it was. Ellie began to walk faster and was glad when she saw the welcoming glow of her dad's house in the distance.

It now stood on its own. A lone beacon on a winter's night. It looked surreal standing all by itself but it still had the power to tug at Ellie's heart strings even in the sorry condition it now found itself in. The front door no longer stood open but was locked tight against the world outside. Ellie had to knock loudly before she heard her dad coming to the door.

"Who is it?" Harry shouted from within.

"Me, Ellie," she shouted back.

Harry opened the door, "What are you doing here?"

"Thought I'd come round to see you," she said stepping inside.

Ellie didn't say, because I worry about you and don't want you to be all on your own. Or asked, are you lonely, have we all abandoned you?

"That's nice but good job you caught me in as I'm going out soon," Harry said leading the way into the living room.

Ellie thought, so much for worrying about you.

"School, okay?" He asked.

"Yeah, it's okay."

"Do you want a cup of tea?"

"No, it's alright dad."

Ellie didn't like her dad's tea. For some reason he used tea leaves as if he didn't know tea bags had been invented and even though he used a strainer there was always leaves that clung to your tongue once you took a sip. To make matters worse he had even taken to buying sterry milk which was horrible, telling her it lasts longer, as if that was important.

"I've bought some lemonade, will that do?" Ellie stared at her dad in shock.

"Lemonade?"

"Yes lemonade," he laughed, "You don't seem to like tea these days so I bought it for you."

Ellie was touched, "Ah thanks dad, that's great."

Ellie settled down on the settee and her dad, after handing her a glass of lemonade, sat in his usual arm chair. If she didn't know better, she could try to make believe that she still lived here and her friends' houses still stood in rows outside and her mum would be in from work soon and everything was back to normal but she knew it wasn't and a sad feeling washed over her. Benny rushed up to greet her and she stroked him laughing,

"What's Benny doing here?" She asked as Benny settled back in front of the fire.

"Came round to see me," Harry said and Ellie wasn't surprised as she knew Benny often popped round to visit Harry as well.

"He can walk home with you," Benny looked up and wagged his tail and Ellie was glad she would have some company on the way home.

"Fluffy still here?" Ellie asked.

"Yes, he certainly is. Cats aren't like dogs, they're more attached to the home than the people," Harry said, "but Benny still likes coming round to see his old man, don't you boy?" Benny's tail thumped once more. "So, what you been up to?"

"Nothing much," Ellie said, "the usual."

"Take your coat off or you won't feel the benefit," Ellie stood up to do as she was told as she knew it was no use arguing with him. Once she settled back down her dad asked once more, "School, okay?"

"Yeah."

"Still hate Miss. Leeson?"

"Of course, she's a right cow."

Harry laughed, "Hope you don't tell her that."

"As if," Ellie said smiling, "She'd kill me."

"Quite right too," Harry said, "you should be scared of the teachers or you'll never learn anything."

Ellie decided to change the subject, "Fiona's going out with Simon tonight," Ellie stared at her dad waiting for his reaction.

"Is she now?"

"Yeah, and they're all helping her to get ready."

"He popped round here the other day."

"Did he?" Ellie was shocked.

"Certainly did. I told him I was going out so he soon scarpered."

Ellie laughed, pleased her and her dad were on the same page.

"Have the Council been in touch?" Ellie asked sipping her lemonade.

"No, but the local paper has." Ellie stared at him incredulously. "Yeah, knocked round the other day and took some photos."

"Get lost," Harry kept his face serious but Ellie could see he was chuffed as he had puffed out his chest.

"Told them until the Council gives me the money, I deserve I'm not going anywhere."

Ellie settled down as she knew now her father was on his favourite subject. She shook her head, tutted at the appropriate moments and threw in a few comments but it was pretty much a one-sided conversation. Eventually Harry stood up.

"Oh well, Ellie you'd better make tracks, you don't want to be walking home too late." Ellie got up to leave and put her coat back on, "Make sure you go down Borough Road, don't be taking the short cut, you don't know who might be knocking around."

"Come on, Benny," Ellie said and Benny stood up and obediently followed her.

Ellie pecked her dad on the cheek and he waved from the front door step to make sure she was walking towards Borough Road. Once he'd gone back inside, she turned round as she had no intention of taking that route and anyway, she had Benny with her now so it wouldn't be as frightening.

"Come on Benny," she said, "I'll race you."

Her and Benny took off down the street. Ellie didn't feel the cold or worry about the dark. She had Benny with her and before long she was back in her own home, settled in front of the tele with her mum and Sally. Gary was in his usual position lounging on one of the arm chairs and as far as Ellie was concerned sitting there thinking he was Lord Muck.

CHAPTER 38
Papa was a Rolling Stone
The Temptations

Ellie was in school when she found out that her dad had made celebratory status by being on the front page of the local paper. Jason Murphy who had once lived in her street came in clutching a paper. Ellie's family knew the Murphy's quite well but they had moved from their street a few years before there was even a hint of their neighbourhood was going to be knocked down.

Jason was smiling when he came up to her and up until that point, she hadn't noticed the paper in his hand, "Your dads on the front of the paper," he laughed.

Jason pushed the paper under her nose and Ellie felt her face going red as she saw a picture of her dad standing on top of a pile of bricks with the caption 'Angry Harry Fights Back'. Her dad was wearing his workie clothes which consisted of jeans, big hob nail boots and an ill-fitting jumper which had seen better times, which although not tight on him still managed to allow his belly to protrude predominately over the belt of his jeans.

"Oh no," Ellie said, looking around in case anyone else had saw the paper, "Put it away quick."

Jason looked at her confused and lowered the paper, "What's the problem? I think it's dead funny."

"I don't, Jason. Please don't show anyone else, will you?"

Ellie didn't hold out much hope of this as most lads would shout this from the roof tops once they realised it embarrassed her. Ellie could imagine everyone laughing at her and was mortified. It was one thing her dad fighting the Council and refusing to move out of his home due to his 'high principles' but it was another thing knowing all her class mates would see where her dad lived.

"I don't know what you're embarrassed about, me mum and dad thought it was great. Me mum told me to bring it into school to show you but I'll keep it to myself if that's what you want"

Ellie couldn't decide if he meant it or if this was just a precursor to a day of taking the Micky out of her. Ellie lowered her voice so no one could hear her, "You know what the lads are like Jason, they would have a field day if you showed them this, especially Bean Head."

As if on cue Bean Head walked into their class. Ellie didn't know how he had earned this nick name, all Ellie knew was he was manic, he had a loud mouth and loved nothing better than chasing the girls round the school and embarrassing them. This, Ellie realised would be a golden opportunity for him, Ellie felt sick with the thought of it.

Jason looked disappointed with Ellie's reaction but then he looked pointedly at Bean Head and smiled as if he knew exactly what Ellie meant. Thankfully Jason put the paper back in his school bag.

"Promise me you'll keep it to yourself?" Ellie asked.

"Yeah promise." Ellie smiled at him and Jason shook his head at her and walked away.

Ellie held her breath in school all day but true to his word Jason did not show anyone else the paper. Jason went up in Ellie's estimation that day. Yes, the Murphy's were a lovely family, her mum always said that and now Ellie understood why.

Later that night when her mum came home from work the first words out of her mouth were, "Have you seen your father on the front page of the paper?"

Ellie's mum was putting shopping away as she spoke. Ellie and Gary had followed their mum into the kitchen both thinking of their tea rather than desperate to greet her from work.

Gary started to laugh, "Yeah seen that. It's in the front room." Gary went into the living room and returned with the paper in his hand. Gary held it up so his mum could see it. Pat shook her and Gary was laughing, and said, "Stupid get, he looks a right idiot."

"I wish he'd just move?" Pat sighed.

"He's a right show," Gary said.

"What do you know," Ellie shouted at him, "at least he stands up for what he believes in more than what you do."

"He just loves arguing with people, that's all he does. Likes nothing better than picking a fight with people," Gary said warmly, raising his voice.

"You two stop arguing," Pat said intervening, "And Gary don't talk about your father like that."

"What? I'm only saying what everyone else is thinking," Gary shouted back.

"I don't care it's disrespectful," Pat said.

Ellie pulled tongues at Gary behind her mum's back but he was already marching out of the kitchen.

"I can't win in this bloody house," Gary muttered.

"I don't know why Gary wants to skit at me dad all the time. He's my dad and I think it's great what he's doing and so does Mrs. Murphy."

"Mrs. Murphy?" Pat asked confused, "Jason Murphy's mum?"

"Yes," Ellie said. "She said at least he's got principles."

Ellie knew that was stretching the truth a bit but her mum didn't know that.

"Oh, when did you speak to Mrs. Murphy?" Pat's mum asked.

"Jason Murphy told me today in class. She said his family all thought what me dad was doing was great, so there."

Ellie left her mum speechless in the kitchen and went up to her room annoyed with it all. Ellie knew she was being hypocritical and hung her head in shame that she too had been embarrassed of her dad in school that morning, but she wasn't going to tell anyone about that. She sat on her bed feeling confused and angry. She picked up a book she had started to read the previous night and was soon lost in its pages forgetting about her dad, or her mum and even Gary.

By the time Ellie was called down for her tea her anger towards Gary had evaporated. Sally was already at the table picking at her food as always but Ellie devoured her tea, as she suddenly realised, she was starving. In between mouthfuls Ellie told her mum and Sally what school had been like that day and how Bean Head got on her nerves.

"He's nearly as bad as our Gary is," Ellie said.

"He can't be that bad," Sally said shaking her head.

"You haven't met him," Ellie said.

"I heard that," Gary shouted in from the living room but there was no malice in his voice and they all started laughing.

"Trouble with you Ellie Thomas, you have far too much to say for yourself," Pat said, smiling at her, "Now eat your tea and shut up."

CHAPTER 39
Welcome Back
John Sebastian

Ellie heard the news with amazement. Fiona was getting married to Simon. Again. Once more the house was full of magazines and talk of the wedding. Fiona, though, was taking a much more pragmatic view of the procedures this time.

"I just want a small wedding, mum. In a registry office and we're having a small Do afterwards. Nothing fancy. I think it was just too much last time, I think I got too carried away and I think the stress just got to the both of us."

Pat smiled, "Whatever you think best, love."

"I don't think it was stress," Ellie whispered to Sally as they sat watching the tele together, "I think it's because Simon's a divvy."

Sally laughed and whispered back to Ellie, "I think it's Simon we should be feeling sorry for."

This sent them both into gales of laughter but their mum and Fiona were too busy talking to notice.

"I wonder," Ellie said already sniggering at her own joke, "If they're going to arrive at the Registry Office on Simon's scooter."

"Yeah, with me dad on the handle bars," Sally said and they both laughed hysterically at the thought.

"Will you two shut up," Fiona said and their mum tutted at them.

"What's going on," Gary who had been out, walked into the living room.

"Our Fiona's getting married," Pat said beaming at him.

"Jesus' tonight," Gary said, "Not all that again."

"You're giving her away," Ellie shouted as her and Sally began to roar with laughter again.

"What?" Gary looked ashen at the prospect.

"You're the head of the household now Gary," Ellie screeched barely able to contain herself. "You have to take your responsibilities seriously."

"As if," Fiona said, "Mum, will you tell them two they're doing my head in."

"Shut up Ellie, if you've got nothing nice to say then don't bother," Pat said sternly to them but even their mum had a smirk on her face and they noticed she too was trying not to laugh.

"You're all doing my head in now," Fiona shouted and stomped out of the room.

"Fiona, don't be daft," Pat said shouting after her, "We'll get Gary a haircut it won't be that bad."

Even Gary laughed at that one.

"He can wear one of me dad's old suits," Sally screamed unable to contain her giggles.

They all carried on laughing ignoring Fiona's tantrum.

Eventually Pat said, "Now stop it all of you, I'll go and calm her down." Pat wiped her eyes and went up to see Fiona.

It wasn't too long before they heard Pat and Fiona laughing upstairs as well, so whatever Ellie's mum had said to Fiona must have worked, Ellie thought to herself.

"Wonders will never cease," Gary said looking up at the ceiling and smiling, "Our Fiona's actually developed a sense of humour. There's hope yet."

Gary laughed at his own joke and then flopped into his usual position into the arm chair he had taken ownership of.

Pat came down the stairs and decided to sit in the kitchen. She had brought home a few notes from work and decided to take advantage of the fact that the kids seemed to be absorbed in whatever they were watching on the tele and she could make a start putting a case together.

She looked at the notes she had taken down. A woman had come in to complain that she was being treated like the office junior by all the men in the office. Asking her, amongst other menial duties, to make tea and coffee for meetings when she held the same position as them. It had been made worse by the fact that she was receiving no support from her manager. Pat was sure it could be sorted out but just wanted to make sure they followed the correct procedure and that she was clear about the lady's job description before she planned which approach to take.

Pat's mind wondered and she smiled to herself thinking about Fiona. She hadn't bothered trying to talk Fiona out of marrying Simon this time. Fiona obviously loved Simon and as long as she was happy, Pat mused, maybe that was the main thing. We all have to make our own path in this world, I suppose, and Fiona would make hers, whether I like it or not, Pat told herself. Maybe it would work out for Fiona and Simon, only time would tell.

Pat looked round the kitchen, at the walls she had painted a pale blue and the little touches she had made to make it warm and inviting. The kitchen was still her domain but now it also acted as her study, so to speak. It was not a refuge like her old kitchen had been but a safe warm environment where she cooked for her family and worked peacefully if she needed a bit of space away from the kids. Pat had never felt so calm.

She shuddered at the thought of the years she had spent arguing and cajoling Harry compared to what she had created for herself away from him. She wasn't against marriage, lots of her friends were very happily married and good luck to them but for her and Harry it just hadn't worked out. Maybe it never had. The kids had taken up most of their youth and now looking back she couldn't even remember if they'd had anything in common in the first place.

The fact was though she no longer hated Harry and she was glad that she hadn't become twisted with bitterness. What good would that do her? In fact, she felt detached when she thought about him. The fact that she was divorced and didn't have to put up with him anymore, helped. Pat laughed to herself, yes it helped a lot.

Harry seemed settled in his little bachelor pad with his mates around him and no wife telling him where he was going wrong. Obviously, it hadn't occurred to him to ask for a two bedroomed flat so the kids could stay over but it suited Ellie and Sally to just drop in and visit, so as long as they were happy with the situation Pat had nothing to complain about.

Life was strange, Pat thought, it came up and bit you on the arse or offered you an escape route when you least expected it. If someone would have told her a couple of years ago, she would have divorced Harry she would have laughed in their faces. At the time she felt as if there was no way out. She had felt as if she was trapped, caught in head lights, with nowhere left to turn. Funny how things worked out.

Pat remembered how she had relied on those pills to get her through the day. Thank God she had managed to wean herself off them. Pat had heard some terrible tales of women who had become dependent on them and realised now she'd had a lucky escape. All Pat knew was that was all in the past now. She felt safe in this house, secure in her job and happy as a mother. At last, she was confident enough to be her own person.

Pat looked down at the notes she had written and then an idea occurred to her. Pat began scribbling down on her note pad with a happy expression on her face. Pat was absorbed, lost in a world of her own.

CHAPTER 40

Go Your Own Way
Fleetwood Mac

It was Easter half term so Ellie and Sally decided to go and see their dad as they were at a bit of a loose end. The air was warm for this time of the year and it reminded Ellie that summer was fast approaching. Last summer seemed so far away now, almost like another life time. Ellie remembered how anxious she had been with the thought of moving but she had to admit it hadn't been that bad in the end.

If she had told herself last year that she would actually like where they lived now, she wouldn't have believed it. Ellie loved her new school and had made loads of new mates. She was always telling Sally she was going to love Gorsey and Sally couldn't wait to start.

The best thing was though Ellie's dad had recently moved from their old home. He had eventually accepted the Council's offer of money, and although she didn't know the exact figure, according to her dad, it was nearly treble the sum their neighbours received, so he had been made up.

Harry had given Pat half of the money and Pat immediately started to re-decorate the house. She told them she was going to buy a new carpet for the living room, stairs and landing. Ellie thought it would look lovely once it was finished. She had to admit although it was a lot nicer living where they were now, she still missed all her old friends who had moved away.

Harry lived in a one bedroomed council flat and seemed really pleased with himself. When Ellie first went there her dad seemed to have made a cosy little home for himself and Ellie realised, he was far happier than she would have ever dreamed possible. He had at least two friends who lived in the same block

Emma Littler

as he did and they had formed, what seemed to Ellie at least, a club of sorts. They always seemed to be popping in and out of each other's flats and helping one another.

There was a couple of pubs round there too which were now her dad's locals. Last week they had popped round to see their dad but he wasn't in. Ellie and Sally decided to go and see if he was in one of the pubs close to his flat. They had peered through the door of the first one, and it was like being transported into another world. The bar was full of men talking loudly and laughing, and smoke hung in the air, shimmering in the light. There didn't seem to be any women in there, apart from the barmaid.

"Who you looking for, love?" the barmaid asked when she spotted them.

"Harry Thomas," Ellie shouted to her.

A man called out, "He's down The Catons."

Ellie thanked the men and re-emerged from the smoke and the heady smell of beer which permeated the air and was grateful for the fresh air outside. Her and Sally quickly made their way to The Catons, the second pub on their list. This pub was even smaller than the first. It didn't seem as welcoming though with its peeling paint work and bare wooden floors.

The air was just as thick with smoke and clung to their nostrils. Ellie half expected their dad to chase them away but he had been quite jovial and greeted them warmly. He even bought them a glass of lemonade and a packet of crisps each.

Ellie and Sally settled in on a low bench against the wall and their dad had pulled up a stool. Ellie was dismayed when a large burly man with a red face came over and said, 'Now come on Harry you know kids aren't allowed in here' but their dad had taken the man to one side and the Landlord had said, "Okay just this one time but don't let them be making a habit of it.'

When their dad came back, he had rumpled their hair and said that they shouldn't really be here and not to do it again but for just this once they could have a little chat while he had a beer. For that hour Ellie and Sally felt really grown up sitting talking to their dad in a pub. Men came over to talk to their dad and their dad introduced them and all in all he seemed to be very popular and well liked.

When they left, he'd even given them fifty pence and told them to 'spend it wisely'. They had run off laughing to themselves and wishing they could do it again but they knew they wouldn't get away with it all of the time. This had been a one off but it had been exciting all the same.

When their dad first moved into this part of their neighbourhood, they hadn't known it very well. Territories were clearly defined in their area and each child knew their designated place precisely. The first time they tried visiting their dad Ellie and Sally had been chased by a gang of kids. It was only five minutes from their new house but they might have been entering a war zone with the welcoming committee they received. Ellie and Sally had run as fast their legs could carry them and arrived home puffing and panting and out of breath.

Ellie and Sally thought that would be the end of it but the other gang hung round outside their house shouting insults and saying 'They'd get them when they came outside.' Thankfully Gary had been in and chased the other kids away, saying, 'He'd kill them if they ever touched his little sisters'. One of the bigger lads shouted, 'I didn't know they were your sisters, Gary' and Gary had shouted back, 'Well they are so leave them alone'.

It was the first time Ellie had felt proud of their Gary and she looked at him in a new light. Who would have thought their Gary would be her hero. It seemed to have worked as well because the next time they went to their dad's they were only met with hostile stares and had been able to walk to their dads unhindered.

***

When they arrived at their dad's both Ellie and Sally were relieved to find that he was actually in. It was a bit hit or miss going round to their dad's as more often than not he would be out. They sat down and talked to him for a bit. Sally always wriggled uncomfortably and didn't talk to their dad as much as Ellie did but then Ellie could hardly get a word in edge ways as their dad always had a lot to say to them even if most of the conversation was series of questions and rebuffs.

Another subject which was often broached at her dad's was Fluffy. The whereabouts of Fluffy were currently unknown. Fluffy had also refused to go with their dad when he moved and had run off the minute, he saw the removal van. There had been numerous searches for him. Fluffy had been spotted though but not one person had managed to capture him.

Harry told Ellie not to worry too much.

"Cats are very hardy creatures, very independent. If he doesn't want to be found there's not a lot we can do about it. He'll either find a new home or go feral."

"Go feral? What's that?" Ellie asked.

"Live off the fat of the land," Harry laughed but Ellie still looked confused so Harry said, "When he's hungry he'll go hunting for food. That cat won't go hungry, believe me and you."

It still hadn't stopped Ellie looking for Fluffy though. Ellie and Shelly went looking for Fluffy after school, and at the weekend but she never even caught a glimpse of him but then her dad told her that Fluffy had been found alive and well. He was living with an old lady who had taken him in. Harry told them that he had called at the old lady's house to see if indeed it was the infamous Fluffy.

Harry said to her, "I knew it was our Fluffy because the minute I tried to stroke him he nearly tore a slice of my hand off."

They all laughed but Ellie still felt Fluffy was their cat and now he had been found he should come home. Harry disagreed.

"No, the old lady's loves him and it wouldn't be fair to take him back." Harry said, "Besides, she's only an old little lady all on her own, Fluffy can protect her better than any guard dog ever could."

Ellie was won over by that argument. She didn't really miss Fluffy she had just been worried about him but now she knew he was safe and sound she was quite happy with Fluffy's current living arrangements and had nothing more to say on the matter.

So, all in all Ellie felt a lot better. She no longer had to worry about her dad, her mum seemed happy, Fiona was getting married and Gary was Gary. The only person Ellie missed was Danny, she couldn't wait to see him. It seemed as if he had been gone forever. They received the odd letter from him and they would all gather round whilst their mum read it out and then they would all write a little paragraph to him to let him know how they were getting on. It wasn't the same as actually seeing him though, but for now it was better than nothing.

CHAPTER 41
Knowing Me, Knowing You
ABBA

Half term wasn't the same as it used to be. This time last year she would have been playing out on the street or riding her bike or building dens. This year Ellie had been shopping over to town with Sally and Shelly, which had been fun. Ellie was more interested in fashion now and had bought a new top. She couldn't wait to wear it next time they went out somewhere special.

They had been the baths and boys had been bombing them and chasing after them and that had been a good laugh too. It occurred to her one day when she went home that she was spotlessly clean and although she knew she was too old to be climbing walls or making dens she still missed it. Ellie felt like she was growing up and she didn't know if she was ready for it yet.

Ellie had also started to read more; she became lost in imaginary worlds and some days she would rather sit in with a good book then actually go out and play. She was sitting in the living room reading a book, oblivious to the noise of the tele or Sally and Gary in the background, when someone knocked on the front door. Ellie looked up but Sally had already gone to answer it.

"Ellie," Sally shouted through, "there's a Matt at the door for you.

Sally looked up, confused, "Don't be daft."

Sally walked back into the living room, "I'll just leave him there, shall I?"

"Oh, you're just winding me up," Ellie said continuing to read. The only Matt she could think of was Matt Williams and why would he be calling for her?

"I'm not joking," Sally whispered, "He's at the front door and wants to see you."

Gary, who had been watching the tele started to laugh, "Who's this Matt then when he's at home?"

"Oh, stop it will you Gary, it's probably Billy and she's winding me up."

Ellie flung her book down and went out to the hall. Sure, enough the front door was wide open, and Matt Williams was standing on the front doorstep staring at her. Ellie couldn't believe her eyes, what the hell was he doing knocking at her house? She walked towards him cautiously, she couldn't imagine what he wanted.

"Hi, Ellie," he said, sounding nervous, "Just thought I'd knock round and see if you were alright."

"Of course, I am, why wouldn't I be?" She asked him incredulously.

Ellie could hear sniggering coming from the front room and prayed that Matt couldn't hear them.

"That's good," Matt stood there, shuffling his feet.

"Is that why you called round, then?" Ellie asked.

"Yeah, and I wondered," Matt stammered, "If you would like to go the pictures with me or something?"

Ellie stared at him as if he's gone mad.

"The pictures?" She asked.

"Yeah."

Ellie was confused, was Matt Williams asking her out on a date? It felt surreal, this was a dream come true for Ellie. She'd had a secret crush on Matt Williams from the minute she'd met him, but she never for one minute thought it was reciprocated. Even now she thought it must be some kind of joke being played on her.

"With me?"

"Yeah, of course," he was going to say something but then he looked as if he thought better of it.

"Oh right, what's on?"

Ellie didn't care what was on, but it gave her time to think as what she really wanted was the ground to open up and swallow her because she was way out of her depth and didn't know how she should act.

"I don't know, Logan's Run looks good."

"I'm going to see that with Shelly."

She wasn't but it was the first thing that came into her head.

"Oh well we can watch something else?"

"I can't I'm sorry, I'm going in now."

Out of pure embarrassment Ellie shut the door on Matt Williams's face. She had felt her face going red, could hear the laughter in the living room getting louder and it was the first thing she thought of to get out of the situation. Ellie felt mortified. She walked away towards the living room; the laughter was growing louder. She ran in and Gary and Sally were looking out the window and watching Matt Williams walking away.

"Get away from the window," Ellie shouted.

She didn't know it was possible if she could have felt anymore embarrassed, but they had managed it somehow.

Gary turned away from the window, "Ah Ellie's got a boyfriend."

Sally joined in.

"No, I haven't he just wanted to talk that's all."

"He fancies you," Gary said.

"No, he doesn't," Ellie said feeling her face burn with shame.

"He does," Sally joined in, "Why else would he call round?"

Pat walked in, with bags of shopping in her hand, "What are you lot going on about now?"

"Our Ellie's got a boyfriend," Gary shouted.

"Oh, get lost you two, no I don't."

"Is it that the lad I've just walked past?"

"Dark hair and a hunch on his back?" Gary scoffed.

"No, he hasn't," Ellie said.

"He must have if he fancies you," Gary said.

"He looked nice, Ellie, take no notice," Pat said.

"You can't even get a girlfriend, Gary, so I don't know what you're talking about," Ellie shouted but Gary just continued to laugh at her.

Ellie ran to her bedroom and slammed the door. She knew she wouldn't hear the last of this now. Why on earth did Matt Williams' call round, she hated him. She wished boys would go away. She was sick and tired of them. Why couldn't they just be friends, but she knew they'd want to kiss her too and she wasn't ready for that.

Ellie had a horrible feeling in the pit of her stomach. She could still hear Gary and Sally laughing downstairs, she hated them too. She knew it was best to ignore them and they would soon get bored, but it was still a pain.

She tried not to think of Matt Williams, or the way he looked at her or his blue eyes and the way he made her laugh at school. She didn't think she'd be able to ever look at him ever again. The worst bit was though she wished she'd said yes and gone the pictures with him. Then she lay on her bed and slowly the embarrassment left her, and she was left with a warm glow as she remembered that Matt Williams had actually asked her, Ellie Thomas, to go to the pictures with him.

She couldn't wait to tell Shelly but then, she realised, he probably wouldn't want to know her now that she had slammed the door in his face. Ellie's face grew warm again, butterflies were whizzing around in her stomach, and she didn't know how she felt about it all.

Why did life have to be so complicated, Ellie thought. It was easier when she just hung round the street and boys were just her friends. Yeah, she had boyfriends, but that was just a childish little game they played, she had just hung round with them and usually she had finished with them after about two hours because they were getting on her nerves. This was a totally different ball game. This felt serious for some reason. Ellie was entering unknown territory, and she didn't know the rules.

Ellie remembered the girl in her class who had French kissed a lad, and it suddenly dawned on Ellie, what if Matt Williams wanted to French Kiss her? Because if he did, that would be even worse. Janet Henshaw, the girl in her class was called, and she was the one who had French kissed Michael Lawler and it had gone round the school in a matter of minutes.

After that Janet Henshaw had suddenly become very popular with the boys. She always had boys asking her out now and walked around the playground thinking she was God's gift. Probably all lads thought girls of her age French Kissed now. Would she look like a big baby if she didn't want to?

Ellie decided to call round to Shelly's. Shelly would listen to her. She crept downstairs and was out of the house before her brother and sister could find anything else to say to her. Ellie ran to Shelly's hoping she was in. She knocked on the door and thankfully Shelly answered. Shelly took one look at Ellie and knew Ellie had something to tell her.

Shelly shouted through to her mum, "Mum I'm just taking Ellie up to my room."

"Alright love," they heard as they ran up the stairs.

Shelly was really lucky. She had her own bedroom as she was an only child. Her bedroom was gorgeous as well, all pink with matching bedroom furniture. Ellie dreamed of having a bedroom like Shelly's.

"What is it?" Shelly asked as they flopped on to her bed.

"Oh my god, Shelly, you are never going to believe it, but Matt Williams has just knocked round at ours and asked me if I wanted to go the pictures with him."

"Get lost. Matt Williams? What did you say?" Shelly could hardly contain her excitement.

"Well, I didn't really say anything," Ellie mumbled.

"What do you mean?" Shelly asked.

Ellie could see how confused Shelly looked but Shelly hadn't been there it had been embarrassing.

"Well, I shut the door in his face."

"You did what?" Shelly screamed jumping up off the bed and glaring at Ellie as if she was stark staring mad.

"I didn't know what to say and our Gary and Sally were laughing in the living room and I just felt mortified and before I knew it, I'd slammed the door in his face and now he'll hate me and he won't ask me to go the pictures with him now. Will he?"

Shelly didn't disagree with her but just stared at Ellie as if she'd never seen her before in her life but then Shelly, who always looked on the bright side of things, smiled at her and Ellie looked at her hopefully.

"No, if he was brave enough to call round to your house, he must really like you."

"Do you think so?"

"Yeah definitely."

Ellie felt a bit better then.

"You don't think I've made a complete idiot of myself then?"

"Probably," Shelly said laughing, "but he'll get over it."

They began to talk in earnest about her next move. Ellie didn't mention her fear of having to kiss a boy, there was some things that she couldn't even admit to her best friend. After a while Ellie began to feel better. Ellie left Shelly's feeling more confident and walked home happily, thinking of Matt Williams and smiling to herself.

Ellie was in a world of her own until she saw a group of boys hanging round and realised that Matt William's was amongst them. Ellie's embarrassment returned. She wished she could turn around and walk the other way, but they would see her and then she really would look stupid. So, instead she put her head down and walked quickly by. She thought she had made it past them without any incident when she heard footsteps behind her.

"Ellie," she heard Matt call to her. She turned around slowly, trying to ignore his mates looking at them from across the road, smirking, but they didn't say anything. Matt was far too popular for them to try and ridicule him and Ellie was grateful for that at least. "I'm sorry I called round. I hope I didn't embarrass you?" He said once he was standing in front of her.

"You didn't," Ellie took a deep breath thinking of Shelly's reassuring words and decided the best policy was to be honest, "It's just I was surprised that's all. My older brother Gary was in, and he loves it when he finds something to skit at me about. Not that he was skitting at you it's just," Ellie felt as if she was speaking far too fast, but Matt didn't seem to notice and interrupted her.

"My mates talked me into it I should have just waited until I bumped into you."

Oh, Ellie thought puzzled, did that mean Matt didn't want to ask her out.

"It's okay," Ellie stared at the floor.

"You didn't give me a chance to say that we don't have to go the pictures we could do something else?"

Ellie was surprised that he still wanted to ask her out and she was dying to say yes but what if he wanted to kiss her and she got it all wrong and he thought she was just a kid? Ellie didn't know what to do.

"I don't know," Ellie shuffled her feet and couldn't bring herself to look at him

"Go on, we'll have a laugh," Matt continued.

Ellie found herself saying, "Yeah okay then but just as mates though?"

Matt laughed but then said, "Yeah, of course."

He smiled at her, and Ellie smiled back.

"So, should I meet you, somewhere? Maybe tomorrow night?"

Ellie thought quickly, "What about the top of my road at about 6 o'clock tomorrow, then?"

"Yeah, that'll be great, I promise I won't knock at yours."

Ellie laughed, "Yeah don't, my brother would have a field day."

"My older brother's the same," Matt said.

They stood for a moment. Ellie didn't know what to say.

Eventually she said, "I'll see you at six tomorrow then?"

"Yeah," Matt paused and then said, "Can't wait."

Then Ellie really did blush. She smiled awkwardly at him and then walked away.

As she was about to let out a sigh of relief Matt called after her, "Oh by the way they're knocking the last of your old road down you know."

"I know," Ellie said, puzzled that he should mention it.

"No, I mean now, they're knocking it down right now, I walked past there before, and the bulldozers are there and everything."

Ellie hadn't even realised Matt knew where she used to live but decided not to ask him, it was a small neighbourhood, so it was hardly surprising.

"Are they?" Ellie felt gob smacked and said more to herself than to Matt, "I suppose it was only going to be a matter of time."

"Yeah, just thought you'd be interested."

"Yeah, I am thanks."

Ellie walked away slowly. She was glad she'd seen Matt and sorted things out and she knew under normal circumstances her mind would be in a whirl about meeting him tomorrow but now the only thing she could think about was her old house. Without thinking she turned in the direction of her former home.

CHAPTER 42
Danny Boy
Various Artists

Ellie heard the bulldozers long before she reached her old street. The sound was deafening, accompanied as it was by the loud crashing of bricks as they fell and the shouts from the men working on the site. Her old street was nothing more than a demolition site. It didn't seem real. Her old street was a mass of bricks and mortar. She stared at the abyss of her old neighbourhood, flattened beyond recognition. It was only the bingo hall at the top of the road which gave her any bearings, otherwise she could have been anywhere.

Ellie watched as large trucks of one form or another were busily working to clear the bricks away and were creating huge fumes of dust in their wake, so she found it hard to see clearly. Without warning a gust of wind blew, the air cleared, and her old home came into view. Ellie was amazed. How could it be still be standing in the middle of all that chaos. It was almost a miracle but there it stood teetering on its own, an island in the midst of a storm.

The sides of the house were revealed with bricks and chunks of cement jutting out, and large dark crevices had opened the house up to the elements. Ellie could still make out the green paint around the window frames and Ellie noticed a spot of colour fluttering in the wind. Then she recognised that they were the remnants of the parlour's blue curtains, which were hanging forlornly in the empty house, a strange reminder of former times.

She had been so happy there, then Ellie thought, well most of the time she had been. It was only in the last year that she had finally tuned into the arguments of her parents, before then they had only been background noise. She had thought that all parents argued and fought, and dads went to work and spent the majority of their time in the pub whilst mums stayed at home.

Ellie had wanted time to stand still. She hadn't wanted her life to change but it had and so had she. She realised that now. However, much you wanted life to stay the same before you knew it had moved on, sometimes for better and sometimes for the worse. Ellie realised she's had no choice in the matter. Although she had wanted to stay in the cocoon of her childhood, she had to admit that a lot of things which had happened were for the best. Both her mum and dad seemed happier; they had all learnt to adapt to their new surroundings.

Ellie sighed and then her attention was drawn to a bulldozer standing in front of her home. She watched as its large lead weight swung and hit the front room windows. The house stood shaking, the large weight swung once more, this time the walls began to crack. After the third attempt a huge hole had been ripped into the front of the house and bricks were falling into a huge pile at its base. Ellie watched in morbid fascination as her house was knocked down before her eyes. She felt removed from it. A witness of her past disintegrating.

"Ellie," she heard a shout behind her.

Ellie turned around slowly to see a figure approaching her. She watched as a man came nearer. Ellie recognised his walk but with the dust in her eyes she found it difficult to quite make out his features but then she realised it was her older brother Danny. Ellie couldn't believe her eyes.

"Danny," Ellie shouted in return and ran to his open arms.

Danny swung her round and round. She felt like a child again. Her big brother was home, their Danny and Ellie realised she was both laughing and crying at the same time.

"Let's have a look at you," Danny said as he set her down. He smiled and rubbed the top of her head, "Look at you, aren't you a sight for sore eyes."

Ellie laughed, sniffing, her tears now gone, "You didn't tell us you were coming home."

"I know, thought it would be a surprise."

"I can't believe you're here," Ellie stared at him as if he was an apparition. "How did you know I was here?"

"I didn't, I heard the house was being knocked down and thought I'd have a last look at the old place."

"It's nearly gone," Ellie said. "Look."

Danny stood for some minutes looking towards where their street used to be.

"Oh well, what can you do, it was a shit hole anyway," Danny said turning once more to look at her.

"No, it wasn't," Ellie said, her defensive stance for their old home returning in an instance. "I loved it there."

"Yeah, I did too when I was your age, but nothing lasts forever." He smiled at her, "Getting a bit upset, hey," he said, rubbing her head once more.

"No, just wanted to see it for the last time, that's all."

"Yeah, me too," he paused, then asked, "So, how are you, kiddo?"

"I'm great."

Danny laughed, "You're still a little ragamuffin."

"No, I'm not. I'm in big school now."

"Oh, all grown up then?"

"Sort of," Ellie felt her heart swell, she loved Danny, she didn't realise how much she had missed him.

"So, how's mum and dad?"

"They're okay."

"Finally divorced hey."

"Yeah, they argued too much."

"You can say that again," Danny said shaking his head but then more seriously he asked, "But, you're okay, aren't you? Finding it better in the new house?"

"Yeah, sort of, Gary's being a pain, though, thinks he rules the place."

"Does he now? Wait till I see him."

Ellie smiled at the thought of Danny sorting Gary out, he wouldn't know what hit him. She looked up at her older brother, marvelling at his features, he was a lot like their uncle Tony she realised and wondered how she had not noticed it before.

Ellie attention was drawn back to her house as with a few more swings the lead weight had knocked most of the upper story down. She looked at Danny, his face was intense and she realised he was as moved by the sight as she was. Ellie was grateful he was here, so they could share this moment. They stared until the dust finally obliterated everything from view.

"It's gone now, Ell. Nothing more to see."

"I suppose so."

"It's a shame though. We had some good times there."

"Yeah," Ellie said and they both stood reminiscing lost in their own thoughts.

Danny pulled himself out of his reverie and said, "As I said, Ell, nothing lasts for ever."

"I'm learning that," Ellie said, sounding older than her years.

Danny looked down at his little sister, she was growing up, he realised. It wasn't so much that she had grown, she had but it was more her attitude and the way she spoke. He wished she could stay just as she was, innocent, and he could protect her but he knew he couldn't. She looked as if she had the world on her shoulders and he wished he could take away her burdens but he knew she would have to deal with them herself, like they all had to. He shook his head and laughed at his sombre thoughts. I must be getting soft in my old age, he thought, our Ellie's alright. She's a little tough nut.

"Shall we get going then?" Danny asked.

"Yeah," Ellie said, sighing once more.

They started walking back towards their new home. Ellie felt safe and protected walking next to her big brother. She suddenly had an overwhelming feeling of joy at the fact that he was there. Ellie stared at him and wondered why he looked so different. Suddenly it occurred to her, Danny had grown up too, he looked more self-assured, more confident. Whilst they had all been arguing and shouting and divorcing and moving to a new house Danny had been somewhere else, in his own world, a world they hadn't shared.

"Have you been home, yet?" Ellie asked.

"No, I've not seen the new house yet. I went and found the old man in the pub and had a pint with him. Knew I'd find him there."

"Yeah, me mum says it's his second home."

Danny laughed, "More like his first," he shook his head, "he'll never change."

"No, I don't suppose he will, mum has though."

"Has she? In what way?"

"She's happy," Ellie said simply.

"About time," Danny smiled and looked down at his sister once more, trying not to let his emotions get the better of him. They turned into their new street, "You know what, Ell?" Danny said.

"What?"

"Family's what's important, not where we live. Just because mum and dad have split up, it doesn't change anything, we're still a family you know."

"I know, Dan," Ellie said.

"So, no more tears hey, let's look forward not back."

Ellie smiled. It was great having Danny home. Mum would be made up to see him and everything was brilliant. Tomorrow, she would see Matt and her heart did a little somersault at the thought of seeing him. Then she realised Gary couldn't skit at her because their Danny would shout at him. She felt the joy bubbling up in her and wanted to bottle it and keep inside herself for ever so she would never feel sad again. All she knew when Danny was home, she felt safe and secure. She felt so happy. It was if everything was falling into place at long last.

They turned into their new street and Ellie felt quite proud pointing out their new house to Danny with the garden in the front and the gate all newly painted. She realised it was a lot nicer than their old house.

"Race yer," Danny shouted and sped off in front of her.

Ellie laughed and shouted, "That's not fair, you had a head start."

Danny slowed down and let Ellie pass him, "Oy," he shouted, "you're too fast for me."

Ellie laughed knowing he'd let her over take him.

"Mum," Ellie shouted as she ran through the front door, "Our

Danny's home."

"Oh my God!" Pat screeched as she ran from the kitchen, towards her eldest child, "Here's my Danny boy, my little hero, are we glad to see you."

Pat wrapped him in his arms, laughing and crying all at the same time. He was still her little boy, however much he'd grown.

EPILOGUE
Get me to the Church on Time
Frederick Leowe - Alan Jay

The big day arrived. Fiona wore a simple white silk dress, with lace on the sleeves and on the collar. She looked beautiful, even Ellie had to admit that. Fiona's hair was piled up on her head with white ribbons hanging down amongst her curled blonde hair. In her hand she held a bunch of pink roses.

Harry walked her down the aisle, in a suit all crisp and new. Ellie thought she saw the hint of tears in his eyes but maybe it was just a trick of the light. Ellie's mum cried a lot. Ellie felt embarrassed for her. Ellie and Sally wore matching dresses, but Ellie's was blue and Sally's was yellow. They weren't exactly bridesmaids but they were pretty close to being so. Ellie didn't want to be a bridesmaid, Sally did.

The morning had been chaotic. If Ellie thought Fiona was a nightmare getting ready for work this took it to a whole new level. There had been tears, tantrums, bedroom doors slamming. Cries of, *"I'm not going, my hair's a mess"* from Fiona, and tears when she said she looked fat in her dress.

An assortment of women, from Fiona's friends to Pat and their aunties had all tried to cajole Fiona from her bedroom with urges of, *'It's only wedding nerves,'* and *'she'll be alright if someone would just pour a drink down her'* but at last Fiona was ready, looking stunning with not a hair out of place. Yes, all the women agreed she looked a picture of loveliness and even Ellie had to admit Fiona scrubbed up well.

Then with a champagne glass in her hand and a smile on her face, Fiona stood soaking up the compliments from all the women, who by that point looked frankly frazzled by it all. Ellie had noticed that when Fiona wasn't looking they had raised their eyes in the air, tutted and patted Pat on the shoulder as if they now knew what she had had to endure for all of these years.

Ellie shook her head. She had been trying to tell everyone for years that Fiona was nothing but a little prima donna but no one had taken any notice of her. Ellie sighed, oh well better late than never. At least now they realised what hard work Fiona is but it was small consolation now that Fiona was actually leaving, their comprehension of the burden they had all had to carry, as far as Ellie was concerned, had come far too late.

At last, the wedding cars arrived and they all spilled out of the house and into the front garden. Neighbours stood around oohing and ahhing as Fiona at last made her appearance. Congratulations were made, and invites of 'Don't forget you're all invited to the Do tonight,' were reiterated and then just as Pat was getting into the car a scream split the air as Pat suddenly remembered she had left her hat on the kitchen table.

Pat fanned herself in the car and glared at Ellie and Sally and said, "I hope you two never get married, I don't think I could cope doing this all over again."

"Don't worry Mother," Ellie said indignantly, "even if I did, I wouldn't carry on like that."

Sally kept quiet and Ellie eyed her up suspiciously thinking there was definitely another Fiona in the making.

Thankfully, it was a warm summer's day, it was early June and the sky was a deep blue, with only the faint wisp of clouds drifting by. Rain had been predicted but hadn't arrived. Birds sang in the trees, the air felt fresh and warm. It was perfect. Fiona had indeed opted for a registry office wedding but it was not a come down, as Wallasey Town Hall was a beautiful building.

The building itself stood overlooking the river Mersey. Ellie could smell the brine drifting up from the shore, blending perfectly with the light summer breeze and competing with the heady scent of roses pinned to every button hole in sight. Seagulls hovered overhead, squalling to one another, dipping and diving in the sky as they always did here on the banks of the Mersey.

After the ceremony pictures were taken on the staircase and then they all moved to the back of the Town Hall and had even more pictures taken on the stone steps which led down to the prom. Groups of people clustered around. She noticed Danny and Gary both puffing away on cigarettes and laughing together at some joke they shared. They both wore suits which matched their dad's, and they all looked really smart. Even Gary managed to scrub up nicely and had had his hair cut so looked respectable for a change.

Everyone had told Gary to behave himself and so far he had exceeded expectations. Danny had come home especially which made the day even more special as far as Ellie was concerned. All their family was there, their grandmother, their nan and granddad, aunts and uncles, cousins and nieces. They were all standing round looking really pleased with themselves. Pat's family stood in abundance and were roaring with laughter, telling jokes and creating a jovial party atmosphere that would only increase as the day proceeded.

A simple wedding had become a very large affair. After the wedding everyone was heading back to Pat's home where she was laying on a small buffet to keep everyone going until the night time. This was only for close family and friends but even this would be a large gathering by anyone's standards. Pat had been worried that they wouldn't all fit into her home but they knew they'd manage it somehow, even if it spilt out onto the pavement outside or into the garden at the back they would manage somehow.

The local Labour Club had been hired for the party in the night time, with even more people attending and Ellie was looking forward to this bit the most. She knew by that point most people would be drunk and dancing, and telling silly jokes. She loved her family's parties they always had a good time.

Ellie looked over to where Simon's family stood. There were far less of them than there was on our side, Ellie was glad to see. They stood in a tight circle keeping their distance and eyeing up proceedings with a distasteful look on their faces. They all looked very serious and she had only seen Simon's mum smile once or twice. Simon's dad didn't look too bad, she had seen him laughing with Harry earlier on but he been brought to heel with a stern look from his wife and quickly returned to her side.

It seemed to Ellie that they liked Fiona but kept throwing dirty looks at Gary and Harry, and Ellie and Sally had agreed they all looked stuck up. Simon's mother had a very posh voice but Pat had said she was nothing but a 'tuppeny half ha'penny snob' who had 'nothing to be snobby about'.

Simon on the other hand looked as pleased as punch with himself, and kept saying 'Let me introduce you to my wife' and Ellie found it quite nauseating. There were a lot of ohhs and ahhs and doesn't she look beautiful and don't they make such a lovely couple and Ellie thought maybe it was best if she kept her opinions to herself.

Cameras never stopped flashing and Ellie kept on being dragged away to be photographed with all and sundry until at last it was time to return home. Cars beeped and people shouted to one another that so and so will give you a lift. It all seemed very confusing to Ellie but at last she was dragged into a car and they soon arrived back home. The house quickly became crowded and drinks were poured and toasts were made.

Once in the house Ellie and Sally had been given Baby Cham to drink. Ellie felt very sophisticated drinking from a fluted glass but found it difficult to maintain her dignity when she was being pushed from pillar to post. A few of the older men made Ellie feel uncomfortable, some seemed a bit leery towards her which Ellie found totally disconcerting. One old man, with a beard kept telling her she was turning into a lovely young lady and didn't she look nice when she made the effort. Ellie frowned and wondered what had gotten into everyone.

Ellie thought that her mum looked particularly nice even though she hadn't stopped for five minutes, she still looked fresh and clean. Pat was wearing a lovely peach suit with a cream blouse with matching shoes and hand bag. Pat's hair had been styled and curled and earlier on in the day a cream hat had sat perched on her head at a perfect angle but the hat was no longer anywhere to be seen. Her mum's hair still looked nice though, Ellie thought, and all in all her mum looked a lot prettier than Simon's mum.

Ellie noticed that her dad's mate, Phil Malone, was paying her mum far too much attention but her dad didn't seem to possess the same observation skills as Ellie and hadn't even noticed. Ellie wondered whether she should tell him but then thought better of it. She watched her dad as he stood laughing with her uncles and drinking his beer.

Suddenly, Ellie saw her mum march away from Phil with an angry look on her face and Phil Malone had shouted, 'You're a free woman now, Pat, no harm in trying'.

Ellie looked round to see if her dad had seen the exchange but his back was turned and Ellie assumed he hadn't. Ellie watched as Phi Malone laughed and then had the cheek to walk up to her dad and start talking to him. Ellie decided she didn't like Phil Malone. He was worse than Bean Head in school and if he kept it up, she would have no other option but to tell her dad.

Later on, they all found themselves in the Labour Club, the room was packed. Fiona and Simon kicked off proceedings with a slowy and then Harry approached Pat.

"Would you do me the honour," Harry had said in a loud voice and Pat had laughed and taken his hand.

Pat had said in an equally loud voice, "Of course, but don't be getting any ideas, Harry, you had your chance and you blew it."

Everyone laughed and Harry said, "Once bitten twice shy, hey Pat."

"Too right," Gary shouted, "Take no prisoners mum."

The party had been great. Lisa, Joan, Steph and Paula were there and when they first walked in Ellie heard her dad shout, "Watch out the Women's Institute have arrived."

Lisa had shouted back, "See your still alive and well and living in the dark ages then Harry."

Then she saw Billy and was surprised to see Matt Williams with him. Ellie hadn't actually invited Matt to the party but she had told him if he happened to turn up, she couldn't see anyone throwing him out.

Matt left Billy and came over to speak to Ellie.

"It's a great party, isn't it? Your family's huge."

"I know," Ellie was about to say something more but then their Danny had suddenly appeared by her side.

"Who's this then?" He'd asked and given Matt the third degree. Then Danny shouted Gary over and said, "Keep your eye on this one, Gary while I'm away."

Gary had said, "Don't worry Dan, got it covered."

Then her two brothers had laughed but Matt had still looked a bit worried and looked up at Danny and Gary as if they were heavy weight boxers or something.

All in all though, Ellie decided the next day, it had been

wonderful and it was the best night ever, and Ellie would remember it for the rest of her life. Ellie felt so happy, she felt as if her heart would burst. The best thing was though her and Sally no longer had to share a bedroom with Fiona. As far as Ellie was concerned, things certainly were on the up and up and she couldn't wait for her summer holidays to begin. It was going to be the best summer holidays ever.

Printed in Great Britain
by Amazon

39286355R00165